The Right Ingredients

Nancy Shew Bolton

Scripture taken from the New American Standard Bible © Copyright © 1960, 1962, 1963, 1968, 1971, 1972, 1973, 1975, 1977, 1995, 1997 by The Lockman Foundation.

THE RIGHT INGREDIENTS © 2014 NANCY SHEW BOLTON
Published by Prism Book Group
ISBN-13: 978-1502443229
ISBN-10: 1502443228
First Edition, 2014
Published in the United States of America
Contact info: contact@prismbookgroup.com
http://www.prismbookgroup.com

ENDORSEMENTS

"*The Right Ingredients* is appropriately named. Nancy Bolton has cooked up something very satisfying...a realistic look at life behind the scenes in a cake shop; a romance that has its ups and downs as in real life; three dimensional characters and family situations; and a spiritual awakening that is very moving. This is a novel you'll be sorry when it ends as you'll grow to love Ann and her experiences." Dvora Waysman, author of 13 books including *The Pomegranate Pendant*, now a movie titled *The Golden Pomegranate*

"This debut novel reminds me of the early Mitford novels. A slice of life story with a gentler feeling to it. Some interesting plot twists surprised me, and I fell in love with the characters." Lena Nelson Dooley, multi-award winning author of the McKenna's Daughters series — *Maggie's Journey, Mary's Blessing,* and *Catherine's Pursuit*

"*The Right Ingredients* is an engaging book with realistic characters. Author Nancy Bolton manages to weave themes of divine, romantic, and family love into a cohesive plot, as the redemptive power of love transforms Ann from a timid wall flower into a mature, confident woman. Grab a tissue to dab at some happy tears while you immerse yourself in this tender love story." Carlene Havel, author of *A Hero's Homecoming* and other love stories

"I had the pleasure of previewing *The Right Ingredients* by Nancy Shew Bolton. I wasn't disappointed. Her story weaves a dream two college friends bring to fruition. Along the way they experience, faith, confidence, trust, and love. A plus are the luscious goodies they make, that will bring a smile to your face and a dash to your favorite bakery!" Diane Dean White, author of *Carolina in the Morning*

DEDICATION

To God, who inspires, teaches, comforts, and counsels me; my parents, who encourage me to write and who give me and my three incredibly creative siblings a multi-faceted orientation to life; to my husband, who fills my heart with joy and romantic love and who still makes me laugh; our five sons and the women they love, and our grandchildren, all of whom are a constant source of joy and amazement, and our extended family and friends who light up our hearts with happiness. You are all part of me, and part of what inspires me to write. You are truly the music of my existence. May God continue to bless you all.

CHAPTER ONE

ANN HOPED THE bakery stayed empty of customers. She needed every bit of concentration to decorate the cake the way she envisioned it. Her eyes scrutinized the last patch of undecorated surface. Almost done. Shifting on the chair, elbows planted on the low icing table, she pressed her lips together and leaned closer. She calculated the perfect angle to hold the frosting bag.

A stray hair drifted into her line of vision and she blew out a quick upward breath to deflect it. How on earth could any strand escape her coiled braid? She should have worn the hairnet. But hairnets were old-womanish. Still, she preferred them to the flimsy paper hats she and Susan wore the first year they opened the bakery. They never fit well, and exasperated her by sailing off her head when she rushed past the ceiling fans.

The bell on the bakery's front door tinkled. Ann sighed and wished Susan would return from deliveries. She glanced through the archway and out the picture window. Maybe she'd appear. No such luck. Oh, well.

"Be right there," she called. Ann set down the icing bag, rose from the chair and angled her hips to slip past the table. As she stepped sideways, two bees zoomed in and flew toward her. She startled, brushed both hands to scare them away and lost her balance.

In helpless shock, her stomach fell as her forearms, palms and chin landed on the cake and sunk in while a groan escaped her. Ann lifted her head and stared in total horror. Loud moans erupted. "No, no, *no.*"

As though a protest would change anything. Tears gathered. She drew away from the cake, and straightened up. One little wobble, and her handiwork was destroyed.

"Are you okay?"

Ann stared at a tall, sturdy man in jeans and a tee shirt. He stood in the archway between the front and back rooms and surveyed the scene. "I'd have stayed out there, but I heard you cry out and thought I'd better check on you."

Ann's lip trembled. She pushed against the tide of emotion. No tears in front of customers. The two bees danced on the frosting, poking around on her ruined cake. "It's all their fault. I tried to do everything right, and see what happened?"

She pointed a frosted finger at them while her tears overflowed. Through the blur, she glanced from the excited insects over to the man. She blinked to clear her vision. His eyes were sympathetic, and his mouth wore a suppressed grin. He stood in a firm stance, yet appeared poised to offer assistance. Ann searched for a clean part of her arm and brought it up to first brush the tears, then the frosting beard off her chin. She must look like some sort of clown.

The merriment left his face. "I'm sorry. I think maybe they flew in when I opened the door. Can I help?"

"That's kind." Ann attempted a smile. "But I don't think you can fix this cake. And please don't feel bad about the bees. They love to break in here with all this sugar."

She strode to the sink and turned on the water to wash off the pastel colored mess. "I'll be out front in a moment."

"Okay."

Ann finished her clean-up, wiped off her chin, hands and arms, and dabbed the towel on her eyes. She tied on a clean apron, straightened her shoulders and stepped to the front room of the bakery.

"Well, you look better." He laughed. "I'm sorry, but that was pretty funny."

Ann imagined her ridiculous appearance before she cleaned up and couldn't help joining him. When their laughter subsided, he asked, "Feeling better?"

"Thank you, yes." She needed a laugh.

"I'm glad. Must've been frustrating." His obvious sympathy unlocked her natural reserve.

"I've decorated it for almost an hour, and now I've got to start the whole thing over from scratch. My business partner isn't back from deliveries and I have more cakes to make." She didn't like to complain.

Take a breath. She shrugged. "Anyway."

He grinned. "You seem pretty young to run a bakery."

"I don't feel young today." She grimaced and shook her head. "I guess it's technically not a bakery, either. We only make cakes and cookies. Susan and I work here together, four years now, since college." She blew out a breath. "Gets pretty crazy sometimes. Who knew the organic cake business would be so popular?"

He chuckled. "I'm not surprised, after all the raves I've heard. You know, I've had days like yours." He stretched out his hand. "My name's Tom Tillman. Sure hope your afternoon gets better."

She clasped his offered hand and gave it a shake. "Ann Shaw. Around here most days are hectic, though I don't usually fall on the cakes. I want to thank you for offering to help."

"Wish I could have. I'm a capable farmer, handy with the livestock, but no good at cake fixing. Or baking, which is why I'm here." He spread his hands out towards the display case.

"Hey, how ironic. A farmer with the last name Tillman. Tillman. Do you get teased?"

"Sure. Especially back in college. They loved to goof on me and make up nicknames. They also told me I had no choice in professions because of it."

They shared a laugh.

"So, that's why you're a farmer?"

Tom shook his head. "No, I'd be one even if my name was...Ann Shaw."

Ann's cheeks grew warm at the way his tone dropped. She'd never connected to a customer so fast. He was easy to talk to.

The bell chimed and three men who wore green electric and gas company uniforms marched in and sat at the counter. Ann nodded at them.

"Hey, guys. Fred, Bill, Skip."

They were what she and Susan called *regulars*. Fred, in his late forties, arrived every morning before work, always sporting his cap with the company logo on the front. Ann wondered if he even wore it to bed.

"You can wait on them first," Tom told her.

"Coffee?" She started towards the carafes.

Fred announced, "We need twenty-one cups to go, and some cake. We're gonna surprise one of the fellows on his last day before retirement."

She'd halted after his first few words and turned to stare at him, then back at the lone, half-full carafe of coffee next to the line of four empty ones. Fred had been there this morning. Why didn't he mention needing coffees and a cake later?

Ann's lifted spirits deflated. "Is it all right if it has no writing? I'd need extra time." She glanced over at Tom, expecting him to be annoyed at the wait. Instead, he looked on with an interested air. She hurried toward the coffee pots and calculated how much she'd need to brew.

Fred's tone sounded apologetic. "Well, it is kind of spur of the moment, but could you put his name on it? We'll wait. Right, guys?"

They nodded in unison.

Ann kept her breaths even. In quick motions, she started the coffee brewing and turned back to Fred. "Okay. Is one sheet cake enough? It serves twenty-four."

"Sure."

"Which kind? We have a chocolate with cream cheese frosting, a raspberry with vanilla, and a lemon with coconut. I wouldn't choose that one, though. It's too hard to write on the coconut." She stayed in business mode while part of her remained aware of Tom.

Fred glanced at the others. "The chocolate one?"

They all agreed and Ann lifted it from the showcase and placed it on the counter. A tall, middle-aged woman rushed in and smiled at her. Ann darted a glance at Tom. She should wait on him first.

Tom gave a slight tilt of his head toward the newcomer and told Ann, "Go ahead."

He appeared to enjoy all the activity. The carafes let out little hisses of fragrant steam, and coffee aroma filled the air.

"What can I get for you, ma'am?"

"We're having an office party. They told me to pick up one of your sheet cakes." She caught sight of the one on the counter. "Ooh. What kind is that one?"

"I'm sorry. I sold it to these gentlemen here." Ann gestured toward Fred and company.

"Hmm." She made a small grimace before her features brightened and she pointed at the showcase. "Is that lemon coconut? I've bought one before."

Ann nodded.

"I'll take it." Ann boxed it, entered the sale and turned toward the coffee area. She exchanged a smile with Tom on the way.

Ann lined Styrofoam cups along the counter where the carafes of coffee were. She poured with efficiency while she held each cup still. The timer in the back room buzzed. Ann blew out a breath and pressed her lips together. Her mind ordered out the sequence of tasks she'd need to accomplish. Get the cakes out of the oven before they burn, hurry and pour the coffee before it cools off, wait on Tom, and write on the sheet cake.

Susan, where are you?

The front bell sounded. This was too much. Ann's shoulders slumped as though someone plunked a loaded yoke across them. She glanced over, first to Tom, then to the short slender man in business clothes who stood next to him and studied the contents of the showcase. Tom walked the length of the counter and stepped around behind to stand next to her.

"Let me help. I'll pour the coffees."

She hesitated, unsure.

He gave a slight raise of his eyebrows. "I can handle it. I know how. I use to work at a diner during college."

"Thank you," she breathed out. Ann grabbed the sheet cake off the counter, informed the new customer she'd be right with him,

[6]

and shot Fred a quick grin. In the back room, she set it down on the clean part of the icing table, and glanced at the squashed one nearby. She allowed a quick scan for the missing bees, and whisked the pans out of the ovens.

Ann ran back out front to wait on the latest shopper.

"What can I get you, sir?"

"Hmmm. They look so good." He pointed at the upper showcase full of small cakes. "Which kind is this one, and that one—oh, you might as well tell me what they all are."

Breathe. Breathe.

She cleared her throat and rattled off the varieties while the customer emitted noises that indicated his pleasure. Too harried to respond to his approval, she waited and tried to appear patient.

"I'll take the chocolate cherry one." Ann boxed it up for him, completed the sale and turned to Fred.

"What's the name?" She glanced at Tom, who grinned at her and snapped the tops onto the coffees.

"Jerry. With a J."

"How about 'Congratulations, Jerry.' I can write the years on, too." Ann poised at the archway.

"Good. Thirty-eight. A whole decade longer than me." Fred beamed at his companions.

"What color do you want the writing in?"

"Doesn't matter." Fred shrugged.

"Of course it does." Ann shook her head at him and delivered a good-natured roll of the eyes.

"You pick it then."

Ann dashed to the back, and chose a bag with mocha icing. It would be attractive on the cream colored frosting. Wow. Thirty-eight years. Yikes. Her entire lifetime plus thirteen. The thought hit her and halted her decorating for a moment. She heard the bell sound again as she finished and hurried to bring the order out front.

"Be with you in a minute," she told the young woman who stood by the showcase.

She slid Fred's cake into a box and observed with pleased surprise how Tom had parceled all the coffees into bags, folded the tops and placed them into one large carton. He'd added packets of sugar, creamer and plastic spoons as well. Ann beamed at him and entered Fred's sale. Tom walked around to the other side of the counter and nodded at Fred and the guys as they passed by with their purchases.

The new customer's eyebrows lifted as she regarded Tom. "Do you work here, or are you waiting, too?"

Tom laughed. "Both, I guess. But you go ahead."

Ann couldn't help a chuckle. She turned her attention to the woman.

"What can I get you?"

"Pick-up for Wilson."

Ann hurried to the office in the back to retrieve the order. The cold, air-conditioned air refreshed her while she located the boxed cake and reluctantly exited, closing the door. A few quiet minutes in the room with her feet up would be bliss. She rushed out and completed the sale. When the customer left, Ann smoothed her apron and breathed out a big sigh. She smiled at Tom. "Thanks so much for your help. I should give you a free cake."

"No, no. Besides, I may have let the bees in, which made trouble and extra work for you. It's the least I could do. Is it always this busy?"

"Often enough."

He whistled and shook his head.

She grinned, took a small breath and fixed her mind on business. "So, what can I do for you?"

"I want to order a birthday cake for my son."

"Oh." A twinge of disappointment surprised her and made her ashamed. She pushed it away. No wonder he's helpful. A family man. "Birthdays are fun. Though I always dreaded mine."

"Why would you dread it?" Tom's eyebrows rose.

Ann gave out a short laugh. "I didn't like all the attention. Getting sung to and everyone watching while I opened presents. I used to wish I could hide."

Tom chuckled. "Ah, an introvert. And you work with the public. You seem to do just fine."

"It took quite a while to get the hang of it, believe me." Ann shook her head. "Susan had to wait on everyone most of the opening year until I managed to without the jitters. I'm probably an extreme version of introvert. Mom says my first sentence was 'Go away.' I think I said it to one of my older sisters."

Tom shared a congenial laugh with her, his eyes warm. Okay. Back to business. Why would he want to hear so much information? Ann's reserve kicked back in.

She reached for her order pad. "I need to know the variety of cake, how many people you're serving, when you want it, and the name, age, and design to put on it."

His features took on a perplexed aspect, brows crinkled as he looked up. "Hmm, name, age and kind I know. I'm not sure on the other things…"

He tapped a finger on his chin, and glanced down. "He likes chocolate. I guess chocolate cake with vanilla frosting."

"All right. Now I need his age and name and whatever toy or activity he likes most." Ann held her pen poised over the order pad and flicked a gaze at him. His eyes were so dark blue, they almost appeared purple.

"Jesse. He loves tractors and goats, and he'll be four." Tom's face held a pleased, proud air as his head lifted.

They figured out what size he needed and Ann wrote it all down with the date.

"So, how much will it be?" He reached into his pocket and produced a wallet.

"You don't need to pay until you pick it up."

"I'd rather settle it now. After all, you're going to do the work." He smiled at her. "If something came up and I couldn't get here, it wouldn't be fair. It's happened to me before. I don't want to do the same thing to you."

Ann peered closer as her emotions moved from surprise to gratitude. She'd become accustomed to dealing with rushed, stressed people who wanted everything their way and right now. Most of them didn't seem to consider her or Susan's efforts. "I wouldn't think it would happen to a farmer."

"You bet it does. I once had a guy order five gallons of goat's milk and eight dozen eggs. I got it all ready for him. He never showed up or called, and I hadn't gotten his number. I didn't make the same mistake again." He shook his head.

"Now you've mentioned numbers, can you write yours here at the bottom of the receipt in case we need to call you?"

"Sure."

He took the pen and pad she held out. She studied his strong, sun-browned hands as he wrote. She glanced up at the edges of medium brown hair curled underneath the rim of the ball cap he wore.

"What time do you want this on Saturday?"

He flashed his grin again. "Is noon too early?"

"Not at all." Ann returned his infectious smile as she placed the money in the register. "We're here by six a.m."

"I guess a bakery's like a farm. I'm in the barn by six, unless Jesse's having a slow morning. He insists on dressing himself now he's a big boy."

"I always thought farmers got up at four or something."

Tom laughed. "Most do. My Dad and I figure six is early enough. We don't work jobs off the farm, so we can start later. I'm sure Jesse appreciates the extra sack time. I'd hate to roust him at four in the morning."

The remark puzzled Ann. Why should a little boy have to wake up when his father did? Jesse must be a light sleeper.

"Well...thank you, Ann. I'll be here at noon on Saturday."

"And thank you, again."

He touched the brim of his cap as if to salute her, grinned and ambled out. After he hopped in his truck and started it, he waved before he drove away. She waved back and stared after the truck until it vanished. Why couldn't all their customers be like him?

He's so calm. Content. Maybe because he's outdoors a lot. Ann gazed out at the bright summer sunlight flickering on the leaves. Thank goodness for the picture window. At least she could view the outdoors. The brief rise of optimism yielded to a momentary image of her pet hamster from years ago. He'd lived his life in a large glass aquarium with a running wheel and a wire top. But she'd kept him safe from the cats and other dangers. She sighed. Safety is important.

Susan drove in the lot. Now things would ease up. She strode in haste to the front door, her smile huge, expression elated. Graceful, tall, and bird-quick in her movements, Susan never seemed to lack enthusiasm or energy.

She burst through the door. "Hey Ann, this is awesome. The restaurant guy called me and said they want to start offering our cakes on their dessert carts. So I stopped in to hammer out details with him. He wants a variety of four different kinds delivered before dinner service starts."

"Tonight?" Ann struggled to keep the dismay from showing in her voice and face. Susan looked so thrilled, how could she dampen it?

"Yeah." Susan nodded with a big grin. "Isn't it wonderful? I've wanted to land some restaurant orders. If this works out, who knows?"

Ann swallowed and tried her best to appear supportive. *Who knows? It may kill me.*

"Well, let's get busy." Susan bustled to the back room. "Gee, what happened here?"

"Two bees startled me and I fell on the cake. I'll clean it." Ann stepped through the archway.

"Are you okay? Did they sting you?" Susan scrutinized Ann's face.

"No, they were more interested in the cake than me." She scanned the room, peering at the ceiling. "They've gone somewhere."

"Guess they ate all they wanted. Good. Satisfied customers." Susan laughed and donned her apron.

Ann couldn't help a grin at Susan's joke. But why couldn't she share the same hopeful excitement as Susan? She cleaned up the mashed cake and the table while her thoughts returned to how kind Tom Tillman had been to her.

When she glanced at Susan scooping flour into four bowls, she couldn't stop the questions. "We're doing them from scratch now?

Why don't we send over four we've already done? We still have other orders to fill."

Susan took butter from the refrigerator. "Goodness, no. I want these to be as fresh as possible, so he'll trust our quality of work. It's a fancy place."

"Susan..." Ann held her palms up in an exasperated bid for mercy.

Susan grinned and put her hands on her hips. "C'mon, let's impress him. We can do it."

Ann sighed and turned back to work. All the product in the showcase had been baked today. How fresh did cake need to be? She knew this would be a long night. Images of her bed waiting at home flashed through her mind while she worked. The back room heated up and the ceiling fans whirred on high speed to release the waves of hot air shimmering out of the ovens.

Susan delivered the restaurant order after they locked the front door at five. Ann continued work on the standing orders for morning. Susan returned and the hours passed while they finished, boxed and placed the cakes on shelves in the air conditioned office. They still had to clean up.

By the time everything was done, the clock showed five past eleven. Ann had been too busy to eat since the quick snack she'd grabbed around five. Now she only wanted sleep. No wonder she'd lost so much weight. Ann trudged out to her car, arms and legs rubbery. She turned the key. The engine labored and stopped.

Please not now. Not tonight. Ann switched from dread and tried encouragement. Maybe it would work.

"C'mon, you can do it. Here we go." Two more tries, and the engine turned over. She blew out a breath of relief and drove to her apartment. She hoped it wouldn't stall out before she got there.

Somewhere in the distance, her life raced on ahead of her, and it took all her effort to try and catch up.

CHAPTER TWO

AT HER SMALL apartment, she sank into her easy chair and let the breeze from the window cool her flushed face. Her weary gaze traveled along the walls at the various paintings and drawings she'd done when she used to have free time. Her eyes fluttered shut and she drifted into half-sleep. Annoying sounds intruded on her peace. Her neighbors were arguing. Again. Forced back to awareness, she tried to ignore them and yearned for sleep. They showed no signs of a cease fire.

She rolled her eyes, stood and shuffled in tired slow motion to shut the window. Better some stuffiness than another lengthy installment of the continuing drama of who should wash the dishes. Why would they fuss about kitchen work at this time of night? She trudged to her room and flopped onto her bed. Pajamas later.

I'll lay here a minute.

As she stretched and relaxed, her body sank into the comfort. She couldn't hear the words anymore, just a low rumble which rose and fell as the argument continued. Perhaps next time she'd wait until the neighbors verbally jousted for a while and yell out, "Why don't you stop bickering and do the dishes? You could have finished them by now." Tempting, but not likely. In her mind she heard what her parents would think. *Goodness Ann, you're acting like some sort of hooligan,* they'd say. Funny word.

"Hooligan," she spoke out loud and giggled. The giggles turned into laughter and escalated. Ann remembered how her father would call her "slap-happy" when her hilarity bounded out of control. Those silly words drove her to laugh harder, but then, as though a switch became flipped inside her, laughter turned to tears. She relinquished herself to them and as they slowed, she sank into exhausted sleep.

ANN RACED AROUND the next morning and muttered, "Too many snooze alarm hits." She rushed into the bathroom to check her hair in the tiny mirror and stubbed her big toe hard against the doorjamb.

"Ouch! Why am I so clumsy these days?" She knew the answer. Not enough sleep. Ann hopped around, hairdo forgotten.

Well, I'm sure awake now.

She limped back to the bedroom to rub her toe. While she winced and massaged, a thought came to her. If anything good ever happened, she'd be so shocked she'd run off screaming. The comical image of herself made her chuckle while she tied her sneakers. How wonderful to have comfortable shoes. They helped her weary feet hold up under long hours on concrete floors. They were worth the expense.

Ann ignored the throb of her toe and rushed out to the car. In the mirror, she spied some stray hairs which must have escaped when she hopped. She pinned them back next to her coiled braid and turned the key. The car stuttered and stopped. After four tries, she quit in frustration and dropped her head onto the steering wheel.

Work, sleep, and problems. Nothing else.

"Please," she begged in a whisper. "I need to go to work. If I don't, I won't be able to pay for your tune-up."

A few more tries and a jubilant shout escaped her when the engine took hold. Her quick flash of joy evaporated as she maneuvered into the hectic college-town traffic. She turned down several roads to follow her alternate route.

Ann pulled in at their small downtown bakery, too hurried to halt for her usual appreciation of the birds as they hopped in the glossy ivy on the side of the building. She did stop to gaze at the bright blue of the cloudless sky, and the sign she'd painted which hung above the picture window. It depicted two women who held opposite sides of a sheet cake with "Sue-Ann's Organic Cake Factory" written on it. A smile flickered across her lips. Ann opened the back door and took momentary pleasure in the lush scent of cakes and coffee.

"Thank God you're here," Susan wiped her floury hands on her apron. "The pick-up time for the big college dorm order got moved up and they'll come by for it in four hours." She scanned the battalion of filled cake pans with the practiced eye of a drill sergeant.

"Why didn't you call me? I could have been here earlier."

"It's okay—you're here now. We can handle it together. Have a little faith." Susan checked the ovens, glanced over and giggled when Ann scowled at her.

Ann put the hated hairnet on. "Well, I have confidence in *you*. Look how much you've done already. What should I do first?"

"You can make the cream cheese frosting for the almond chocolate cakes. I'm about to take them out. Then fix a batch of

French vanilla icing for the raspberry cakes, and set the bowl in the refrigerator. I'm baking those next." Susan swept her hand toward the pans on the counters.

Ann tied her apron and assembled the ingredients. The familiar adrenaline surge kicked in. *Feels like wolves are chasing me.* "When did you start? It's only six now."

"Around four-thirty. Right after I got the call." Susan slid some cakes onto the cooling rack.

"Good thing you live upstairs." Ann grabbed a large bowl.

The bell on the door rang followed by the oven timer.

"Can you get the customer?" Susan asked.

"Sure." Ann set down the butter and cream cheese, hurried through the archway and adjusted her apron. "Hi, Fred."

He sat down and let out a weary yawn, his arms on the counter.

She poured his coffee. "So, how did the retirement party go yesterday?"

"Outstanding. The cake tasted great and we had a fun time. Jerry said he might stop in sometimes and see what we're up to. Says he's been coming to the workplace so long, the car would probably drive itself." Fred chuckled. "He sure looked gloomy about leaving."

After thirty-eight years? Ann couldn't fathom it.

"Stay somewhere for so many years, it gets to be home, I guess." Fred shook his head, thanked her for the coffee and stirred creamer into his cup.

How sad. Ann wanted to change the subject. "Anything else? Orange juice?"

"I'll have a piece of cake. Smells awful good in here."

"You'll be in trouble with your wife if you keep ordering that for breakfast." Ann pursed her lips.

"Why? Those silly cereals she buys are full of sugar, so what's the difference? I say life's not worth living if you can't eat what you want." He shrugged and picked up the coffee.

"You told me last week she's worried about your health and weight."

"Well, you must eat the cake, and you keep dropping pounds, so maybe it'll work for me, too." The steam and aroma from his coffee floated upward as he grinned at her. He took a short sip. She couldn't help a smile at his mischievous smirk.

"Well thanks, but after baking them all day for years, I don't have an appetite for them anymore. Plus we work so hard and it's hot, too. I guess it's why I keep…melting." She joked, glanced down at her flat stomach and back at Fred. "Anyway, what kind would you like?"

He studied the cakes in the showcase. "Carrot cake's pretty healthy, right?"

Ann laughed as she brought a piece to him.

"It's good to see you laugh. You're always so rushed and worried. You know," he lowered his voice, "I'm going to give you some advice. I hope you don't mind."

A nervous twinge started in her stomach. She swallowed and waited. Had she done something wrong?

Fred continued in a serious tone, "One of these days you'll look in the mirror and be my age, and it'll get here pretty fast, too. So be sure you're doing what you want with your life."

Ann stood rooted as an icy awareness swept through her. She viewed him as if her eyesight sharpened and highlighted every detail. Gray hairs were visible at his temples while wrinkles creased his forehead and the area around his concerned eyes. Ann cleared her throat and stared off. "Um…thanks, Fred. Be back in a minute."

She hurried past Susan and escaped to the small bathroom. Ann shut the door, closed the toilet lid and crumpled down. The familiar work rhythms in her mind stopped and derailed. The focus of her thoughts underwent a quick shift in a different direction and made her unsteady.

It reminded her of the sensation she'd had as a small girl walking to school, trying to navigate the parts of the sidewalk cracked and heaved up by tree roots. Other unsettled memories tried to surface. No, not now. She fought to push them away.

Besides, she should be done with things from the past. Ann forced her focus back to Fred's words, and defiance rose inside. Did Fred do what he wanted, year after year at the same job?

Doing what I want?

Who's allowed to do that? She sat still and struggled to sort herself out and go back to her usual mindset. She had to help finish the big order. Hiding in the bathroom was not permissible. She took some deep breaths and stood up to splash cold water on her face.

After she dried off and hung the towel, she stared in the mirror and studied her blue eyes. She searched them until unease grew in her middle. Ann straightened up, lifted her chin and declared aloud, "You're young, you work in your own business, and there's nothing to be upset about. You've settled on something, and you're fine. What else matters?"

She gave her reflection a quick nod and exited the room. But the entire morning while she worked, an odd sense of inner awareness haunted her, as though part of her still stared into her own eyes.

"Are you all right?" Susan asked after the cakes for the dorms were picked up and they had time for a small break. They sat in the office in the back room and hoped to finish lunch before more customers arrived.

"I don't know." Ann glanced at her for a moment, shrugged, and set down the rest of her tuna sandwich.

The bell on the door sounded. Susan jumped up, plunked down her half-eaten sub and announced in a cheery voice, "I'll go."

Susan never resented interruptions. Each order and interaction with customers made her chipper. So what was Ann's problem?

"I guess I shouldn't react to every word anyone says to me," she mumbled to herself while her mind ruminated on Fred's comments. She stared at her lunch.

Susan poked her head through the doorway. "Hey. We've got orders for a wedding cake and assorted desserts for the rehearsal dinner. Guess we'd better plan it out tonight. They want it next week."

The bell tinkled again, and Ann tried to sound cheerful. "You go ahead and eat. I'll get this one."

By late afternoon, the humidity rose, and the inside of the bakery felt like a sauna. Whenever they opened the ovens, a blast of heat assaulted them. Ann amused herself by thoughts of movie scenes with workers on ships or trains shoveling coal into furnaces, their faces streaked. Moisture trickled from Ann's damp head, down her neck and back. Susan started to sing a line from "Old Man River." Ann laughed and joined in.

"You and me, we sweat and strain, body all achin' and wracked with pain... Tote that barge and lift that bale." They finished the song right before a customer walked in.

"Thank God for music." Susan grinned and strode to the front. Once they closed, Ann and Susan sat in the office in front of the air-conditioner and finalized plans for the wedding cake. Relief washed through Ann as her skin cooled.

"Too bad we can't put air conditioning near the ovens. Today was brutal." Ann pinned up a few loose, damp strands of escaped hair.

Susan laughed. "If we installed AC by the ovens, we wouldn't take much pay home. We'll get a thunderstorm soon, I bet. The humidity's atrocious. Feels like we're underwater."

"And tomorrow it could be clear and thirty degrees cooler." Ann rolled her eyes.

"One of the perks of living in upstate New York." They shared a wry laugh and returned to brainstorming.

After they finished plans for the order, Susan made her way to her upstairs apartment. Ann researched pictures of goats and tractors as inspiration for Jesse Tillman's cake. She worked hard to make every cake unique. She'd place four little goats jumping around the number four and the same number of tractors under his name. Ann finished by eight o'clock, pleased with the results. She hoped Tom Tillman liked her work.

Ann boxed the cake for pick-up the next day, set it on one of the shelves in the office, and drove home. She turned the radio up loud to boost her energy and prepared a quick supper of a grilled cheese sandwich on rye. Some thin slices of red onion furnished a tasty addition. She heated up a cup of tomato soup and sat down, relieved to eat.

The next day near noon, Ann darted glances out the window in anticipation of Tom Tillman's arrival. Thirty minutes later, a middle-aged woman pulled up in his pickup truck and bustled in.

"I came for Jesse Tillman's cake," she said. Ann figured she must be a relative. She possessed the same broad smile and kind blue eyes. Ann fetched the box and opened the top.

The woman's hands flew to the sides of her face.

She cooed, "Oh, how lovely. What a wonderful job you've done. He loves tractors and goats."

Ann beamed in appreciation at her reaction. "Mr. Tillman said he did, so I put them on there for Jesse." The lady started to open her purse and Ann said, "He already paid when he made the order."

The woman tapped the side of her head. "I think he told me, but I get so distracted at times. I always make the cake for his birthday, but this week has been so busy." She rolled her eyes and closed her pocketbook. "I'm a grandma and sometimes it's hard to run around after Jesse and help with the farm, too. Times like those, I miss Judy the most. That's Jesse's mother."

"Where is she?" Long work hours, or maybe the military?

"She died after she delivered Jesse." Ann's stomach dropped. Guilt for asking the question spread through her in a chilly flow. How awful.

"Poor little thing. We miss her so." The woman's eyes grew soft and sad. She breathed out a sigh, and glanced at Ann. "But we have Jesse, and a lot to be grateful for."

How could anyone deal with the loss of a loved one in such a sudden, catastrophic way? A twinge of shame flickered through Ann when she pondered the woman's genuine remark about gratitude.

I couldn't be thankful after such a tragedy.

Mrs. Tillman picked up the cake and smiled. "Thank you again so much. I'm sure Jesse will be thrilled. Good-bye, dear."

Ann nodded and tried her best not to appear deflated. After Mrs. Tillman drove off, Ann wrapped her arms around herself and imagined the awful scene while deep sorrow for all of them flooded her. How horrible. How did Tom stand it? A shiver clenched her shoulders.

"Relationships are not for me," Ann declared aloud and shook her head. Heartaches and loss didn't happen if you stayed unattached. Besides, almost everyone she knew in a relationship always complained about it. And she had too many memories of all the agony and dating dramas her two older sisters endured. Break-ups. Distressed sobs and frightening depressions. Threats of suicide which shook Ann's soul. It sounded about as much fun as jumping into a volcano. An arena to be avoided at all costs.

The Tillman tragedy haunted her throughout the day, and long into her evening. If God was real, as Susan maintained, things like that wouldn't happen. At times, she experienced flashes of anger. It wasn't fair for the Tillmans to have to carry such a heavy burden. She wondered how they managed to be normal and functional. Calm and…chipper, almost lighthearted only four years later? How was it possible?

Images of Tom's understanding eyes and amused expression when she'd pointed at the bees crossed her mind. How considerate and helpful he'd been. The friendly wave when he left. Poor guy. And she thought her own problems were rough.

She ordered some food for delivery and followed the usual Saturday ritual of staying up late to watch a movie. While the end credits rolled, her eyes scanned the quiet, tiny apartment. It struck her in a flash. She was the only living thing here. Not even a pet or a plant.

A strong flash of loneliness unsettled her, and she pushed it away. Perhaps she could buy some goldfish or a bird. The possible places to put them would be the bookcase or the end table. But where could she store the stacks of history books which covered both surfaces? She got up and straightened the two landscape pastels hanging above the television. They'd been fun to draw.

Ann strolled into the kitchen to rinse out the cup she'd used for peppermint tea. Thank goodness it did the job and calmed her indigestion after dinner.

"Why did I order spicy Chinese take-out?" Ann realized she'd asked the question out loud. As though to humor her recent divided awareness of herself, she joked, "I don't know. Why did you?"

Ann chuckled and flipped off the light.

CHAPTER THREE

AFTER ANN WOKE and dressed the next morning, she poured some juice and grabbed a power bar. She parked herself on the tiny porch for her Sunday reading. Nothing like a good history book. A scan of the trees held her momentary attention. The slight sway of their branches made a peaceful sound, and the reflection of the sunlight danced across each limb.

When autumn approached, the leaves would begin their glorious transformation. Ann anticipated it every year. What a visual treat. She settled herself into the peace of the outdoors and smiled while the breeze teased the little loose hairs around her forehead.

Ann became so engrossed in her book, it took a moment to register the new sound. *Please, no.* Her neighbors had come out and launched into verbal combat on the adjacent balcony. All the apartments had tiny private porches, but if a person sniffed or moved, anyone on their own porch could hear. Their argument centered on who should do the laundry. Ann rolled her eyes and kept trying to read.

The peace of the morning faded. She tilted her head back and stared at the awning above her. Ann found herself pleading with them in her mind.

Please. Go away. Just do the laundry. It's not hard. I'll do it for you if you'll stop arguing.

When she was a young girl, their house ran pretty well as far as chores were concerned. She and her sisters had designated jobs and did them whether they wanted to or not. Neither one of her parents would have tolerated their daughters arguing about their duties. By round two of the argument, her patience wore out. Ann stood up, and spouted, "Oh, for crying out loud."

She stomped into her apartment and whipped the sliding door closed with a firm thunk. She wondered if the message got through. A stab of guilt paralyzed her. She stared at the blank glass of her small television, then to the picture centered on top. The faces of her family at Thanksgiving smiled back at her.

"Guess what, everybody. Now I slam doors and yell at people." Ann wanted to go somewhere and do something. Go where?

The sound of gleeful children at play in the yard across the street drifted in through the open window. She stepped over and parted the curtain. A catch swelled in her throat at the sight of their delighted soccer game. Ann sunk down into a kitchen chair to read, but her mind wouldn't stay on it. She scanned the same page over and over until she realized it and stopped.

"What's wrong with me?" Her words echoed through the silent apartment. She remained still as if to wait for the answer and shook her head at her odd mood. She needed a change of scenery and thought of possible destinations.

I'll drive to the lake and feed the ducks.

She pinned up her hair and grabbed a loaf of bread on the way out. The sun shone hot and the atmosphere inside her car breathed out heat like one of the ovens at the bakery. She longed for air-conditioning, but the expense put it out of consideration. Even opening all the windows didn't help much.

The drive to the lake should have taken a short time. *What's with the extra traffic?* Realization dawned. Stupid Finger Lakes Berry Festival. Ann never enjoyed big crowds and parades. They sparked an awkward, out-of-place sensation in her, and she didn't like being bumped and jostled.

She drummed her fingers on the steering wheel and became more frustrated as the cars ahead of her crept along. Sweat beaded on her forehead and neck, and dripped down her spine. It tickled. She twisted her arm and torso so her fingers could reach the itch, and her foot slid off the brakes. A sharp thud jolted her as her bumper hit the car ahead of her. The occupants in the back seat whipped their heads around. They stared at her with eyebrows up and mouths gaping open.

How she wished the ground would swallow her. Ann flicked a fast glance in her rear-view mirror, and backed up a little. She sat for a moment and tried to steel herself for the explosion of anger and harsh language. The car she'd hit traveled onto the shoulder and the driver waved at her to follow.

After she parked and stepped out to face the music, a voice sounded through the window of the jeep passing alongside her.

"What did I tell you? Women drivers."

Ann pressed her lips together and resisted the urge to glare as the car passed. She swallowed the lump in her throat and dread rose as a man stepped out of the vehicle she'd hit. Dressed in a white dress shirt and gray slacks, he was tall, slender, and looked around sixty.

"Are you all right?" Gentle concern filled his voice.

Surprise coupled with relief washed through her and replaced the tight dread. Her mouth had popped open, and she closed it a moment before she answered him. "Yes, I am. Are all of you okay?"

"We're fine, young lady. No harm done," he assured her with a chuckle. They examined both bumpers. His sported a dent.

Guilt heated her face. "I'm so sorry. I didn't mean to. My foot slipped off the brake by mistake. I guess I better give you my insurance numbers for the repair claim."

"No need. It's a small dent. I can fix it myself." He nodded and shot her a smile. "Besides, it would make your insurance go up. You're young. Bet you pay a lot already."

Wonder filled her. "Aren't you mad at me?"

"You're worth more than the bumper or this car ever could be. Don't you know that?" He studied her, his voice kind.

Ann stared at him as awareness dawned in her. No, she didn't know it. The majority of people she knew appeared to value their cars, jobs, and houses as though they were the most important things in life. What sort of folks did this man hang around with?

"I'm Jim Cortland." He extended his hand, and she shook it.

"I'm Ann Shaw."

"Pleased to meet you, Ann. We're all on our way to church services, so I'd better get going. You should come and visit sometime. We're on the next street over and two blocks down on the right. It's 210 Greene Street."

"Thank you for your kindness. I appreciate it."

"You're welcome, Ann." He turned to leave and glanced back. "Have a good day and always remember God loves and cherishes you."

Ann stared as he entered his car and waved at her. She returned the wave. What a kind man. Lightness lifted inside her on the drive to the lake. The pressed-down, unsatisfied sensation which seemed to dog her every step faded. She imagined herself as a musty house and someone opened a window after a rainstorm. Now a quiet, fresh breeze flowed through.

She parked near the water's edge and found a bench to sit on. She eased down and stretched her legs in front of her. The slow rhythm of the rippling current matched her breathing. Her eyes drifted to the sky, deep blue and cloudless, then back to the lake. Its slight waves broke on the pebbled shore. Pieces of driftwood, bleached, sinewy and large enough to sit on, were scattered at intervals near the water.

How does he know God loves me, cherishes me? Is it true?

After hearing so many different things over the years, the topic sounded too conflicted and hard to figure out. Jim Cortland made her curious. He seemed quite sure, and genuine. How did he get that way?

As a teenager, Ann engaged in many disagreements with Susan about God. She recalled one of their last ones. "If God created people," Ann maintained, "and people are scary, He must be even scarier."

"You can't judge God by people," Susan responded. "The only one you can judge Him by is Jesus. He's the one who shows us what our Creator is like. Why don't you read His words?"

"I went to Sunday school. I know the stories. Besides, my parents say that's what they are. Stories."

Susan refused to discuss it after a while, which suited Ann. Her parents told her being a decent person was enough. She shook her head. There had to be more to strive for than being a good person. Why else would God be such a big topic of conversation everywhere?

Ducks swam nearby and her hand reached to extract slices from the bag next to her. Ann stood and threw pieces of bread into the water. Delight filled her as they paddled and quacked, gobbling her offering. The warm, gentle breeze touched her face. She stretched her arms up to run her fingers over the feathery leaves of the willow branches swaying above her.

Ann laughed out loud at the eager ducks as they swam about, flapped their wings and waited for more. She wished she could pet them, but they wouldn't let her approach. A memory popped into her head. Her grandmother once told her God put the fear of man into animals. Perhaps it was the reason people can walk in the woods and not see anything but birds. If it were true, how had He done it and why?

The bread supply exhausted, she raised her hands. "Sorry, guys, all gone."

Ann strode to her car and drove away, for once unaware of anyone's bad driving behavior. Her mind pondered new thoughts instead. Had God placed the fear in animals to protect them from people? The thought comforted and delighted her.

Ann tried to remember and organize everything she'd heard about God. She decided to drive past the place Jim Cortland mentioned. Ann parked across the street and studied the building. It appeared to be a regular house with a big parking area. Music and song rose through the open windows. She leaned her head back and listened. Beautiful.

After a while she opened her eyes. *I might visit here sometime.* Ann surprised herself with the thought. She spent the rest of the day on chores while she mused on what Jim Cortland said to her, and how it made her cheerful and peaceful. She couldn't remember the last time she'd experienced those feelings.

Ann hummed with the radio and assembled a casserole of macaroni and cheese topped with bread crumbs. She sautéed some green beans with fresh, minced garlic. The scent of the vegetables as they simmered in olive oil filled the little kitchen. After Ann ate and cleaned up, she settled down by the open window to read before bed. Tonight, instead of annoyance at the sound of her neighbors bickering about dishes, she felt sorrow for their endless conflicts.

THE NEXT MORNING at work, she brought Fred his coffee. He fixed her with a quizzical expression, one brow raised. "You look different, like you've been on vacation or something."

Ann laughed. "I haven't had one of those in years. Carrot cake today?"

"I'll have chocolate almond this morning." He grinned at her.

"Coming right up." She stepped over to the showcase.

"I figured you'd scold me. Are you okay?" Fred stared at her.

Ann brought him the cake and nodded. "Actually, yes. I think I am. Yesterday a man told me God loved me."

"Didn't you know that already?" His eyes widened.

"No. Guess I didn't." Ann shrugged.

"Well, now you do. Looks like it's done you some good, too." Fred flashed a smile and started in on his treat.

Later, the girls sat in the office and ate lunch, and Ann began to tell Susan about Jim Cortland. The bell rang.

Ann leaped up. "I'm done. I'll go."

"Wow. Someone's hyper today."

Ann chuckled and made her way to the front of the store.

Tom Tillman was there at the counter and beamed when he caught sight of her. He wore jeans with a flannel shirt and his blue eyes stood out in his tanned face. "Well, hello, Ann Shaw."

Ann grinned. "Hello."

"I wanted to stop in and thank you for the great job you did on Jesse's cake. He almost didn't want to eat it, just stare at it. He's talked about it all weekend. We even took a picture before we cut it." Tom laughed. "He's out in the truck with my Dad. Mind if I bring him in to say thanks? He said he had to see the lady who made his cake."

"Sure."

He strode out the door and over to his truck. He unbuckled his little boy, lifted him into his arms and carried him in. What a cutie. Jesse had black hair and brown eyes with dark lashes. Despite the different coloring, his features favored Tom. He wore jeans and a flannel shirt like his father.

She almost exclaimed, He must have his mommy's hair and eyes, before she stopped herself. Any reference to his wife would be painful. She said instead, "He's like a miniature you. Isn't he adorable?"

Oops. Tom might think she'd meant he was adorable since she'd said Jesse resembled him. She hoped her face didn't get pink. Ann kept her eyes on Jesse. Maybe Tom hadn't noticed. The awkward moment passed as Tom set Jesse down. He ran around the counter to Ann.

"Hello, nice girl." With a big smile, he reached his arms up to her.

She picked him up, and he bestowed an exuberant hug on her.

"My name is Ann." She grinned at him when he leaned back and studied her. So much life in those eyes.

"Thank you for the tractor goat cake, Ann." Tom and Ann laughed. Jesse gave her a kiss on the cheek. Her face warmed, touched to the core by his gesture.

After giving him a hug, Ann set him down. Tom gazed at his son, eyes soft with a face full of pride. "Come on back over here, pal."

Jesse hesitated, scanned the cakes in the showcase and glanced at Ann. He pointed to the lemon cake with coconut frosting, and entreated his father. "Daddy, can I have some?"

"Sure, but we can't take long. Grandpa will be done reading his newspaper soon, and he'll want to get home. Come sit over here with me."

Jesse dashed to his father, and Tom settled him onto the stool next to his. "Well, guess we'll need two pieces, please." Tom lifted his hands in a gesture of mock helplessness. "I'll take another one for my Dad. To go. Make it *two* to go. Can't leave Grandma out."

She brought them each a piece. "Did you want any water, soda, or coffee?"

"Water's fine, thanks." Tom nodded. "We'll share a glass."

Ann delivered the water, bagged up the extra pieces, and set them on the counter next to Tom. After registering the sale, she busied herself with little tasks in the front so she could watch the father and son together. Ann had never been around a single father with a small child before.

Tom took his son's hand before they ate. In a low voice with both heads bowed, he murmured a short prayer of thanks. How interesting. Tom helped Jesse whenever he wanted a drink and spoke in quiet tones with him. His attentiveness to his son was captivating. Jesse ate with care and glanced often at Ann. What a sweetheart.

"This is yummy cake, too, Ann," he piped at her in his bright little voice. "Why don't you come live with us? You can make cake at our house."

Ann laughed. "Thank you, Jesse. I'm glad you like it. But I have to stay here and help my friend make cakes."

"You live here?" he glanced around.

"My friend does. My place is a few blocks away."

[34]

"Do you make cakes at your house, too?" Jesse's curiosity and animated facial expressions tickled her.

Ann giggled and shrugged her shoulders. "No. I pretty much only sleep there."

"Don't you or your friend have any toys?" His little face wore concern, his eyebrows raised.

"I have a lot of books. I like to read."

Jesse's demeanor brightened. "Daddy reads to me at night before I sleep. Someday, I'll read books, too."

"I'm sure you will."

Tom's obvious love as he watched Jesse warmed her inside. How he adored his son.

Susan stepped out with a tray of cakes for the showcase and shot Tom and Jesse a smile before she bent to arrange them. Ann reached to retrieve their empty plates and water glass.

Tom thanked her and Jesse echoed, "Thank you, Ann."

"And you're welcome, Jesse." She touched the tip of his nose.

Susan stood next to Ann while Tom scooped Jesse up. The little boy squealed in delight, and they both called out, "Bye, Ann."

Ann waved before Tom drove away.

Susan asked, "Who are they?"

"Tom and his son Jesse. He's the man who came in and ordered the birthday cake for Jesse last week. They stopped in to say thanks." Ann wiped the counter.

"Did you meet them before then?"

"No. Why?"

Susan shrugged. "I don't know. It seemed to me like you were already friends."

"Nope. I bet it's because Jesse's so outgoing. He came over to hug me and kiss me for making his 'tractor goat cake.' Isn't he precious? And he's only four and so well-spoken."

[35]

"He sure is a cutie. So is Daddy."

Ann fidgeted with her hair and didn't reply. They returned to work. Ann's mind circled back to Tom and Jesse throughout the rest of the day. The short interaction with Jesse thrilled her heart.

I might have my own child someday.

The thought of getting married dampened the hopeful thought. Not likely.

If the business grows, I might be able to adopt.

She pictured again the tender love written all over Tom's features when his eyes were on his son, and wondered if her parents gazed at her the same way. She thought of the many pictures taken of them with their little girls, and the attitude of delight on their faces. Guess they did.

At home later, she checked out the refrigerator and freezer and sighed. Too bad the choices were sparse. She'd need to shop again soon. She didn't want to defrost anything or make eggs, so she settled for a tuna sandwich and heated up some onion soup. Ann enjoyed cooking but never had much time except on Sundays. The first couple of years as they established the bakery, she cooked all day Sunday, assembled a week's worth of different kinds of homemade dinners, and froze them.

She'd prepare chili, pot pies, beef stew, various soups, and chicken and dumplings, reveling in the aromas and the bounty of her results while she stacked them in the freezer. Ann would gaze at them with contented satisfaction when she decided which meal to have every night.

Maybe she should use the slow cooker again. What a comfort to step into her apartment with the aroma of dinner lacing the air. It made the small place seem more like a home instead of somewhere to sleep between shifts of work.

At least she helped run a business, she thought as though to defend herself. The recent uncomfortable awareness about her life bloomed into a surge of anxiety. The image of the retirement cake she'd decorated with the words "Thirty-eight years!" on it surfaced in her mind. She experienced a vivid mental picture of herself decades later in this apartment alone, heating up something to eat, gray hair at her temples. The empty loneliness of it appalled her. Was that her future?

Ann's appetite disappeared and an icy, trapped sensation seeped through her. She wanted to run somewhere, anywhere, and be somebody else. She covered her face, and it shocked her to realize her hands trembled. She tried to calm herself down.

She couldn't walk out and leave Susan with all the work. A flash of anger hit, and she pounded the table. "What about me?" she cried out. "Don't I matter?"

The fury dissolved, replaced by a sense of heavy sadness.

Oh, God, what am I going to do?

She pushed her plate aside and laid her head down on her arms as tears rolled like water. Her eyes closed, she whispered, "I don't even know who I am... What I want."

After a time as the emotions subsided, her mind ran through images and memories. She pictured herself first as a little girl, engrossed with artwork in school and at home. Then later as a young teenager in art class, turning most of her attention to projects she took pride in. Ann halted the memories, and remembered her parents' constant discouragements to her.

"How will you provide for yourself? Even the best artists rarely live off their work. We're only thinking of you. Concentrate on something you can make a living at. Steady, useful work with good

[37]

pay and benefits." Over and over, every time she shared her enthusiasm for artwork. The future she'd imagined slipped away into the air.

Ann experienced again the sting of disappointment and grief she'd known as she transferred her efforts to something more sensible than art. She concentrated on her "regular" classes when she attended college. Part of her turned quiet afterwards, like a wild bird trapped in a cage.

Her tears slowed and stopped, and her breaths became even. She stood, made her way to her bedroom closet and browsed through boxes until she found what she searched for. She located them—her old art supplies lined up in the box. Ann hesitated before she took out a sketch pad and some pastels and sat at her small desk. After an hour she viewed the picture she'd created of a woman feeding ducks at a lake. "Hmm, not bad."

She should never have let herself get so obsessed with worrying about work. She found some thumbtacks and put the drawing up on the wall. After she studied the waves and sky, Ann delighted in the fine details of the duck feathers and pieces of bread as they dropped from the woman's hands into the water. The peace she'd experienced at the lake infused the picture and filled her heart.

Ann strolled back out and finished her dinner. Decorating had been the best part about the bakery...whenever someone wanted a special cake, like the one she did for Jesse. Her face softened into a smile as she remembered his sweet little personality.

CHAPTER FOUR

ANN TOOK HER sketchpad, some pencils, and pastels with her in the car the next day. She placed them on the passenger seat with care, as though they were her friends. If she ever had time to spare, she could sketch. She hummed with the radio while she drove to work and parked.

"Good morning," she sang out to Susan. The warm scent of vanilla filled the air.

"Morning." Susan grinned and slid pans into the ovens. "You sound lighthearted today." She placed her hands on her hips. "So, right now I'm working on the base for the wedding cake. They dropped off the pillars and stand for it last night when they picked up the rehearsal dinner desserts."

She poured batter into prepared pans lined up on the table before her. "I figured we can frost and decorate at the reception hall kitchen and leave it right there. They gave me a key so we could go over whenever we're ready."

"Okay." The front bell sounded, followed by Fred's hearty *hello*. Ann tied her apron and bustled out to wait on Fred. She set a steaming cup in front of him. "I know you want coffee, but I'm never sure what else. I keep expecting you to start a health kick."

"I'm already on one. These cakes are organic." They shared a laugh. "So, today I'll have chocolate cherry."

She cut him a piece and set it in front of him. "Hope you enjoy it."

"I will. Best cake in town." He chuckled and forked some into his mouth.

Later while they ate lunch in the office, Ann told Susan about Jim Cortland and her little car accident.

Susan's face lit up. "I know Jim. I've visited there before."

Ann tilted her head in surprise. "When did you visit?"

"The last time would be almost a year now. I went with my parents. Their church sometimes does outreach with Jim's group. We helped with the holiday food drive, and afterwards both churches held services together." Susan paused and smiled. "Quite beautiful."

"You never told me about it." Susan's blissful expression and description indicated an experience Ann puzzled over. Church services could be beautiful?

"I didn't think you were interested." Susan's honest eyes caused Ann pain.

"I'm sorry." Ann dropped her gaze, ashamed.

"For what?"

Ann glanced back up and swallowed. "For not listening much and usually making fun of your beliefs."

"That's okay." Susan reached over to pat Ann's shoulder.

"You can tell me things if you want to. I'd like to understand more."

Susan's features warmed while she studied her. "I'll answer questions, too. Anytime."

"And maybe you and I could visit there together sometime?"

"Sure we can. Whenever you want," Susan said, eyes shining. Ann half expected her eager friend to quote chapters and verses from the Bible and make plans to take her to church right after work.

"Thanks. I'm too shy to go alone." Ann took a deep breath and let it out. "I hoped you'd want to."

"Is this why you seem happier lately?" Susan gave a slight lift of her eyebrows.

"I've been lighter inside ever since Mr. Cortland was so kind to me and told me God loved me. Before that I had this weird tense sensation on and off, almost like panic. Yesterday, it all crashed into me at once and sort of...broke open."

Ann traced a finger along the slight scar of an oven burn from a few weeks earlier. She sighed. "I'm so used to doing whatever's expected of me and concentrating only on that. Now, these different thoughts about my life are shifting everything, but I do feel better. I did a pastel sketch last night for the first time in years."

"Wonderful!"

The bell on the door sounded. Susan gave Ann's arm a soft squeeze. "I'll get it."

She overheard Susan informing someone about when the wedding cake would be completed. Ann exited the office to frost and decorate a chocolate cake for an anniversary party. She left the shop early and took all their supplies to the reception hall to begin work on the wedding cake. Susan joined her after she closed for the day, to finish it together. When completed, they stood back to admire their efforts.

Their creation had four levels, on pillared platforms with the largest tier on the bottom. They'd piped on various blossoms, stems and leaves in pastel shades of frosting up the sides of each level and on the tops as well. At the pinnacle, little bride and groom figurines stood under a tiny canopy with flowers piped all around their feet.

Pride and satisfaction spread through Ann while her eyes traveled over the cake. Her gaze fastened on the tiny smiling couple, their hands clasped as they prepared to step into their future. Ann experienced a sharp twinge of sadness. She pushed it into the storage room inside her mind, and slammed the door.

The weary girls sank onto chairs in the reception hall kitchen. "I think they'll be thrilled with it." Susan sighed, flashed a pleased smile, and raised one eyebrow at her. "Remember our first wedding cake?"

They burst into laughter. Ann said, "Oh, it's burned into my brain. We doomed it with the meringue-style frosting."

"Well, it was my idea," Susan asserted. "I thought it would be more unique."

"It was. Maybe too unique." They laughed again as Ann remembered the cake. Four tiers from largest to smallest, piled one on the other, rather than on pillared platforms, so it would be easier for the customer to transport.

After they worked long hours on it, they finished the elaborate decorations near midnight. Their completed product stood resplendent as a prom queen on a counter in the back, ready for pick up the following day. They returned the next morning to find that the meringue frosting had melted in the humid summer heat, causing the top three layers to slide off and break on the floor.

They'd stood still in appalled shock, then got busy, cleaned the mess, and worked all morning to get another cake ready. Ann was as harried as though someone with a stopwatch yelled and chased them, but somehow they'd finished the new one in time.

"Well, we've learned a lot since then." Ann shook her head.

"Thank God." Susan gave a weary stretch. "Let's go home. I think we've worn this day out."

"I agree." Ann yawned.

They locked up and filed to their cars. Ann called out, "See you in the morning."

"Bright and early," Susan answered in a playful voice and opened her door. Susan had a much newer model car than Ann, who still drove her used one from college. The bakery showed more of a profit now, but the utilities and supply costs continued to rise. Ann took comfort in being as frugal as possible.

They waved as they drove away, and Ann's mind relaxed while she traveled along at a slow pace. She allowed herself to enjoy the peaceful sensation which arrived with the dawn or the dusk. Pink clouds shimmered with a bit of gold around them as the blue of the sunset sky deepened.

Ann stopped her car on the shoulder of the road to gaze at the sight. A small Thai restaurant across the street emanated spicy, exotic aromas which drifted by on the gentle breeze. She leaned back in her seat. People strolled in and out of the building. Her eyes became fixed on the sky and peace as sweet as soft music filled her.

After the colors faded, she drove the rest of the way to her apartment, replaying the mix of hues in her mind's eye. If she'd had a strong enough light inside the car, she'd have made a sketch of them. Ann arrived home, but the prospect of fixing dinner held no appeal. She ate a peach and a banana and shuffled off to bed.

The next afternoon, she decorated a sheet cake for an office party while Susan called in a flour order. The front bell signaled a customer. She stepped out to see Tom Tillman as he stood at the counter in jeans and a dress shirt, the usual ball cap not on his head.

"Hello." Ann glanced out at the truck. "Where's Jesse?"

"At the pediatrician's with my mother."

[43]

"Is he all right?" Concern gripped at her middle.

"He's fine. Only a checkup. He doesn't need shots this time, so he's happy."

"Good. He seems as though he's always happy."

"He is. He told me, 'I like the doctor but I get mad a little when he shoots me.'"

They shared a laugh. Ann said, "It amazes me how well he speaks."

"I think it's because he's usually around adults and we never baby-talked much. My folks told me he'd learn faster if I spoke with him in complete sentences." He shrugged and smiled. "Guess it worked pretty well."

He continued to stand.

She gestured at the display case. "Did you want some cake or anything?"

"Uh, sure." He sat down and studied her as she waited.

Moments of silence passed. She stood poised in front of him. "Which kind would you like?"

"Well…um, I guess some of that." He pointed to the chocolate cherry cake. She brought him a piece.

"Coffee?"

"Water's good." He offered a polite smile.

Ann set down the glass, processed the sale, and returned to wipe the area around the coffeemakers. She decided to stay busy near him until he finished. He might want to talk some more. Ann cleaned the showcase windows and removed a small speck of frosting from the counter in front of it. She glimpsed his face reflected in the glass. He watched her with a steady gaze.

Nervous tension erupted, and Ann hoped it didn't spark a blush. She averted her eyes from his reflection and concentrated on polishing the other showcase. He cleared his throat after a few minutes and she glanced over. His cake and water were almost untouched.

"Isn't it good?"

"No. I mean yes. It's fine, but...I didn't stop in to eat cake."

She waited. He appeared uncomfortable.

"Should I take it away? Do you want it to go instead?"

This is weird.

He pressed his lips together for a second, and asked all of a sudden, "Would you like to have coffee?"

Confusion mixed with her unease. She glanced at the coffee pots. "I don't care much for it unless I'm tired," her voice trailed off. "Um...did you want some?"

"I mean...well," he looked down, and back up. "Would you like to have something...dinner or something with me?"

Ann stared at him a moment and took a breath. Shocked surprise hit, followed by an unfamiliar sense of freedom. "I would."

His shoulders relaxed and he smiled. "Awesome...tonight?"

"Sunday is my only day off. I work until late every night. Even though we close at five, we're here until almost seven. Later, if we have extra orders."

"We can eat when you're done." Tom shot her a grin.

"I might not be good company by then," she warned.

"I don't mind." His eyes were steady on her face.

She liked the take-a-chance sensation which grew inside. "Okay."

"What time should I come for you?"

"Eight o'clock?"

"Sounds fine." His smile spread. "Where do you live?"

"I'm in the apartments on Wyckoff Lane. Apartment seven on the ground floor." A short pause ensued as each studied the other.

Tom stood. Ann pointed at the cake. "Do you want to take it with you?"

"Sure." He nodded at her and waited.

Ann packed it into a bag, and caught his stare when she turned around. Her cheeks grew hot. Shyness coupled with nervousness crept in and overshadowed her previous bravery.

"I'll see you at eight." Tom smiled. Ann managed a small nod. He stepped out the door, sauntered to his truck, and waved at her. She waved back.

What have I done?

Ann stewed all afternoon and her nerves built as the hours passed. Conversation topics would be a problem, since she didn't know him well. What was a person supposed to do on a date, and what were the expectations? She'd need to be entertaining, wouldn't she?

Questions darted through her mind. *Where will we go? Do I pay for my meal, or is he supposed to since he asked me? What if I can't think of anything to say?*

He might bring Jesse with him. She brightened with delighted hope for a second. No, that wouldn't happen. People don't take their kids with them on dates.

Ann said nothing to Susan, though Susan would have been a source of useful advice. Almost twenty-six years old, and she had no dating experience. She wasn't sure if she wanted to go now, and drove home in nervous exasperation.

Two dresses hung in her closet, both of them from when she weighed more. Figuring jeans or slacks on a dinner date wouldn't be the right thing, a sigh of frustration escaped at the limited options. She picked the ankle-length blue one with short sleeves and a lacy collar. Ann tied the waistline in with the built-in ties, but the dress still had a loose fit. She preferred clothes which weren't tight, so it suited her taste.

Ann unbraided her hair and brushed it. The soft waves reached to the middle of her back. Leave it down, or put it up? A trip to the bathroom mirror to check sounded smart. She peered at her reflection from various angles.

Guess I'll pass.

What a relief she didn't wear makeup. Her tension level had soared beyond the ceiling, and she never would have managed to apply it. After experiments with different kinds in high school, she always rubbed it off without realizing, and gave up trying.

Glued to her living room chair, Ann took slow breaths and began to calm down. The doorbell rang and startled her. Nervous tension spiked and gnawed at her middle. Might as well get it over with. Hold on a minute. It might be fun. The thought energized her. She stood up, stepped to the door, took a breath and opened it.

Tom's eyes sparkled with his broad smile. His gaze dropped, taking in her outfit and her hair. Ann relaxed a bit at his obvious approval.

"Ready?" He asked. His jeans and dress shirt, with the addition of a denim suit coat, matched the color of his eyes.

"Yes." She shut the door and walked with him to his truck. He opened her door before he walked around to his. Ann settled her dress around her, and realized with surprise that some of her nervousness stemmed from anticipation, not just dread.

He started the engine, and turned to her. "Where would you like to go?"

She hadn't expected the question and drew a blank. "Um...I'm not sure."

"Well, where do you usually go to eat?"

"The kitchen," she replied without thought. He burst into laughter, which made her smile.

"I mean when you're out." He waited.

"I don't go out much. I get take-out food sometimes." What a lame response. What could he do now? Take her to a drive-thru? Bet he didn't realize what a dud he'd asked out.

"Want me to choose?" His genuine, amused smile relieved her.

"Yes, please." She breathed in.

"Okay. I know a fantastic place."

Thank goodness he worked the problem out. Now she'd try to relax. He put the truck in gear and drove while Ann wondered what sort of meals he liked. He might love spicy food. She'd get indigestion and look sick and he'd think she was a real load of fun.

She sat still and quiet, worrying. Her gaze traveled to his right hand when he shifted gears, then to his leg as he pumped the brake. The outer muscle in his thigh moved under the denim and she averted her eyes, embarrassed that he may have seen her staring. She took in a breath.

He darted a glance at her. "Rough day?"

"Kind of hectic." Dread over the date had been the most difficult part.

"I've wondered how you manage. I'd probably go nuts if I had to deal with lots of people all day and live in town with the constant traffic. I'm a real farm boy."

"The city I went to college in was a lot worse and pretty big, but I guess if you're always in the country, any town seems too busy." What a brilliant observation. She almost rolled her eyes at herself.

"So what'd you take in college?"

She let her gaze travel over his handsome profile. "History, human development, and psychology."

He peered at her with lips pressed against a smile. His brows rose as he asked, "How did you end up in a bakery?"

She laughed. "I planned on either being a history teacher, because I love it, or a guidance counselor. Susan and I loved to bake for ourselves and our college friends, so we decided to start a business." She returned his grin. "My parents and both sisters were upset with the decision. All of them are teachers, including both brothers-in-law. They wanted me to choose a steadier job with benefits. They're fine with it now, though."

"I took some courses at the Ag school at Cornell." He flipped on the turn signal and waited for the light to change. "My dad used to work there, so I got a big break on the tuition. What I learned helped me make improvements on our farm."

He shot her a grin. "I always knew I wanted to be a farmer. A lot of the people I met in college kept changing their majors, trying to figure out which career would pay the most."

He shook his head and shrugged at her before he made the turn. "They thought I was silly to go back to farming. They told me I'd make a lot more and not work as hard if I specialized in something else. But I love it."

What would it be like to love your work? She liked it in the beginning, except waiting on strangers. Now it was so hectic and fast. Too chaotic for her. She glanced at Tom's profile again and a flash of fascination surged inside. He drove into the parking lot of a small Italian restaurant.

"Wow," he exclaimed. "Lots of cars. It's a popular place, especially with the college students." He parked and turned to her. "Do you like Italian food?"

"Yes I do, very much."

"They make it all from scratch, even the pastas and the ravioli. It's all tasty, and they don't overcharge, either."

He stepped out of the truck. Ann reached to open her door, but realized he was circling around to do it for her. Her gaze met his through the open window. His closeness made her cheeks warm. She drew in a breath and climbed out.

"Thank you." She nodded, keeping her eyes on the pavement.

Wonderful aromas filled the air as soon as they walked inside. Tom asked for a corner table and the waitress seated them at a round candle-lit one with a deep red cloth. Gentle light suffused the cozy room and the diners ate and conversed in quiet tones. Now as they faced each other across the table, she endured a fresh surge of nerves. She couldn't meet his gaze longer than a second or two.

The waitress asked them in a chipper, confident tone what they wanted to drink. Tom nodded at her to order first.

"Do you serve iced tea?" Her voice sounded so timid.

"Yes, ma'am. You, sir?"

"The same."

She gave them a quick nod. "Be right back."

"Isn't this a fine place?" Tom's eyes circled the room.

Ann examined the surroundings and tried to let the peaceful aura absorb into her. She nodded her agreement. He'd get livelier conversation from a mime.

"Ever been here before?" Tom asked. He appeared comfortable. How did he manage?

"No, but some of our customers have mentioned how good the food is." She twisted her napkin in her lap as the waitress showed up with their tea.

"Thank you," they said in unison.

It relieved her to have something to do. She concentrated on the menu and sipped her tea.

For goodness sake, speak.

She darted a glance at him. "What do you usually get?"

[50]

"Well, I don't come here a lot. I eat in the kitchen, too...or the dining room," he added with a playful grin at her. She returned it with a shy smile.

He studied the choices. "I've gotten the lasagna, the manicotti, the spaghetti with meatballs, and the linguini with pesto before. They were all tasty." An excited expression crossed his features, reminding her of Jesse. "Plus they serve it with garlic bread. I'd probably eat a big plate of it by myself, it's that good."

Ann loved lasagna, and wondered what pesto tasted like. She'd never tried it but heard raves about it from her mother. She better not order food she'd never had, in case she didn't like it. He might think she was one of those picky complainers.

She glanced up. "Guess I'll order the lasagna."

"Good choice. I might have it, too...but...well, I think the manicotti is calling my name tonight."

She had to think of something entertaining to say.

After a minute of quietness which dragged like an hour, Tom asked, "Ever had the Thai iced tea they serve at the place near the lake?"

"No. Is it good?" Thank goodness he had no difficulty speaking.

"It's amazing. It's got such intense tea flavor, and this layer of creamy stuff floating in it. It's more of a tea milkshake."

"I parked near the restaurant the other night to enjoy the sunset, and it smelled wonderful. I hear Thai food is quite an experience." Some of her tenseness faded.

"You've never been there, either? I figured a single person in a city running their own business would eat a lot of meals out, especially someone as busy as you."

"Nope. I haven't tried Thai because sometimes hot, spicy food bothers me." Ann didn't want to admit most of the reason she

[51]

avoided restaurants had to do with her frugality. Susan often teased her and called her a tightwad.

"Well, all their food isn't hot, but full of different flavors. We'll go there sometime."

He said it with such ease. While they ordered, Ann wondered how he knew he'd want to take her out again. He was probably being polite, or maybe he only wanted to be friends. If that's why he asked her out, she should stop responding with such nervousness. Interesting thought. She'd never had a close man friend before.

The waitress brought two small bowls of mixed salad. The colorful greens were without large chunks of carrots and celery. Oh, good. She felt like a goat or cow when she chewed big hunks of hard vegetables. These were soft, flavorful mixed greens, shred into manageable pieces. Various dressings in pretty, labeled bottles stood on the table.

They picked out their choices and added them to the bowls. She glanced at him and realized he'd bowed his head. Unsure what to do, she kept her eyes down until she glimpsed his face rise up. They exchanged a smile and started on their salads.

Ann wished she was in the know on the unwritten dating rules most people learned as teenagers. She'd been too busy with all the challenges to her sanity to pay attention to an activity she figured she'd never do anyway. How did it work? If someone was nervous when they asked you out, did it mean they liked you, or they were afraid you'd say no?

He seemed quite relaxed now, although he hadn't been when he'd asked her. Ann sighed. She'd drive herself crazy in her attempt to figure it out. All at once she decided to let it go. She visualized the pastel she'd done of the water and the ducks. Ann closed her eyes for a moment, and remembered the sensation of peace at the lake.

"Tired?" His voice sounded gentle.

Ann looked at him. His sympathetic expression and kind eyes relaxed her and she ceased being afraid of him.

"Not too much. It's a peaceful kind of tired. Probably the same way you feel at the end of the workday."

"Yeah, but I don't work twelve-hour days or more all year." He shook his head. "If you only get one day off every week year-round, it's not much of a break."

"The pace slacks off in colder weather. There aren't as many weddings and celebrations. We get an overlap, though, because of less business with the colleges over the summer, but more local orders. When those slow down, the colleges start ordering again. We try to take as many jobs as we can during the busiest months to see us through the slower ones."

Tom beamed. "Guess I'm right. Running a bakery is like farming in some ways."

He lifted his tea glass to her. She smiled and raised hers and they both took a sip. The waitress returned with their orders. Ooh. She stared at the beautiful food displayed on shiny plates. Fragrant steam rose from the entrees, melted cheese visible on the sides under the tomato sauce, and more sprinkled on top. Their server placed a basket of garlic bread in the middle of the table.

"Thank you," they chorused.

"This is so yummy," Ann said after the first bite. She savored the rich flavors. "Wish I knew this recipe."

"You like to cook?"

"Yes. I just don't have a lot of time to."

"No, you sure don't. I like cooking, too. Sometimes I watch cooking shows, or as Jess calls them, 'cooker shows.' He watches with me."

Ann pictured it as though she watched one with them. Why did that pop into her head? She focused her attention back on her meal. Tom told her some Jesse stories while they enjoyed their food.

"Mind if I nab the last piece of garlic bread, or do you want to split it?" Tom's hand poised over the basket. His hands appeared so capable and strong.

"No, you take it. I'll be lucky to finish the rest of this."

"That's one problem I don't usually have." He gave her a big smile.

"Well, you work hard, so you need a lot of fuel."

"You work hard, too. How do you stand it all summer? Always inside. Standing near ovens. At least I get a breeze most of the time where I'm working." Tom shook his head. "It surprised me how hot it was in the back the day I ordered Jesse's cake."

She remembered him standing in the archway. "It can get pretty extreme. It's weird, though. Sometimes even when it's sweltering and hectic, it's like we fall into such a rhythm we don't feel it anymore."

"Yeah. I hear you. Hard work can be...hypnotic."

"Yes." She grinned. "That's the perfect word for it. Whenever we can grab a break, we take turns and escape to the office where we've got AC. It's our oasis."

"I'm glad you have one." His gaze softened.

Ann glanced back at her plate to keep from blushing. By the time he drove her home, she was at ease, as though she'd known him for months.

"Sorry to keep you out this late." Tom parked in front of her house. "Guess you'll be tired at work."

"I don't mind. I'll drink some coffee." What happens now? Her shyness returned.

"Can I have your phone number? I want to call you tomorrow if that's okay."

"I'd like you to." She wrote it on a piece of paper from her purse.

He slipped it into in his pocket and smiled. "Thanks."

"Thank you for such a wonderful dinner."

"Glad you enjoyed yourself." Tom climbed out and walked around to open her door. He strolled next to her. "I want to make sure you get in safely."

Ann unlocked the front door and stood in the doorway. They regarded each other for a moment, and he nodded. "Goodnight, Ann. I'll call tomorrow."

"Goodnight." Tom walked to his truck and waved to her. She returned it and breezed inside.

"I had fun," Ann declared to her apartment and almost skipped to the bedroom.

CHAPTER FIVE

AT THE BAKERY the next morning, Ann daydreamed over the date. Little details about his hands and the sparkle in his eyes when he laughed popped into her mind. What an easy manner he had during conversation. And the way his expression grew warm when he looked at her. She wondered if he'd call later.

Whenever the phone rang, a short thrill flashed through her until she realized it was only another customer. Besides, she'd given him her home number, so he probably wouldn't call her at work. Every time the front bell dinged, she caught her breath and imagined he stood out at the counter.

After hours of this, she became impatient with herself. This was silly. She forced her mind to concentrate on the job at hand. Then she'd remember something he said or how his features appeared, and she'd make a quick try to quench the thoughts. She had to stop the junior high behavior.

That nightmare phase of her life still haunted her. She'd endured merciless teases and taunts about being overweight, then the added cruelty after she got her braces. "Tinsel teeth, metal mouth," the boy she had a secret crush on would crow at her in sing-song whenever he caught sight of her. Her heart sank as she blushed in embarrassment, and the other boys laughed with glee. She didn't let herself remember the more painful memories. Ann swallowed and fixed her attention on her decoration skills.

Despite her efforts, the stress continued to build inside. As soon as she had a free minute, Ann rushed into the bathroom and leaned back against the wall. Emotions coursed through her so fast she couldn't identify them.

Deep breaths. Breathe.

So what if he didn't call? So what? She'd been fine up until now. She didn't need to hope for something which would only hurt her anyway.

Grow up and go back to work.

Ann splashed cold water on her cheeks, dried it off and squared her shoulders.

Do your job.

Okay, this attitude would help get her focus where it should be. She exited the bathroom.

Susan opened the back door to take out some trash and let out a shriek which caused Ann's shoulders to jerk.

"What is it?"

Susan held her hand pressed against her face. "Rats. They're out next to the trash bin."

Ann's heart rate slowed and she stepped to the icing table. She'd kept a mouse once as a pet and didn't react to rodents the way Susan did. She couldn't stand them, but hated the thought of traps to maim or kill them, either. Last week, they'd spoken with Fred about the problem. He told them if using a trap bothered them, they could set out a bowl of fresh soda. The rats would drink it and because they couldn't burp, they'd bloat and die.

Susan stared at him in horror and said, "At least they die quickly in a trap if they don't get injured instead. If that bothers me, how do you think I could stand it if I knew they suffered a slow, painful death? I can't be responsible for it. I only want them to stay away." Ann nodded in agreement.

Fred gaped at them as if they were crazy. "Suit yourself, but as long as you've got bags of stored flour and sugar in here and leftovers you throw in the bin, they'll be around somewhere, no matter how clean you are."

Neither of them had an answer for him, so Susan consulted the office computer to find a better way. Her previous solution to bang on the back door before she opened it had worked for a while. But not today.

Susan set the garbage bag down and took a deep breath.

"Why don't we move the bin farther away from the building?" Ann suggested.

"It doesn't matter," Susan answered in a hopeless, resigned tone. "They'd still be around wherever we move it."

"I'll take the trash out from now on. They don't bother me." Ann placed the finishing touches on a birthday cake for a young girl who loved to play tennis.

"Thanks, I appreciate it. I can't help my reaction. They give me the creeps." She walked over to study Ann's work. "Bet she'll love it."

"I hope so." Ann yawned and plunked down on a chair. She stretched her arms up and another yawn hit.

"You should drink some coffee."

"Yeah, it would help. I'm kind of tired today." Ann pushed away thoughts of Tom and planned the next set of orders she needed to do. First she'd better eat lunch. After she poured her coffee, she assembled a cheese sandwich.

"Want me to make you something?" she called out. No answer. "Susan?"

Ann couldn't locate her inside the bakery, and the bag of trash had been taken. She opened the back door and spotted Susan by the bin. Her eyes were closed while her lips moved. Ann almost called to her but something stopped her, and she eased the door shut.

I think she's praying. I wonder why.

She might be asking for the rats to go away, or not to be afraid of them anymore. Ann wouldn't ask her about it. Prayer was a private matter, she figured, but couldn't help her curiosity. How do you know when to pray, or what to say? Do you speak the same words every time? People recited prayers on the radio, and others gave thanks to God for their food before they ate. Tom did. And the songs sung in churches. Were they prayers, too? She knew so little.

Her father delivered a short speech of gratitude every year before their Thanksgiving meal. Though he didn't mention God, she assumed that's who he thanked. Her parents taught their girls to mind the golden rule and respect others. Regular prayers and discussions about God were not familiar or usual. Day-to-day concerns, community problems, and local and national politics were the topics talked over in their home.

Hard work and good citizenship were emphasized. Ann couldn't be sure what anyone in her family thought about on the topic of God or prayer. She should ask them sometime. Their responses might be interesting.

Ann made her way back to the office to eat her sandwich. The bell dinged. She sighed, set down her food, and walked out. Jim Cortland stood at the counter and gave her a delighted grin. "Well, hello, Ann. I didn't realize you worked at the bakery."

"It's wonderful to see you again, Mr. Cortland." She smiled back. "I've been here four years now. Susan and I are partners."

"How time flies, especially at my age." He shook his head. "I came in a few times the first year you were open, but I didn't see you. My wife's been in often. She's the reason I'm here. We're giving a surprise party for her sixtieth birthday this Sunday. I need a big cake." He held his arms out wide.

"Okay." Ann giggled and took down the details on her pad.

When he finished his order he told her, "I'd love it if you and Susan would attend. We want to surprise her after services. I figure I'll pick the cake up late Saturday right before you close and hide it in my office. We start at eleven, if you girls would like to be there."

Such a caring, genuine person. "We talked about visiting a few days ago. Sunday's our day off, so I'm pretty sure we can come. I'll tell Susan."

"Wonderful. I'll look forward to it." He walked to the door. Stopping, he shot her a mischievous smile. "I'm so glad you bumped into me. I've wondered how you were, and prayed we'd meet again, and here we are." They chuckled.

"Good-bye." He delivered a quick wave.

"Bye." She waved back. Ann thought about the differences in her life in the short time since she'd first met him. His unexpected kindness and the simple assertion that God loved her began a shift inside. She remembered how the change started even before that, when Fred's words jolted her. Amazement filled her mind at the way it all fit together.

Susan returned inside. Ann wanted to ask her what she'd been doing, but told her about Jim Cortland instead.

"Sounds fantastic. So let's plan on going Sunday." Susan grinned at her.

"Good. What should I wear?" People dressed up for church, but she didn't own much dressy stuff.

"I don't think it matters. Whatever you're comfortable in, I guess." Susan shrugged.

"What are you going to wear?" She needed ideas.

"Probably a skirt and blouse. Nothing fancy."

"*Blouse.*" Ann teased. "Everybody says shirt now."

"I think blouse sounds pretty." Susan smiled. "Did you have lunch yet?"

"I was about to when Jim came in. Want me to make you a cheese sandwich?"

"Nope. I've got tuna salad I need to use up. Go ahead and eat. I'll be in soon."

Ann strode toward the office, stomach rumbling. When the front-door bell dinged, she turned around, letting her shoulders slump as she dropped her head back and blew out a breath. Susan giggled and said, "I'll get it."

Ann sat and started on her lunch. People sure ate an awful lot of cake. She never knew when things would be slow or crazy. Lunch was almost always a challenge to finish. Life should have a sound track, like movies did. That way, the music could give her a clue about what was coming, and the kind of day it would be. She grinned at her whimsical idea.

The phone rang, and hope rose in her for a second. Tom? Nope, an order. She squelched the thought of Tom and wrote down the details. Ann studied her half-eaten sandwich, appetite gone. She sighed, stood up, wrapped it, and set it in the refrigerator. Back to work.

Ann didn't arrive home until after eight o'clock. She ate some scrambled eggs with spinach and feta cheese followed by a piece of cinnamon toast and got ready for bed. Well, so much for him calling. Guess she could stop thinking about it. She fell into exhausted slumber.

The next morning while she showered, Ann thought the phone rang. When she turned the shower off, only silence greeted her ears. Must have been her imagination. After dressing, she decided to pull a small roast from the freezer to place in the slow cooker and hurried to add water, seasonings, onions, carrots, and potatoes before she left.

The day marched by as they moved from one order to the next. Whenever her thoughts wandered to Tom and the now familiar stab of disappointment twisted inside, she forced him out of her mind. No point in thinking about him, she admonished herself, almost glad to let go and get back to life as usual. At least she knew what to expect with that. Well, sort of.

Ann arrived home around seven-thirty and flopped into her chair to rest her feet and enjoy the aroma of the roast. After a few peaceful minutes, her doorbell rang. Probably a salesman. Why not ignore it? Every day in the bakery, she had to answer a bell. She waited. Maybe they'd leave. Another ring. She blew out a breath and trudged with reluctance to answer it.

A glimpse through the peephole made her gasp. Tom stood outside with a worried expression. She paused a moment to adjust her mind to the fact of him standing on her doorstep. Ann smoothed her clothes and took a deep breath. When she opened the door, he appeared relieved.

"Hello." She gave him a smile and hoped she didn't look too horrid.

"May I come in?"

"Sure." She stepped back as he entered, and walked ahead of him to the living room.

"I asked my folks to stay at the house with Jesse and thought I'd drive in and see if everything was all right. I wondered if something was wrong when I didn't hear back from you."

[62]

She regarded him, puzzled. "Hear back?"

"Didn't you get my messages?" His brow furrowed.

"Messages? Oh, goodness, I completely forgot. My machine doesn't work right. It won't play back. Guess I should buy a new one." Now he'd know how few calls she got. Embarrassing.

"I left one last night and one this morning. I didn't realize you wouldn't hear them."

"I'm sorry. I really am. I should have remembered when I wrote down my number. Guess I should buy a cell phone one of these days." He probably thought she didn't care about his calls. "What did the messages say?"

"I just said it was me and gave you my number so you could call. The morning message asked you to call me today around lunchtime when you had a minute. I know how busy you are at work, so I didn't want to bother you there." He chuckled and adjusted his ball cap. "Guess I should get a cell phone sometime, but I'm usually home when I'm not outside. I don't like to be interrupted when I'm working, so I decided not to buy one."

She grinned. "Me, too. I'm at home or at the bakery most of the time, so the only time I'd need one is in the car. I never got one, either."

He glanced around the room, and she asked, "Would you like to sit down?"

"Well, I guess you haven't been home long and probably want to eat and relax."

Ann smiled at his thoughtfulness. "It's okay. I'd like you to stay if you want to."

"Sure." He settled down on the small couch. She sat in her chair, and they observed each other for a moment before he cleared his throat. "How was your day?"

"Busy." She rolled her eyes. "Like usual." His handsome face shot a thrill through her, followed by dismay at her own appearance. By now her face would be tired and washed out, and she'd be sporting plenty of loose strands. She touched her hair and blurted, "I must look frightful."

"No, leave it. You look pretty."

She blinked in shock and almost laughed. "You need glasses, right?"

"Nope. Don't you know you're pretty?" His features wore genuine surprise, eyes widened, lips parted.

Her cheeks grew hot and she glanced down. "No."

"Well, you are." Tom's voice held a gentle note.

A painful, vulnerable sensation swept through her. Ann kept her eyes down, not sure how to manage the rush of unfamiliar emotion. Her fingers fidgeted together, and she couldn't think of anything to say. Silence.

"Should I go?" His tone sounded sad.

She glanced up. "No, don't. I'm not used to compliments. They make me self-conscious, I guess. I'm sorry."

Why am I such a head case?

"Don't be. You didn't do anything wrong. Let's change the subject."

"All right." She smiled at him in relief and unclenched her hands.

"Jesse did the cutest thing today. He chased a grasshopper around the yard while I fed the chickens. When he clapped his hands together to catch it, it jumped, and he squashed it. He brought it to me and said he had to be spanked for killing it."

Tom took off his cap, ran a hand through his hair, put it back on, and sat forward. "So I told him it was an accident, but he was determined. He said I had to spank him because the poor

[64]

grasshopper died on account of him. I understood how guilty he felt. I gave him a small swat. He hugged me and ran off to bury the grasshopper. Isn't he something?"

"He sure is." Warmth spread through her. How lucky for her to have met Tom and Jesse.

"I think I'm holding you up." Tom stood. "Your dinner smells ready, and you must be hungry after your long day." He tilted his head toward the kitchen. "You should go ahead and eat."

"I have plenty. Would you like some?"

Please stay.

He paused a moment and responded, "I ate a couple hours ago, but it smells pretty good. I'll have some if you want me to."

"I do." Ann stood.

He followed her into the little kitchen and sat at the table while she fetched the dinnerware. When she opened the top of the crock pot, the steam and aroma of the food spread through the room. They said "Mmm" at the same time, met each other's eyes, and laughed.

"Shall I say grace?" Tom asked once the plates and glasses of water were on the table.

"Please do." Did he pray only at meals? She wondered so many things concerning him.

He reached for her hand, and shyness overtook her as she bowed her head.

"Father we thank you for the blessings of food, this time together, and for the gift of Your Son. Amen." They exchanged a smile.

"Wow. Tasty," Tom proclaimed after his first bite. "The meat's so tender you don't need a knife."

"Well, it's nothing special. A roast and some vegetables." She speared a piece of potato.

"I taste herbs in this, too. Seasoning makes the difference." He ate another forkful.

Ann grinned at his perceptive words. "Sorry there's no bread. I forgot to buy some."

"This is fine." He regarded her with an amused expression. "I wanted to ask you something I'm curious about. Did you ever lose your temper with a customer?" He watched her as he reached for his water.

Ann laughed and shook her head. "No, but I've come pretty close. Even Susan got irritated once, and she doesn't rattle easily."

"What happened?"

"We were clobbered with a bunch of walk-ins. Some were sitting at the counter, and I waited on them. Susan took care of the people lined up by the register. This man pushed through the line, and people complained."

Tom's intent gaze fascinated and unsettled her. She cleared her throat and sipped some water. "He snapped at them and said he was in a hurry. Then he stood in front of Susan. She told him he'd need to wait his turn like everyone else. He said 'The heck I will. My time's important.' Susan stared right at him and said, 'So is mine, and everyone who's waiting here. Patience is a virtue, sir. I suggest you exercise some.'"

Tom laughed. "What did he say?"

"Nothing. He seemed surprised. Susan waited on all the people who'd been ahead of him, and when she waited on him, he was polite to her. Afterward, Susan said she was sorry for him, having such a stressful life that he could get worked up over a short wait at a bakery."

Tom nodded. "Lots of people in town act like that. They beep the second the light turns if you don't zoom off right away."

Ann grinned. "That's true. And I think they all end up at our bakery. I used to say if aliens landed, the first place they'd come would be our shop."

They shared a laugh. After the meal, they chatted on as evening gave way to night.

When she stifled a yawn, Tom placed both of his palms on the table. "Listen, this was wonderful. Thanks for asking me to stay. I don't want to wear out my welcome and keep you up too late." He stood and took their plates over to the sink. "Can I wash these?"

"Sure. Put them in the drainer afterward. I always air-dry. I'll turn off the crockpot and store the leftovers. Say, would you like to take any of this home for Jesse?"

Tom beamed at her. "It's sweet of you, but you should save it for your dinner tomorrow."

"Okay." Ann placed the rest of the meat and vegetables in a storage container and into the refrigerator, then cleaned off the table. When he finished the dishes, he filled the slow cooker with warm, soapy water.

"Thanks," she said. How thoughtful.

"No problem." Tom wiped his hands on the dish towel and smiled at her. She'd never entertained a man in her kitchen before, other than family. Shyness rose as he studied her. He exuded an aura of quiet vitality and strength. She was entranced and almost stepped closer.

"Well, guess I better go." He made no move to leave.

"Okay." She hesitated for a moment, and glanced up at him before turning to walk toward the door. Her awareness of him intensified, making her breaths shallow. He stopped near her by the doorway.

"Goodnight, Ann." His long, steady gaze mesmerized her. She forced herself to remain still.

[67]

"Goodnight, Tom." He walked out, turned to wave and climbed in his truck. She waved, shut the door, and leaned back against it. He caused such unexpected strong reactions in her. There should be a signal or warning inside her ahead of time so she'd know what to expect. It was impossible to control any of it, because she never knew what she'd feel or when. Now she understood her sisters' extreme responses to dating, and the attraction toward it. She'd entered unknown, fascinating territory.

CHAPTER SIX

THE TWO GIRLS were busy as usual on Saturday and still had Jim Cortland's cake to finish by afternoon. The day flew by as they worked to get everything done. After Jim picked up the order, they finished cleaning. In the office, they filled out the supply orders for Monday. When Ann left, Susan called out, "See you tomorrow at eleven."

"You bet."

Home at last. Ah, her chair. She could relax, put her feet up and not think about anything. Despite her intentions, her thoughts were full of Tom. Then the yawns began. She woke with a start at the sound of the telephone. "Hello?"

"Hi. Tom here."

"Hello." A smile spread across her lips while she stretched.

"I got Jesse to sleep and thought I'd call you."

"Does he cry about going to bed?"

"Not at all. He's great. He likes to turn in, probably because he's racing ninety to nothing while he's up." Tom laughed. "I have to tell you what Jesse said to my Grandma earlier. She came for a visit and Jesse stared at her while we talked. He asked her, 'Are you old?' My grandma laughed. 'I guess I am.' Jesse thought for a minute and said, 'I'm still new.' Boy, did we laugh."

Ann chuckled along with him and wished she'd seen his expression when he'd said it. She loved Jesse's face. Did he resemble his mother, or know much about her? She wanted to ask Tom about Judy, but couldn't imagine starting such a conversation without hurting him.

"So what did you do today?" he asked.

She told him various details then described Jim Cortland's cake and how she and Susan planned to visit his church in the morning.

"I know Jim. He's a friend of my Dad's."

"Have you ever gone there?" Perhaps he'd want to go with them.

"I visited once with my folks when I was a kid. I haven't been to church since shortly after Jesse's birth."

Wonder if he's mad at God. Maybe he's too busy.

"Oh. Why?" She couldn't help the question.

"Jesse's awful young to sit quietly so long. I didn't want to leave him in the nursery with someone I don't know. I can teach him what my parents taught me, and read his children's Bible to him right here. I need to be the one to answer his questions."

His pause dragged out and made her wonder if he'd continue. He sighed. "Church people seem to argue with each other, in my experience. They tell you you're wrong if you don't agree with them about everything. I don't like it."

His calm tone clashed with the decisive words. He sounded bitter. Had his wife's death hurt him too much? Her mind cast around for a response. "We didn't go to churches while I grew up, but how do you know they're all like that?"

[70]

"I don't. I'm being logical. How many denominations are there? Hundreds? In some places, I've heard they have separate black and white churches, as well as other ethnic groups. Maybe there's something wrong with the whole church thing. Otherwise, they'd worship and study together as fellow believers, wouldn't they?"

Oh, dear. She knew nothing about this. "Well, you've got a good point. I don't think we have separate churches in New York, though, do we? Maybe people get comfortable doing things a certain way, and they don't question it."

Tom emitted a short sarcastic laugh. "I think you're overly optimistic. I have a big problem with any kind of racism anyway, but to see it in a place which should be free of those attitudes, well, it really turns me off."

He sighed. "I'm sorry, I don't mean to sound harsh. Some things get me upset. I want Jesse's mind to stay free and unhampered. He's so open and friendly. I hate the thought of anyone putting cruel or hypocritical thoughts in his head. Or telling him his mother died because she must have done something wrong."

Her breath caught. *What?* "Did someone actually say that?"

"Yes. More than one person." Ann and Tom went quiet. Her stomach ached at the pain in his tone. Well, she'd wanted to know more about him and Judy, but hadn't expected anything like this. She drew in a deep breath.

"To your face?"

Tom's voice sounded constricted, as though speaking hurt him. "No. But it got told to me."

She listened to him breathe while dismay cycled through her insides.

He cleared his throat. "The people there knew Judy, so that's why we attended. I couldn't get over the shock, and I wouldn't go back. I won't let Jesse hear such things. And I've never told him she died right after delivery. He might blame himself."

Ann's eyes filled up and her own throat tightened. He'd endured so much. She swallowed hard to bring herself back in control. No wonder he harbored bitterness about church. She managed to speak. "I'm sorry...so sorry you heard such horrid words. I hope you don't blame God for what people say and do. I used to."

"I don't, but like I said, I want to be the one who answers Jesse's questions about God. I won't trust anyone else for it, other than my parents. Not after what happened."

How awful for someone to even think such a thing, especially a person who attended church. She could understand questioning God about a tragedy, but not saying hurtful words like those to other people. Anger rose, and she wished she could find the people and tell them how awful their words were. However, the damage was done. "I don't think Jim Cortland would ever say anything like that. But I understand your concern."

Tom remained quiet for a minute. "Thanks. I appreciate that."

"You're welcome." They were silent again. Though painful to hear, part of the gloom faded because he'd been willing to share it with her.

He drew in a breath. "I wonder if you'd like to spend tomorrow afternoon with Jesse and me. We could go to the park by the lake after you come back from services."

Her heart lifted, and she smiled. "Sure. How about if I buy some day-old bread to feed the ducks?"

"Good idea. It'll be fun. Give me a call when you're home, and we'll come and get you. It's supposed to be warm tomorrow, after our first chilly night. We may get light frost later, so I covered some of the garden vegetables after dinner."

[72]

"It'll be cold this early?"

"Yep. It's September. I always keep my eye on the weather."

Ann laughed. "Upstate New York. I guess I should be used to it by now. Anyway, I suppose it's kind of a preview of coming attractions."

"I agree. It gives everyone a heads up...us, the animals, the trees. My cat has quite a time keeping up with all the mice trying to move into the barn before the cold sets in."

"Ooh, a kitty. What kind is it?"

"A big silver tabby with green eyes and seven toes on both of his front paws. He's a great mouser and gentle with Jesse."

"What's his name?"

"Abner."

"Cute. We had a tiger kitty when I was growing up. And we had a tortoiseshell cat, too. I miss pets. They're such a comfort." She remembered how the cats would curl up on her bed at night. She'd been so thrilled the first time the tabby purred as a kitten. The same delight flooded her whenever she spied a cat.

"Can't you have one at your apartment?"

"Yes, but they charge you more. I'm not home much, and it doesn't seem fair to a pet to leave it alone most of the time."

Tom chuckled. "I guess you're right, although cats are pretty independent."

"True. I'd feel guilty, though."

"I wish more people were as thoughtful of animals." He paused and stifled a yawn. He sounded so cute. Ann pictured herself curled up on a couch next to him, head resting on his shoulder, as she and Jesse petted Abner.

She tried to imagine his living room and realized her heartbeat had increased. In her mind, she lifted her head and gazed into his eyes. Warmth flooded her. Oh, dear. She needed to calm down.

Tom said, "Guess I'll go clean up the kitchen. So, give me a call tomorrow when you're home, all right?"

"I will."

"Sleep well."

"You, too."

Ann let out a deep sigh. She admired the way he navigated such painful waters and retained his faith, though perhaps not in people. She leaned back in her chair and wondered about his interest in her. She was so boring compared to him. He expressed himself with much more ease and wasn't reserved. Ann couldn't fathom why he often observed her in a searching way, as though he wanted to ask her questions. She wondered what possible things he might want to learn about her. She hoped not everything.

CHAPTER SEVEN

THE NEXT MORNING Ann slept until almost ten. She hurried to dress and grab something to eat. The sun shone clear and bright after the cold night and small clouds scudded in a light blue sky. She could see her breath a little when she sat in the car and waited for it to warm up. Late summer was so weird. Sweltering one day, chilly the next. After she arrived, Ann stayed in her car while people strolled in. When she spotted Susan, she hurried to accompany her.

"Hey." Susan greeted her with a big smile. She studied Ann's expression and took her arm. "Don't worry," she joked. "They won't bite too hard, I promise."

"I know." Ann chuckled as they ambled in together. It appeared more like a home than a church. A large room with a lot of windows shone with the morning sun. Rows of wooden chairs were arranged in a semicircular pattern around a piano and chairs in the middle of the room. The sight of a few small amps, microphones, and guitars surprised Ann. Whenever she'd gone to churches for weddings or funerals, the inside area had been much more formal. Well, this would be interesting.

She and Susan chose seats near the back and smiled at the people who glanced their way. Susan waved at a person across the room. A happy buzz of muted chatter filled the church. Ann figured there must be around fifty attendees, all ages and a mix of colors. If Tom were here, he'd see not all churchgoers were the way he thought.

Jim Cortland stepped in from a side door with a woman she assumed must be his wife. Recognition flashed through her. She'd waited on her before and remembered her as sweet and patient. His wife settled at the piano while Jim sat on a chair and tuned a guitar. A younger man with a similar appearance to Jim made his way to another chair and picked up the second guitar.

I didn't expect this.

When they finished tuning up, Jim said, "Folks, let's clear our minds of concerns and think about our blessings as we play for you. We'll prepare our hearts to welcome whatever God has for us today." The piano started and the guitars joined in. It was a lovely, gentle instrumental and as it continued, relaxation spread through Ann.

She closed her eyes and remembered how she'd experienced the same peace after she first spoke with Jim. She basked in the welcome sensation. Disappointment rose when they stopped. She glanced up when Jim spoke.

"Let's pray." He bowed his head and remained silent for a few moments. "Father, please guide me to speak Your word clearly and deliver Your message to us for this day. Bless each heart and mind to receive Your truth, and give all of us ears to hear, and the strength to release our will and let Yours be done. Help us to become more like Your beloved Son, our earthly example. We ask this in Jesus' name. Amen."

Murmurs of *amen* sounded as she lifted her head. Earthly example? She'd never thought of that. What she understood of Jesus was his role as an important teacher who started the golden rule. She knew so little, and wondered if she'd understand the things Jim would say.

He scanned the room. "Good morning, everyone. I'm glad you're here. Let's sing."

His wife began a joyful tune while people clapped and sang with it. The song was unfamiliar to Ann, but she clapped along with the catchy melody, caught up in the liveliness. Some people raised their hands on and off during the music. She'd seen this before in a documentary about religion. Though unsure of the meaning for the action, it interested her.

When the first hymn ended, somebody started another one and the musicians followed, adding the accompaniment. This continued with each choice while Ann marveled at how it all flowed together. The last song held a jubilant, triumphant tone and made her want to stand up and cheer.

Ann startled when a few people jumped up and waved their hands. They shouted things she couldn't hear, since everyone sang with such energy. It both unnerved and fascinated her. Ann's parents always taught her to be reserved and quiet in public, but she found the obvious jubilation around her compelling.

Susan stood and clapped and sang with joy. Ann wished she were uninhibited enough to stand. Instead, she clapped, regarding everyone with curious interest. When the music ended and people sat back down, Jim set his guitar aside and stood up. He offered thanks for the "cleansing blessing" of the song service.

What a fitting way to describe it. She imagined the music driving away the dull, gray film of concerns and leaving behind a bright, shiny room of people ready to be filled with something better.

Jim cleared his throat. "I realize there are parts in Scripture we find difficult to understand." He let out a small laugh which got echoed by some of the listeners. "And I don't pretend to be able to explain it all. But there are enough simple truths to guide you your whole life. Starting with "you shall love God with all your heart, soul, mind, and strength, and your neighbor as yourself." What does it mean exactly? What does it look like?"

He scanned the room. "It looks like Jesus. It's how He lived, thinking of God first and His ways and listening to His guidance. It's a simple thing to say the words, isn't it? Yet, it's not easy to accomplish. But this is the way we're called to live. And we study the Word not only for ourselves, but so we can explain it to those who seek and need solid answers to their questions."

He stopped to take a sip of water and Ann's attention became diverted by the sound of a small thud followed by a child's loud whisper.

"Mommy, I dropped my truck."

Jim chuckled along with everyone and sent the child and the mother a fond look before he continued. "We're on the same path and can all learn from each other." He opened his Bible and told them, "Since we're working our way through the book of Matthew this month, let's open to chapter five, and you follow along as I read."

Ann didn't have a Bible, so she looked on with Susan. The chapter heading said, "Sermon on the Mount." He began and Ann followed with him. The sound of conviction in his voice paired well with words which resonated through her and lit up her mind. He paused a moment after the last lines.

"Pretty strong stuff. Not only are we to love our neighbor, but our enemies, too, and pray for them. A lot of people think this makes you a weakling, but the Scriptures say weakness is giving in to anger, fear, selfishness, and hate. A person who can control himself is greater than one who takes a city, according to the book of Proverbs. So, our idea of strength is not what God's is, and His is the correct one."

"Amen," a few voices responded.

Jim nodded. "Jesus says at the end of the chapter we are to be perfect as our heavenly Father is perfect. Many people have told me we can't. Now, Jesus wouldn't tell us to be something we couldn't be. So what does this word mean? Jesus talks about showing love to the just and the unjust equally, not loving only those who are your friends or family. So, it's in that sense that we can be perfect."

Ann marveled at the new thoughts percolating in her brain. She hadn't expected to be so stirred up by a church service.

Jim asked, "Would anyone like to be prayed for? Whatever the need is. Salvation, healing, strength or help, come up. Prayer group please join us."

Movement started toward the front of the room. What was happening now? Jim and his wife stood together and spoke in quiet tones to whoever stepped up to them. Then Jim and Evelyn and some of the other people who'd come forward put their hands on them one by one. They murmured prayers she couldn't hear.

What were they praying about? They all seemed calmer than she. She scanned the room. Susan and many others sat with heads bowed, she assumed in prayer. When someone returned to their seat, Ann noted the serene expression on those who'd been prayed for. Their countenance held...peace. Maybe she should be prayed for, but she wasn't a member.

More people moved forward. Her curiosity became displaced by a pull to join them. Ann sat still as an unfamiliar internal struggle began. Stay here. Go up for prayer. After a few long minutes, the tension inside her built up so much it startled her when Susan announced, "I'm going up."

Susan stood and waited with the others. The inner wrestling intensified. No, she wasn't getting up. She couldn't process any more internal changes. Ann remained seated, with her hands gripping the sides of the chair as though to keep it from moving forward. A decision had to be made. Go up or leave? She rose, hesitated for a moment, took a deep breath, and trudged toward the prayer line.

Ann stopped behind Susan and started to fret.

What am I doing? I don't know how to pray or what to ask for.

She chafed inside while the people ahead of her continued in quiet prayer.

Calm down. Breathe. Think.

Her mind drew a blank while she stood there. What should she ask for? Ann wished she could disappear. Susan stepped forward to receive prayer. Ann would be next. She tried to access the peaceful sensation again, but worry crowded it out. Minutes crawled by.

Susan turned, her eyes widening when she spotted Ann. Susan flashed a smile at her before heading back to her seat. Ann stepped up to the Cortlands. Jim asked her, "What do you need prayer for, Ann?"

Ann stood still and stared at him. She blurted out, "I'm not sure." She swallowed. "I'd like not to be so nervous and scared all the time."

"Well, those are good things to ask about," Jim reassured her.

Ann confessed in worried honesty, "I don't know how to pray."

Jim's voice was soft. "You know how to talk, so you know how to pray. That's all it is. You open your heart and mind to God and talk to Him. You don't have to say anything out loud, if it makes you nervous."

He and Evelyn placed gentle palms on her shoulders and other hands touched her upper back. People all around her prayed in quiet tones as Ann lowered her head, overwhelmed at the love and compassion she perceived.

A wave of gratitude washed through her and caused her eyes to fill up as she opened herself. Ann realized she'd hidden in shadows for a long time and the light of this unfamiliar freedom nearly overwhelmed her. A small part of her wanted to run back to the place of safety inside, but the rest of her clamored to embrace the new awareness.

As soon as she decided not to resist, her body relaxed and she spoke to God in her mind. *If you're there, please help me. I don't know how to really live. I'm always nervous about something, and I don't know what to do with my life. I want to be a good person, I try to be, but it's not enough. I want to understand what all this is. I want to understand myself. I want to know You, if it's all right with You. I'm not important, and I understand if I'm not very acceptable, but please hear me.*

She kept her head down as she emptied her concerns to God. Her breaths shook and her eyes filled with tears. Evelyn pressed a tissue into her hand. As Ann wiped her face, a light and free sensation grew in her, coupled with relief. She dabbed her eyes and spoke with grateful sincerity to the Cortlands and the people around her. "Thank you so much."

Jim said, "No need to do that. God's the one who hears and helps. Try to make time for prayer and study every day. You'll be surprised at what you learn."

Ann nodded, overcome, and breezed over to her seat. She could almost have flown.

Susan gave her a quick hug after she sat down. "You look contented."

"I am," Ann whispered back. Contented didn't do the inner change justice, but she had no words to describe it.

Ann's mind tried to process everything and put it in a recognizable context. Yet the experience stood alone, unconnected to anything familiar.

After the prayers, Jim spoke. "We have a surprise planned." He held a hand out to his wife. "Evelyn?"

She rose from the piano and took his hand. He cracked a smile. "Happy birthday, Evelyn. Thank you for being a wonderful wife and companion to me all these years."

Ann thought it was cute the way Evelyn almost glared at her husband, as if she wanted to kiss him and strangle him at the same time. The people around her clapped as two women who wore delighted smiles wheeled the cake out.

Evelyn's mouth dropped open. Jim laughed and began singing "Happy Birthday." Everyone joined in.

"Thank God we made such a big one," Susan whispered to Ann as they watched Jim and the two women cut it into pieces and pass them out. After they'd finished, a few people circled the room and held trash bags open to receive the paper plates and plastic forks.

Jim stood up.

"May God bless all of you as you go through the week. I hope to see as many of you as can attend the upcoming events we've planned. They're listed on the sheets of paper on the side table." Jim spoke a short closing prayer and asked for safe travel home for everyone. He turned to unplug his guitar as people meandered over and conversed with him.

Ann stood and steadied herself, placing a hand on the chair in front of her. She drew in a deep breath. "I want to get one of the papers."

Susan rose up and looped her arm through Ann's. She leaned in close. "Are you okay?"

"Yeah. A bit overwhelmed, but I'm good. I have a lot to think about." She patted Susan's hand. "Thanks for being here with me."

"I'm glad I was. You go ahead and grab a sheet. I'm going to say hi to some people I know." Susan wended her way over to a small knot of churchgoers.

Ann stepped to the table, picked up a paper, and read it. She noted dates and times listed for activities like food and clothing drives, volunteers needed for various helping projects in people's homes, and group visits to hospitals and the county jail.

She wondered if it would be scary to visit locked-up people or those who were horribly ill. Ann remembered the wrenching experience of visiting her grandmother in her last days at the hospital, and how little she'd been able to help her.

A hand touched her shoulder and Ann turned. Evelyn's sweet smile greeted her. "I'm so happy you and Susan visited today," she said in her soft voice. "Thank you for the wonderful cake you girls made. I love all your cakes."

"You're very welcome. And I'm glad I stopped in today, too."

"I hope you'll come and visit again soon."

"I will."

Evelyn gave her a warm hug. "God bless you, dear."

Ann smiled, and Evelyn walked toward a small animated group of chatting people. A quick fold of the sheet, and Ann slid it in her purse before turning to leave. At the doorway, she turned to take in the room once more. Unable to put a name to her experience or even explain it, nonetheless, she'd return.

[83]

CHAPTER EIGHT

ON HER DRIVE home, Ann glanced around at the bright blue sky, the few trees which showed early flashes of brilliant colors, and the strolling pedestrians. Something was different. It was as though her heart had expanded beyond herself, and now everything around her was somehow connected to her.

She marveled at all the internal changes, and the calm way she navigated them. At home, she changed into some slacks and a loose-fitting shirt and sweater. She ate a sandwich for lunch, and called Tom.

Ann sat in the living room waiting, and let her mind ponder what she'd experienced at church. Everything she'd heard and seen created warmth in the center of her being, and the rest of her curled near it like a cat on a hearth. At the sound of a knock, she rose, grabbed the loaf of day-old bread she'd bought for the ducks, and opened the door.

Tom stood with Jesse, both faces wearing smiles.

"Hi Annie, Annie, Annie Ann," Jesse sang to her. Tom laughed in delight. Ann beamed at him.

"Hi Jesse, Jesse, Jesse Jess," she chorused back. Jesse giggled and reached his hands up to her. She picked him up and his little arms wrapped around her. Tom's face softened into a fond expression, his eyes intent on her. Self-consciousness filled her and the strong awareness of Tom's presence hit her as she set Jesse back down.

"Let's go feed the ducks," she announced. Jesse reached for her hand and took his father's in the other. They ambled to the truck as Jesse talked in his animated way. Ann glanced at Tom, touched by his reaction to her.

She stayed quiet as they rode to the lake, content to listen to Jesse and Tom interact. She stared out the window at the blue sky and high clouds and her eyes scanned for any leaves with colors. What a beautiful world.

"Penny for your thoughts," she heard Tom say after a lull. She turned. Both Tom's and Jesse's gazes fastened on her as they waited at a stop light.

"It's so beautiful in the fall. I wish it were this way all year."

"Me, too," Tom said. "Even though harvest time is super busy for me, it's my favorite time of year for sure. Especially in a few weeks when the leaves are the brightest and most of my field work is done. I love to go outside with Jesse and take it all in. Know what I mean?"

Ann nodded. "Yes, I do. I sit on the porch on my days off and just stare instead of reading. So when is your outdoor work finished?"

"Almost everything will be harvested in the next weeks, and I'll plant the garlic and onions. Afterwards, I can relax a little and spend more time with Jesse." He paused as though to add something. He studied her with a steady gaze, and a car behind them beeped.

Jesse pointed. "Green light, Daddy."

"Oops." Tom drove forward. Jesse giggled and grinned up at Ann. She returned it and marveled at the sense of ease she had with Jesse, as though she'd always known him. She experienced such liveliness with him, as vibrant as when she was little herself and greeted each new experience with joyful amazement. She used to be a lot like Jesse. Only shy.

Tom parked near the shore and reached for Jesse as Ann climbed out with her loaf of bread.

"Here we are." Tom set Jesse down. "Don't go too far."

"Okay, Daddy." Jesse scooted toward the water.

Ann grinned at the energetic display. "He's adorable. And so well-behaved. You've done a wonderful job."

"Thanks, but he's a great guy on his own. Such a joyful fellow." Tom's gaze at Jesse touched Ann to her core. So much love in those eyes.

"Well, I think being loved, appreciated, and cared for makes anyone happy. So I still say you've done a great job."

Tom glanced down, a shy grin on his face. "Thanks. I try my best. He means everything to me. I can't imagine life without him."

Jesse sped along the shore, jumped up, and laughed while he circled back.

"I see ducks," he chirped as he raced to them.

"Well, let's feed them," Ann ruffled his hair, delighted at his excitement. She offered him a piece of bread. He grabbed her hand with his free one and pulled her towards the lake.

"Jesse," Tom admonished in a firm but gentle tone, "ask her to go with you, don't pull her."

"Sorry, Ann," Jesse stood still and regarded her. "Will you come with me?"

"Of course." Ann walked with him to the ducks, impressed with Tom's parenting skills. Jesse hopped up and down when they drew closer.

Tom chuckled and pointed at a big log near the shore. "Let's sit here and feed them."

"Can I stand by the water while you sit?" Jesse asked.

"Sure, pal. If we take your sneakers and socks off, you can even stand at the edge where the water is."

Jesse scampered over and parked on Tom's lap. Tom helped him remove his sneakers. Jesse peeled off his socks and tucked them in the sneakers before handing them over. He snuggled his head against Tom's chest a moment before he jumped down and sprinted to the shore with his piece of bread. Ann broke off some pieces and threw them to the nearest ducks. Jesse let loose a delighted squeal when a duck swam close to him and stretched its neck to gobble bread near the water lapping his toes.

Ann's attention drifted to Tom, and she met his steady gaze. For once she didn't glance away after a moment, but held his eyes and smiled. He returned it, and her breath caught. He was so handsome. Why did he want to date her? His interest might stem from how much Jesse liked her. She endured a disappointed twinge, secured more bread and held out a piece to him. "Want to feed them?"

"Sure." His voice sounded soft. He took the slice and let his fingers rest against the backs of hers for a moment. She bent her head to hide her warming cheeks and vulnerable eyes. His voice lowered. "You don't have to be afraid of me, you know."

Ann lifted her head and threw some pieces of bread before she took in a breath. She glanced over, glad his eyes were on the ducks and Jesse. "I know. I'm not afraid, really. I feel...I don't

[87]

know…different or something. Kind of like I'm scared, maybe because I'm tense and don't know what to do."

"You don't have to do anything. Just enjoy yourself. I don't mean to make you nervous."

She nodded at him, and they continued to throw pieces to the ducks. They laughed at Jesse's animated reactions when he scooted back for more slices and acted out the way the ducks stretched their necks.

"The big one won't share," Jesse dished out a momentary scowl, "so I throw his piece way far away so I can feed the other ones before he comes back."

"Pretty smart, pal." Tom flashed him a thumbs-up. Jesse copied the gesture to his father before he dashed to the shore.

"He's a sharp cookie for sure," Ann said.

"Judy was quick at figuring things out, too. But she was pretty shy. Jesse isn't shy at all. He says hello to everyone."

"Does he ask you much about his mother?" She hoped he didn't mind the question.

"Sometimes." His features and voice turned serious. He regarded the horizon and answered Ann in a quiet tone. "I've shown him pictures and told him all about her and how thrilled she was to have him."

"You must miss her terribly." Ann's voice lowered in compassion.

"I do." Tom continued to observe the sky. "She was my first love, and I'll always miss her and be sorry for all the times she never shared with Jesse and me. But as Mom says, Judy wouldn't want me to spend my life grieving for her, so I've worked hard to accept what happened."

Tom sighed and his gaze dropped down. "The hardest part was letting go of the sadness and how unfair it all seemed. I realized I had to get past it and be cheerful somehow." He stared up at his son. "Jesse's been my healing. He taught me to be happy again."

Ann struggled hard to stifle tears while she listened, but her efforts failed. Tom's eyes traveled back to her, and he straightened up and said, "Ann, I'm sorry. I didn't mean to make you cry."

"It's all right." She brushed her hands across her cheeks. "I'm just sad you went through it. I've only ever lost one person I loved. I felt such horrible grief when my grandma died, but at least she got to have good, long years and enjoy her family. I'm glad you have Jesse. He's so full of life and joy."

Tom grinned at his son. "He sure is." He patted her shoulder and pulled a tissue out of a packet in his shirt pocket. He gave a gentle smile and handed it to her. "Got to keep these around for little boys' noses."

She wiped her eyes and dabbed her cheeks. He stood up and stretched. "Let's walk along the water line and see if the ducks swim after us. Jesse'll get a kick out of it." He raised his voice a little, "Hey, pal, come put your socks and sneakers on and we'll walk by the shore."

"Okay," Jesse agreed and started towards them. "But can I feed them the rest?"

"Let's do that while we walk and see if they follow us." Tom sat back down, rubbed the bits of silt off Jesse's little feet and assisted him with his sneakers and socks.

"C'mon, Annie Annie Ann," Jesse held his free hand out to her. The three of them meandered along the shore and stopped every few feet to let Jesse throw bread. The ducks paddled behind, their legs churning to keep up.

The largest duck swooped ahead of another duck to grab the bread away from its outstretched beak.

"I see what you mean about the big guy," Tom said.

"Bad duck," Jesse reprimanded it with a frown. "Daddy, he stole the other ducky's bread."

"I know, buddy," Tom soothed. "Here, give Daddy a whole piece. I'll throw it way back there. Maybe it will take him a while to finish it while the others eat."

Tom threw the bread like a Frisbee and the big duck sailed after it. A few ducks started to follow but soon circled back when Jesse threw the last pieces in the water near them. He cheered when they finished before the big one returned.

Jesse jumped up and down. "You fixed it Daddy, you fixed it."

Tom picked him up, tossed him in the air and caught him. "And you made sure they all had a good lunch."

Tom grinned at Ann. A thought struck her. He probably wished Judy stood there instead of her. A sharp jolt of pain stunned her. She turned her face away as though to admire the lake and tried to let the beauty of the day fill her and remove the hurt.

The water and sky were so blue and endless, and the rhythmic sound of the slight waves as they washed against the shoreline created a peaceful music. They failed to wash away the painful, deflated sensation. It settled itself in her even though she tried to push it away. She sighed.

Tom asked, "Beautiful, isn't it?"

She answered in a manufactured bright tone, "It certainly is."

"Want to get some ice cream?"

Jesse exclaimed, "Oh, boy, ice cream."

"Sure." Ann walked back to the truck with them, relieved that Tom hadn't noticed her mood change.

"So did you have a good time at services this morning?" Tom drove toward the ice cream stand.

"Yes, it was so unusual. I've never been to a place quite like it." She remembered the serenity and joy. "I had a wonderful time."

"Unusual how?"

"I guess because it felt so alive and nothing like what I've been to before, but I haven't been to a lot of churches. So maybe it's not that unusual." She shrugged.

"My parents said something similar after they visited last time. They attend sometimes and always enjoy themselves."

"Why don't they go every week?"

Tom paused before he replied. "My Dad's family has gone to the same church for years and he thinks it's where he should stay a member."

"Oh." There were so many aspects about churches she didn't know.

"Here we are," Tom announced when he parked.

"Yay." Jesse sat up straighter and gazed out the window. "Mmm." He stared at someone walking by with a cone covered in sprinkles. "Daddy, can I eat one of those?"

"Absolutely. What flavor do you want?" Tom chuckled at his little boy and rubbed his hair.

"Chocolate and vanilla with chocolate sprinkles." Jesse's eager demeanor delighted Ann.

Tom's gaze rested on her. "How about you?"

Cones always dripped on her shirt. Not a good choice. She reached for her purse. "Chocolate malt milkshake."

Tom held up his hand. "My treat, all right?"

"Okay."

He exited, walked up to the line, and turned to wave at the two of them. She smiled at Jesse when he looked at her after they waved back.

"I love Daddy." Jesse's expression and words sent warmth through her.

"And he loves you so much." Ann touched the tip of his nose.

[91]

"Yeah. I'm his pal." Jesse nodded his head. He reminded Ann of a chipper little bird.

"I know you are." They sat together in companionable silence and waited for Tom.

"Here comes Daddy," Jesse proclaimed to her and clapped his hands.

Tom climbed in and handed out the treats. "Don't tell Grandma I got you a big-boy one."

"I won't," Jesse assured him while he worked on his cone.

"She doesn't like him to eat sweets?" Ann asked between sips.

"It's not that. We eat at my parent's house today. She makes us our Sunday dinner every week after chores. If Jesse's appetite isn't good, she gets disappointed. But that hardly ever happens. Right, Jesse?"

Jesse gave an emphatic nod and continued to work his way around the outside of the cone. His tongue caught a drip. "Thank you for the ice cream, Daddy."

"Yes, thank you, Tom. This is yummy." She let the frosty liquid thrill her taste buds.

Tom crunched the top rim of his cone. "You're both very welcome. Hits the spot, doesn't it?"

"Right here," Jesse patted his stomach, and then pointed at his mouth. "Here, too."

Tom and Anne chuckled and reached to pat his head at the same time. Ann drew back while a nervous laugh escaped her. Tom shot her a curious gaze and stretched a hand toward hers. He halted when his gaze took in her startled face. His brow crinkled while a puzzled air flickered over his features.

They finished their snacks, and Tom took the napkins and empty cup over to the trashcan then hopped in the truck. "Guess I better drop you off now. We need to head back and do chores before we go to my Mom and Dad's. Did you have fun?"

"Yes, thank you. I did." Until the sad reality hit.

"Me, too," Jesse added and smiled at Ann. "You love ducks, Annie?"

"You bet I do. And swans. They're so pretty."

"What's swans?"

As Ann answered Jesse and described them to him, she glanced often at Tom. He drove and didn't speak much and his countenance appeared pensive. Maybe his mind traveled back to the happier days when Judy rode places with him. Did he think of Judy's face whenever he looked at hers? Her stomach began to ache, and she pushed the thoughts away. He liked her and so did Jesse. Most of today had been wonderful.

CHAPTER NINE

AFTER TOM AND Jesse dropped her off, Ann decided on a walk. Her mind wandered over the different emotions of the day and fastened on her experience at church. Something inside her changed, or opened up today. An awareness of the life force in the trees and the earth filled her in a manner she hadn't experienced since childhood. She stopped to enjoy the antics of two squirrels on a tree branch cracking nuts.

She continued her stroll, her thoughts full of wonderings. According to the Bible, God provided and cared for the entire earth. God's love for everyone and everything captivated her focus. The fact that He loved humans even if they were awful puzzled her. The rest of nature was innocent, blameless and worthy of love. And so many people were wonderful. But what about all the bad things humans caused? And still God loved them? A difficult concept to understand.

Her thoughts became interrupted when she glanced around and realized she didn't recognize the street she walked on. Her eyes darted in all directions, but nothing familiar appeared.

Where on earth am I?

She resisted the sudden flash of panic.

I'm not lost. Don't worry. Keep walking.

A beautiful leaf with mixed colors lay on the sidewalk. She picked it up, and twirled it while ambling along. A wiry man with dark, slicked-back hair and a large bruise below his t-shirt sleeve sat on a porch just ahead of her. He lit a cigarette and asked, "Nice day, isn't it?"

"Yes." she gave him a bright smile. "Can you tell me what street this is?"

"Sure. West Lincoln." He kept his eyes on her, took a long drag and blew out blue-gray smoke. His expression, intense and predatory, made her uneasy. "What's your name?"

"Ann." She accelerated her pace and at the end of the block glanced back to be sure he hadn't followed. He was standing now, as he smoked and scrutinized her. Ann turned the corner with a swift step. She darted periodic glances behind her while she hurried down the sidewalk.

After a few blocks she recognized a gas station she'd gone to before and sighed in relief. Her stomach rumbled. The thought of something scrumptious for dinner compelled her. At the small market near her apartment building, she bought supplies.

Ann returned home and walked straight to the kitchen. Sautéing boneless chicken breasts with garlic, onion, and mushrooms, she inhaled the aromas rising from the pan. She boiled, cooled, and sliced potatoes, humming along with the radio. In a casserole dish, she alternated layers of everything she'd prepared, poured on some cream and chicken broth, topped it with cheese and slid it into the stove.

While her meal cooked, she straightened up the apartment and started a load of laundry. When the food smelled ready, Ann

[95]

opened the oven door. The cheese topping had melted and turned light brown. The cream, broth and cheese had created a bubbly sauce, not too thick or thin. Yummy.

The phone rang after she'd completed dinner clean-up. "Hello?"

"It's me," Tom said. "What are you up to?"

His voice sent a thrill through her. "Nothing much. Just finished cleaning the kitchen."

"Jesse's staying with my folks tonight, so I thought we'd get something to eat."

"Darn. I ate already." Ann frowned, wishing she'd known.

"How about coffee and dessert instead?"

"But it's not a good replacement for dinner."

"I had dinner, but we eat so early on Sundays, I always have something later. Dessert or coffee's okay."

"How about this? I have leftovers from tonight, and different kinds of tea. Why don't you come over here for a while?" *Please say yes.*

"Sounds fine to me. I'll start over now if it's all right."

"Sure." Delight swirled through her.

Ann spooned some of her casserole onto a dish for him and rushed to fix her hair and check her clothes. She stared at herself in the mirror. "He's lonely without Jesse, and they both like you. Calm down."

She grimaced at her reflection, stuck out her tongue, and laughed. Striding to the kitchen, she popped the dish into the microwave, set it on warm, and breezed over to wait in her chair. When the doorbell rang, she bolted up to answer.

"Hi." Tom smiled. Could he get any cuter?

"Hi. Come in."

"Thanks. I do believe I will," Tom responded in a playful tone and sauntered inside.

Ann giggled as she led the way to the kitchen. She picked up the teakettle and brought out a basket of teas. "I've got the casserole heating up. I've gotten out of the habit of cooking over the last year. We've been so busy expanding our client base. But I decided I wanted something tasty tonight. I'm inspired to cook when the nights are cooler."

"I know what you mean." Tom sat down and thumbed through the tea assortment. "After fall really hits, you start craving those comforting meals. Stew, chili—"

"Chicken and dumplings, potato soup..."

They shared a laugh. She poured them each a cup of hot water and they slid the teabags in. Ann loved the way the clear liquid changed color as the tea infused but looked at Tom instead. His well-defined hand dipped the teabag. He had such thick eyelashes. The oven dinged and halted her perusal.

Ann set the plate of food in front of Tom.

"This looks delicious." Tom leaned in and inhaled. "What is it?"

"I invented it. Guess I should think of a name."

He tasted a forkful and nodded his approval. "How about 'Annie's Famous Chicken?'"

She giggled. "It's not famous. This is the first time I've made it."

"It's already famous with me." He took another bite.

"Glad you like it." How gratifying to have nothing else to do but gaze at him and sip her tea.

When he finished, Ann asked, "Why don't we sit in the living room? I'll wash these later."

Ann set the dishes in the sink and followed Tom out. He plunked on the couch, and she took a seat in her favorite chair kitty-corner to him. An end table stood beside it with a stack of books. Tom relayed funny anecdotes Jesse said to his parents about the ducks and the "big hoggy one." They both laughed.

Tom's expression grew serious when he leaned forward. "Why did you get sad all of a sudden when we were at the lake? Right before we left, and you looked out at the horizon? You were so lighthearted up until then. Did Jesse or I say or do something to upset you?"

Oh, no. An uncovered, transparent sensation flooded her insides. It unnerved her how he'd noticed. She didn't want to reveal the thought that sparked her unhappiness.

"Well, I..." Her cheeks flushed with heat.

"What?" Tom's curiosity changed to concern. "It's all right. You can tell me."

No, she couldn't. Ann fidgeted with her hands and shifted in her chair. If she told him, he'd have to deny it to spare her feelings. Even if she assured him she understood, he'd see how it saddened her, and he'd be uncomfortable around her. She didn't wish to lie. What should she do? Ann rose from her seat and paced.

"What is it?" Tom stood. "What did I do?"

"Nothing...nothing...it's, it's..." Ann stopped in front of him. She didn't want to hurt him, but decided to speak the truth. He probably wouldn't come around anymore, but it would be unfair not to tell him she knew how things were. "It's only something sad I realized."

His brow furrowed while his eyes carried out a frantic search of her face. Ann swallowed past the lump in her throat. "I figured while I watched you and Jesse together, you probably wished you were there with Judy, not me."

Tom's concerned expression paled to shock, and he slumped back down. Ann hoped he wasn't too distressed with her. She imagined his agony at having his wife brought up at all, much less twice in one day.

She trudged to her seat. "I'm sorry. I know how hard it must be to speak about her. I didn't mean to cause you pain."

Ann couldn't see his face. His head slanted down as one of his palms pressed against his forehead. She waited and fidgeted with her fingers, stomach aching. He dropped his hand and glanced her way. What she wouldn't give to be able to read his thoughts. He raised his head.

"I thought you understood." His eyes studied hers.

After moments passed and he'd said nothing more, she asked, "Understood what?"

He sighed and pressed his lips together. "I said I missed her and always will. It won't change. We miss the people we love who die ahead of us. I don't mind at all if we talk about her. We do at home. It's better that way."

Tom fixed her with a steady, expectant expression. "I told you I'd worked through the sadness and regret. I did that so you'd know." He hesitated and contemplated her with an intense gaze. "I'm not searching for a substitute or a replacement. For that matter, I wasn't even looking. I like you, Ann. You."

The unexpected declaration launched her into confusion. Her heart raced, and she trained her vision on the floor. She'd been all prepared to assure him of her understanding. She'd planned to say, of course you wish she were here. Don't feel bad about it, et cetera, et cetera. Now her mind went blank.

What should she say? The way his eyes probed hers, what did it mean? The silence grew heavy between them. He probably expected her to raise her eyes to him and speak, but she couldn't bring herself to do either. His sigh echoed through the stillness.

"I guess I'd better go. Sorry if I upset you." He'd walked down the hall before she stood up.

"Wait, please." He turned around, strode back and stopped a short distance from her. She cleared her throat and stared at her shoes, her senses so heightened she could pick out every tiny detail. "I like you too, Tom."

When she managed to peek upward, gentle eyes were fixed on hers.

"May I kiss you?" he asked, just above a whisper.

She trembled and blurted out, "I'm scared."

Tom stepped forward, drew her to him and leaned his head down against the top of hers.

Her tears fell as her anxiety escalated.

He led Ann to the couch and guided her down, his arm around her shoulders. He gently rocked her while she covered her face with her hands and wept.

"Tell me what you're feeling." His voice sounded so tender it intensified her tears. He held her tighter and murmured, "Oh, sweetie."

"I'm so scared," she sobbed. Words poured out of her. "I don't want to hope, don't want to be hurt. It's too hard. I couldn't stand it."

She burrowed her head on his chest, and the fears she'd harbored for years buffeted her. All the recent shifts and changes in her life rose up before her like a mountain she'd never be brave enough to climb. She'd have to sink back to the familiar safety of the shadows.

"I'm scared, too." This admission from him broke her even more. Her focus shifted from her own fear to an awareness of Tom's vulnerability. How courageous he was. How could she risk hurting him? Desperation swept through her. She wanted to run. With a shock, she realized she wanted to run to *him*. Her trembles eased.

The gentle pressure of his head against hers, his arms around her, put her at ease enough to admit, "I've never been kissed before."

"You don't have to if you don't you want to." His hand stroked her hair.

Ann wiped her face on her sleeve and sighed. Warmth surged through her, and she let herself relax. "I want you to kiss me."

She raised her head to look into his steady, deep eyes. His gaze dropped to her mouth. He dipped his head, her eyes closed, and their lips met. Tentative at first, the caress deepened as her shyness receded. Ann stretched her arms up around his neck and shoulders. His firm strength sent a thrill down her back.

The fingers of her right hand explored his hair. The kiss grew and intensified. Instead of being satisfied by it, the longer it continued, the more she wanted.

He stopped and held her a forearm's length from him. She opened her eyes and blinked away the daze. His magnetic expression drew her, and she leaned into him again and met his lips. He soon ended it and rested his head against hers.

Her emotions got the better of her and tears flowed. He pulled back and studied her.

"What is it?" He wiped her cheeks with his thumbs while he cradled her face.

"I don't know. I think I'm...really happy." She reached to touch his hair, then his features as if to memorize him with her hands.

Their lips met again, and the kiss bloomed into a deeper level of fervor. When he pulled away, Tom spoke softly against her cheek. "We have to slow this down."

"Why?" She yearned to stay close to him.

"This is new to you. You need time to sort it out." Ann opened her mouth to protest and Tom placed a gentle finger on her lips. "I'm thinking of you. I'll go home and phone when I get there."

Ann wished she were as stable as Tom. She floated inside and couldn't think straight. She stared at him, her mind still dazed. Tom laughed and embraced her before he rose.

She followed him as though she'd leave with him. He turned after he opened the door, cupped her chin, tipped it up, and gave her a soft kiss. "I'll call you."

Ann stood as the door closed, and her body swayed. Moments later to the closed door, she said, "Okay."

She turned in slow motion, made it to the chair and plopped down. Wow. What an incredible day. Nothing was the same anymore, nothing at all. She experienced gratitude mixed with some apprehension. Could she handle this?

A line from an old song her grandmother would sing played in her head. "What a difference a day makes, twenty-four little hours." Quite an understatement. Ann laughed. She closed her eyes and replayed the sensation of his kiss and his tender concern for her. Time melted away as she relived all the moments with him. The phone rang.

"Hello?"

"Hi. Are you still nervous about this?" His voice held a smile.

She laughed. "I'm not scared now. It's more like I'm floating. So much has happened to me today, so fast, and I don't feel normal anymore...I really don't know what to expect or what to do."

"I have no expectations. You be you and I'll be me and we'll go from there. And Jesse will, of course, be Jesse." They laughed. "Jesse's adored you from the beginning. He mentions you constantly and not because of his cake."

"Is it the reason you liked me? Because Jesse did?"

"Nope. I liked you from the first time I saw you. Crying and covered with cake and frosting. How about you?"

"Me, too, but I didn't realize how much, because I thought you were married until your mother came to pick up the cake. Even then, I never figured I'd be in a relationship, or someone like you would be interested in me." She sighed and smiled.

"Why did you think *that*?" He sounded surprised.

How much should she tell him? "Boys were cruel to me. My weight, my braces, being shy. I sort of gave up on the whole thing. Especially after I went through my sisters getting their hearts broken. I was really surprised when you asked me out, because you're so open and friendly and handsome, and I'm plain and...boring."

"You honestly think that about yourself?"

"Yes. All I do is work and come home, read, and sleep. Well, I draw sometimes, and cook."

Why am I saying this?

"I can see I've got my work cut out for me." Tom sighed.

"What do you mean?"

"Somehow I'll have to show you you're not plain or boring. You're a lovely, interesting woman. Say it for me."

Ann stayed silent, uncomfortable.

"C'mon," he encouraged her. "Say it, please."

"Oh, dear...I'm a lovely, interesting woman," she recited in a quick monotone. Was this true? Did he think of her in those terms?

"I don't hear much conviction. Try again."

"Tom, do I have to?"

"Yep. Let's hear it."

She took a deep breath. "I am a lovely, interesting woman."

"Much better. And it's true, Ann. It's what I see when I'm with you."

She closed her eyes and let go of the familiar normal of lonely nights alone, all the years of not expecting anything more. Tears of joy seeped through and left warm trails on her face. She floated above her old life as though she were in a hot air balloon watching the former landscape slip away.

Please God, let this all be real.

Tom's quiet voice in her ear made her picture his face when he'd bent to kiss her. "I think we should say goodnight now, sweetheart." He chuckled. "It's been quite a day."

"The understatement of the decade. Mine, anyway." Ann smiled.

"I'll call you tomorrow. Goodnight. Sweet dreams."

"You, too. 'Night." Ann sat in her chair for a time and let herself float and remember. No dream could be sweeter than this day.

CHAPTER TEN

The next day, everything wore a shine. Even the bakery appeared beautiful in the morning sun. Ann stepped out of her car and gazed around. When did the world get so marvelous? God sure knew how to create.

"Morning," Ann sang out to Susan when she walked in. Raspberry and vanilla aromas filled the air.

"Hey, you're chipper today." Susan grinned at her and turned back to the mixing machine.

"Yes. The world is new, and so am I." Ann surprised herself with the declaration. She'd never been one to share deep emotions easily, even with Susan.

"I like the sound of those words." Susan stopped her work to study Ann for a moment. Her face relaxed into a smile. "Praise God."

Ann's happiness surged and she strode over and gave Susan a hug—another action she didn't do often. "I think my heart grew a few sizes yesterday."

Susan returned the embrace and laughed. "I'm so thrilled for you. I've prayed for your happiness for years."

The bell sounded and the girls broke apart. They exchanged fond glances before Ann stepped out front, and the day began.

AFTER WORK, ANN rushed to get home. She'd fix some dinner and spend the evening on the phone with Tom. While she prepared her meal, ate and cleaned up, her thoughts danced back and forth. She'd imagine Tom and Jesse in the barn or their house, then images of Tom's kisses and all the emotion they evoked would hit. Anticipation of his call made it hard to settle down and wait.

The phone rang, and Ann grabbed it. "Hello?"

"Is there a lovely, interesting woman named Ann available?"

"She stepped out. You'll have to make do with me." Ann grinned.

"Very funny. Make do? I thought I asked you not to think of yourself that way."

She settled into her chair. "Okay, the lovely, interesting Ann is back."

"There you go." He chuckled. "How are you tonight?"

"Right now I'm sublime."

"And playful. Wish I were with you." He let out some breath.

"Me, too." She closed her eyes and imagined him next to her. "So, tell me how you are."

"Good and tired. Dad and I made the barns ready for winter. Kind of the equivalent of fall cleaning, I guess." She listened to the chores they'd done and reveled in the sound of his voice as her mind created mental pictures of him at work. No wonder his neck and shoulders were so strong. "I got a big, ugly bruise on my arm from bashing it on the barn doorway. Jesse says it's shaped like a rooster."

Ann giggled. Then she remembered the strange man with the bruised arm. "I saw a guy with an arm bruise yesterday when I went for a walk and got lost. Maybe he's been doing barn work, too."

"You were lost? In town? Where were you?" Tom sounded worried.

"Apparently I was on West Lincoln, according to what he told me. His attitude was weird. It made me nervous." She remembered how afraid she'd been at the thought he might follow her.

"Why did he make you nervous?"

She paused to think. "I guess it was the way he stared at me and asked my name, as if he had the right to stop me if he wanted to. I didn't like it."

"Don't take long walks alone, okay? I don't want anyone to hurt you."

Her eyes widened at his unexpected reaction. "Nobody's ever bothered me before. I'm sure he didn't mean anything by it."

"You don't know how some people are. Please promise me you won't walk around by yourself anymore. If you want to take a stroll, call me, and I'll go with you."

She laughed. "You're silly. I wouldn't bother you for something so little."

"It's not a bother, and it's not little to me. I'm serious."

The firmness in his voice seemed out of place to her. "You are, aren't you?"

"Absolutely. I want you to be careful."

She wondered if his over-concern about her safety stemmed from the loss of Judy. It wouldn't sound kind to say it, so she stayed silent.

[107]

"And don't think I said it because Judy died," he added as though he read her mind. She let out a small sound of shock and he laughed. "That's what you thought, isn't it?"

"Actually, yes." He always saw through her. How did he do it?

"Well, it's not why. But losing Judy did make me more aware of being cautious." He paused a moment. "I used to be kind of unconcerned about possible problems. I figured if I worked hard and did my best everything else would work out. Judy thought the same way too, and didn't think she needed to go to the hospital for Jesse's birth."

How odd. "I didn't realize anyone still had babies at home."

"You'd be surprised. Judy was born at home and thought it would be a more memorable experience. Everything checked out, and we had a good nurse, but Judy's bleeding went beyond her ability to fix. After Jesse was delivered, Judy seemed all right, weak but so thrilled. Then she started bleeding so fast, by the time we got her to the hospital, she was already gone." Ann pictured the horror of the scene and closed her eyes in pain.

He remained silent for a moment. "Sometimes you need to pay attention to signs like your uneasiness. I had the same sort of feeling. I thought we should've gone to the hospital before the birth, but Judy insisted he be born at home. I think you should act on it when you get those feelings."

"Where do you suppose they come from?"

"I believe they're warnings from God. We just don't listen enough."

Ann pondered his answer. "Well, maybe if people listened better, fewer bad things would happen. Animals seem to pay attention. They hardly ever get hurt in natural disasters unless they're trapped and can't escape. I always wondered about it.

Scientists tell you it's because of one thing and spiritual people will say it's something else."

"True. And sometimes the same folks who say those feelings come from God will also tell you everything happens for a reason. So why get the feeling if what's going to happen is supposed to happen anyway? It's something I wonder about a lot."

They were both silent before Tom added, "Someone at Judy's funeral told me everything happens for a reason. I know she meant well, but all it did was upset me and make me wonder what possible reason there would be for her to die and never even hold Jesse." Ann imagined how bleak and heavy the day must have been for him. *Oh, Tom.* She wished she could block out all his painful memories.

"My mother knew how the statement made me feel, and she told me most things happen because of our own decisions and choices. She said not to blame God for it, but to ask Him to help me bear it."

Silence stretched out as Ann swallowed and took a breath. "I'm so sorry you went through all of it."

"I know, and I'm glad for the time that's passed. The first year was pretty bad, and one day my mother stared at me and said, 'Thomas Andrew Tillman, you don't honor Judy's memory by all this moping. If she were here now she'd say the same thing to you. Part of Judy is always with you in Jesse. Wake up and live the life you've got and stop thinking about the one you wanted.' After that, I worked through my feelings and concentrated on being the kind of father Jesse needed."

"How did you work through it?" She hoped he didn't mind her questions, but she wanted to understand this part of him.

"I prayed a lot. I read some books about dealing with grief and let myself cry when I was sad, and accept it when I was angry. I

[109]

tried not to run away from the emotions. I'd take flowers to her grave and come home and talk to her pictures. I'd tell her how upset I was at the way she didn't listen to me and go to the hospital. Maybe it sounds silly, but it helped."

"No, not silly at all. You needed to let it out somehow."

"Exactly. After a while, I realized it didn't hurt so much to mention her, and now I can even joke about some of the goofy things she did." He paused. "She's in my memory like anyone else I love. She used to exist only as my dying wife who I didn't ever want to let go of. But now she's in my mind as a whole person who I love and remember as she was."

Ann cried in silence while she listened to him. The depth of pain he'd struggled through and endured with bravery staggered her. She tried to hide her tears but her breath caught during a quiet moment.

"Oh, sweetie." His voice held such compassion, it made her cry harder.

"I'm sorry. It's all so sad." She took in some air.

"I know."

Ann could hear the tightness in his throat and compelled herself to stop crying. After her breathing evened out, he asked, "Better?"

"Yes." She wiped her eyes and settled down. "I like your whole name. It fits you. Thomas Andrew Tillman."

"I'm pleased with it. What's your full name?"

"Ann Carol Shaw. Pretty plain, huh?"

"It's short and sweet, like you."

"My, you're good." She giggled.

"Why, thank you, my dear... Well, time to grab some shut-eye, I think. We both have an early start. I might stop in around lunchtime and say hello if I get the chance. I need to buy a tractor part in town. Is it a slow time for you?"

"Usually, but I can never tell from one day to the next. Sometimes it crawls around noon, and other times we're swamped. We don't have any big orders lined up, so it should be a good time."

"Good. I'll probably see you tomorrow. Goodnight, Ann Carol Shaw." The merry tone in his voice delighted her.

"Sleep well, Thomas Andrew Tillman."

As she lay in her bed later, she whispered to God, her head under the sheet. "I'm so used to protecting myself from people and relationships. And getting hurt, like Tom did. I want to stop shielding myself. I won't get close to you or Tom unless I do. It's scary how deep emotions go, but I need to learn not to fear them. I don't ever want to hurt Tom. Help me learn a better way to live, please."

THE NEXT MORNING rolled by, smooth as a marble across glass. Ann and Susan followed their usual hectic routine, yet with a light heart everything seemed easier to Ann. The closer the hours marched to noon, excitement rose in her at the prospect of seeing Tom. At 11:52, he pulled in. Susan had gone to the office to call in a supply order. Not another customer in sight. *Goody.* Tom strode into the bakery and smiled at her as he approached.

"Hi, sweetie." Her cheeks warmed and he grinned. His presence created such powerful emotions in her.

"You're too cute," he declared and embraced her. They kissed with tender intensity. The world faded, and only the two of them were in it.

Susan called out, "Did anyone pick up the order of cupcakes yet, Ann?"

They broke apart, and Tom stroked her cheek before he made his way to sit at the counter across from where she stood. Ann called back, "Yes, they did."

"Did you tell her about us?" He reached for one of her hands and held it.

"Not yet. I didn't want to jinx it." The admission embarrassed her.

He raised an eyebrow. "You're superstitious?"

"No, just a scaredy-cat." She grinned. "I thought she'd worry, and think I'd be less focused at my job. She's so serious about this place."

"More than you?"

"Yeah." She nodded and lowered her voice. "I work this hard mainly for her. She's my best friend and always dreamed about running her own business."

"What about you? Is this what you want?" He leaned forward.

Ann hesitated a moment. "Well, I love to bake and cook. When we graduated, and she wanted to open a bakery, I thought it would be a good idea. I needed some sort of career."

"Hmm." Tom studied her features.

"What?" She tilted her head.

"It's definitely not your dream."

Ann shrugged. "I usually think of it as her business. She's always coming up with ideas. It's her passion."

"What's your passion?" The question made her cheeks grow hot. He shook his finger at her and teased, "That's not what I meant."

Ann laughed at the admonishment on his face.

He asked, "What do you wish you were doing instead of the bakery?"

"Easy answer. Artwork." Her quick response was followed by his chuckle.

"Did you paint the sign out front?" He pointed outside.

"Yes…How did you know?"

"It's similar to the style on Jesse's cake."

How perceptive. "I'm surprised."

"Why, because I'm a farmer?" Tom raised his brows and grinned.

"Of course not. People who come in here all the time never mention the style of the sign looking like the one on the cakes. That's why, silly."

They shared a laugh. Tom moved his hand back when Susan breezed in.

"Hello. Where's your little boy?"

"He's with my mother right now." Tom stood up. "Well, guess I better get going. I've gotta pick up a part. Talk to you later."

He glanced at Ann, nodded to them both and left. Ann returned his wave.

"Didn't he buy anything?" Susan asked.

"No. He stopped in to see me." She took a deep breath. "Susan, we're dating."

"Really?" Susan beamed. "That's wonderful."

Ann's shoulders relaxed. "Good. I figured you'd be worried."

Susan's eyes widened. "Why on earth would I be? He seems like a good guy."

"Well, I thought you'd be afraid I might concentrate less on work."

"Maybe you should. You don't love it the way I do."

Ann stared at her in shock, and Susan burst out with a laugh. "Did you think I didn't see it? After all these years of knowing you?"

"Well, I figured...I'm not sure what I thought." How embarrassing.

"You were probably sure you did a good job of hiding it, but your face is as readable as a clock."

"It is?" Ann's eyebrows stretched up.

"Yes, it is, to anyone who understands you." Susan patted her shoulder. "You need to enjoy yourself more."

Did Tom and Susan understand her more than she did herself?

Susan took Ann's arm. "Hey, we've got a minute. Come in the office for a sec."

Susan gestured at the couch. "Sit down." She retrieved something from the desk drawer. "This is for you." She placed a hardcover Bible in Ann's hands. "It has side tabs to make finding each book easier. Do you like it?"

"How wonderful. What a thoughtful gift." Ann leafed through the pages.

"In the back are study maps and a good concordance, so you can look up word meanings. It's like the one I keep in my apartment."

Ann stood and gave her a big hug. "Where should I start?"

"With the book of Matthew and work your way through the gospels. You'll get acquainted with Jesus."

"I want to." The bell rang. Ann set the Bible on the desk, and gazed at it a moment before they went back to work.

Ann's emotions ran cheerful and energetic all day. On her way home, she stopped at a store and bought herself lamb chops, broccoli, and supplies to make twice-baked potatoes. While the meal cooked, she perched at the table, wrote her name in her Bible, and began to read. The rich smell of the meat and warm cheese aroma from the potato filled the room. She wished Tom and Jesse could eat with her tonight.

After she finished and cleaned up, Ann snagged the Bible, sat in her chair and continued the book of Matthew, savoring the words as much as she'd relished her dinner. Halfway through, the phone rang.

"Hello?"

"Hi, sweetie. I got Jesse to bed and wanted to hear your voice."

She leaned back and smiled. "Hi."

"How was your day?"

"Red-letter. Susan gave me a Bible. It's got maps and tabs for finding the books, and all sorts of good stuff." She ran her hand over the cover.

"Mine doesn't have tabs. It has maps, though. Jesse and I like to look them over. I also use my study Bible. Read anything yet?"

"Yep." She opened the Bible. "Susan told me to start with Matthew and continue through the four gospels."

"Good advice. You should keep a pen and paper next to you and jot things down when they jump out at you. It helps if you think of questions, too. You can write them down."

"Hey, what a good idea. And I'll ask you or Susan the questions."

"I won't have all the answers, but I'll do my best."

"I told Susan we're dating and she was glad. She thought I was funny to be surprised by her reaction and said I needed to have more fun." Ann stopped to remember. "Susan already knows I don't love the business like she does, because she said my face is as readable as a clock."

Tom let loose a hearty laugh.

"What? That's what she said." Why was it so funny?

"She's right. I can practically read your mind by your expression. And your eyes."

That's how he managed it. "Well, you two are the only people who've ever said that."

"It's because you keep everyone at arm's length. Except Susan and me, I guess." He chuckled. "And Jesse. Such a careful girl. I'm glad you let me in."

She smiled and pictured his gaze, steady and deep. Yearning ached through her.

I wish he were here. "Me, too."

"Are you? I've been afraid you'd resent me for upsetting your well-ordered life."

"Upset all you want." She giggled.

"Ah-ha, so I have upset your life. I knew it."

"Yes, you have. And I like it."

He laughed. "And I like your honesty."

They conversed until they were exhausted.

"I'd better go to bed before I pass out in the chair," Tom said. Ann yawned so hard she thought her jaw would break.

"Me, too."

"Get to sleep, my girl. I'll call tomorrow."

The next day Ann's mind focused on thoughts of Tom to the exclusion of her usual efficiency. She didn't want Susan to guess why her performance wasn't up to its normal standard. It might make her negative about Tom, though Susan rarely became annoyed with anyone. Ann drank two cups of coffee, but by eleven she moved at a snail's pace.

Susan peered at her. "Are you sick?"

"No. I'm pretty tired today."

"Go ahead and lay on the cot in the office for a while. It's slow now and the orders for later are put up."

"You're sure you don't mind?" The thought of a nap sounded heavenly.

"Of course not. Some sleep will perk you up."

"Make sure you call me if you need me." Ann trudged in the office and closed the door. She stretched out on the couch and listened to the hypnotic hum of the ceiling fan. Relaxation seeped through her limbs. She curled onto her side.

Ann woke and glanced at the clock. Wow, an hour and a half later. She smoothed her hair and rubbed her eyes before going out.

"Hi," she greeted Susan. Ann stretched her back and arms. "Thanks for letting me nap. Guess I needed it."

"Tom said the same thing. He stopped in a while ago."

"Why didn't you wake me up?" Ann filled with instant disappointment.

"He told me not to, and that it was his fault you're so tired because he kept you up last night talking. He'll call you tonight. I told him you'd be home earlier than usual since we don't have extra orders."

"We don't?" Anticipation brought her fully awake. He might come over later.

"Not until tomorrow, nope."

"Well, sometimes we get last-minute orders."

"Unless it's some huge thing, I'll handle it." Susan delivered a decisive nod, and added, "Hey, guess what? I had a cool idea to help the rat dilemma. Instead of throwing out stuff we don't sell, I decided to donate the cake to the pantry downtown. They take baked goods and perishables. I called, and they said it would be appreciated. Wish I'd thought of it before."

"Wonderful. I hate throwing away food. It's so wasteful." The bell sounded and Susan headed out front.

They finished by six and Susan smiled at Ann. "Just like I figured. See you in the morning."

"Bright and early." They waved and parted for the day.

At six thirty, Ann's phone rang. "Hello?"

"Hi." Tom's voice sounded chipper. "Did Susan tell you I came by earlier?"

"She did." Ann slid into her chair, closed her eyes and pictured his face.

"So, can I take you out to dinner?"

She hesitated. He'd grow stressed over all this extra expense.

He asked, "Are you too tired?"

"No, I'm fine." How should she begin the subject?

"Well, it's something. So tell me."

"Okay. You've got Jesse to provide for, and now you keep paying for food and treats when you take me out, plus the gas to drive into town. I don't want to cause you any stress or hardship."

Tom chuckled. "Well, you're a frugal little thing aren't you?"

"Yes, I guess I am. I was raised to be." *Hope I didn't put a damper on things.*

"Don't worry. The farm does quite well. We switched to organic years ago and stuck to pasture-raised animals, so we're fine. You won't break the budget if you go out with me."

"Okay. But we could eat here, and I'll fix something."

"You've worked all day. Besides, I think the wiser choice is to go out, my dear."

Her face grew warm at the thought of them alone. "Guess you're right."

"Let's visit the Thai place. I'll tell you which dishes aren't too spicy."

"Okay. I'll be ready when you get here." She hung up, changed her clothes and brushed out her hair. She shrugged into a light coat after she heard his knock.

He swept in, embraced her and stroked her cheek. "I didn't get my noon kiss—"

Before he could finish, she raised her face to his and pulled him to her.

He ended the caress first and teased, "I thought you were shy."

She kept her gaze on him and in a sudden motion, he drew her against him and kissed her with more intensity. He stopped soon after and clasped her hard. "Time to go."

Though her knees were weak, she nodded and followed him out. He took her hand, and they walked to the truck. She settled in and asked, "Where's your pal?"

Tom fired up the engine. "He's at his cousin Jason's. I take him over a few times a week to play. Jason's six months older. They have a blast. Usually I stay and help my brother Tim with projects, but I asked if he and Sharon would mind watching Jesse. When I told them why, they were delighted."

"The brothers Tim and Tom. Cute." She grinned at him.

"It seems more dignified with our whole first names. Timothy and Thomas. Tim and Tom sounds like two sock puppets."

Ann burst out in laughter.

He cracked a smile at her and continued, "They'd be happy to watch him anyway because they love Jesse, but they were pretty thrilled about me going out on a date. They've tried to fix me up with different girls for a while now. I wasn't interested in any of them."

He shot her a loving glance. Warmth spread from her middle and filtered through her limbs. In the parking lot of the restaurant, Tom gazed at her and leaned toward her before he sat back and stepped out.

Why didn't he kiss her? He'd wanted to. He strolled around, opened her door, took her hand, and kissed it as they walked along. When they strolled through the entryway, the wonderful warmth and aromas hit.

"Ooh," Ann exclaimed. "Something smells good."

"Everything I've tried in here is mighty tasty." The waitress seated them after they hung their coats.

"I'm glad you're not nervous like the first time we went out," Tom told her as the waitress returned with menus and glasses of water.

"Thank you," they chimed.

Tom took a long drink of water. "I figured you'd been through some pretty bad dating experiences, and that's why you acted so scared."

"I had nerves all day. I'd never been on a date before."

His eyebrows rose. "I'm honored. Imagine that. I'm your first date *and* first kiss."

Ann smiled, gratified at his words. While she sipped her water, he pointed at the menu and told her which dishes were good. She let herself stare at him. He caught her gaze, stopped speaking and took her hand, his thumb tracing slow circles on the top of it.

They didn't hear the waitress until she cleared her throat. She grinned when they looked at her.

Ann's face heated and she dropped her gaze. "You order, okay?"

Tom held fast to her hand while he ordered their food. The waitress left. His thumb continued the hypnotic stroking.

"All right?"

Ann raised her head. Connection with his eyes caused her to take in a quick breath. How deep did this go? She couldn't manage speech and nodded.

He continued his gentle touch, their two gazes locked as he took her other hand in his. He glanced a moment at their hands, then back to her eyes. Words were unnecessary. She'd thought only beautiful music could transport her and speak to her this way. Such beauty lay within his gaze. The waitress returned with their appetizers and broke the focus.

He released her hands, swallowed, and said, "Guess we better try this. Looks good."

The scent of ginger and cilantro wafted up and Ann studied the food. She'd almost forgotten where they were.

"Yes, it does." Ann took a slow, deep breath to recover her faculties. Every little detail of Tom's features and voice affected her. When she stared into his eyes, once so hard to do, it now served to nourish something inside her. What unfamiliar, wondrous terrain. Ann could have sat with him forever. But the meal ended. Time to join regular life again.

Tom parked in front of her apartment. "I'm not coming in. I'll kiss you goodnight here and watch you go in."

She unbuckled her belt, and couldn't help her puzzled discouragement. Didn't he want to come in, if only for a moment? He'd asked to kiss her but at times acted like he'd rather not.

Maybe he doesn't feel as much as I do. The thought intensified her disappointment.

"You don't have to, you know," Ann replied.

"Well, I need to make sure you're safely inside before I leave."

"Kiss me, I mean."

"What?" His eyes widened while his mouth parted.

"You act like you don't want to."

Tom erupted into laughter.

Now she was surprised. Ann couldn't help a smile when he roared even harder after he'd viewed her baffled face. Ann had to ask. "What? Tom, what?"

He held onto his stomach and continued to laugh. He finally stopped and drew in some air. "I can't believe you thought that. You're so funny."

"Why? You *do* act that way."

Tom took another breath and turned serious. "Ann, I've been married. I'm not used to dating anymore and I don't want to...well...go too fast. You've never even had a boyfriend or kissed anyone before. Things can get out of control mighty quick."

He stopped and studied her. "Neither of us are the casual sort. I don't take any of this lightly. Trust me. I want to kiss you, more than you realize." She glanced down. He dropped a warm hand over hers. "And now you're shy again."

Tom reached, drew her next to him and kissed her with fervor. She stopped first, almost breathless.

"Understand?" he asked her.

She gave a slow nod, and blinked a few times. "But I like it."

He laughed and embraced her. "I do, too. Which is why we need to be careful." He nuzzled her hair. "These things tend to have a life of their own if you don't keep your wits about you."

"I don't have any when you kiss me. They disappear. I told you I don't know how to manage this. How could I guess how strong the feelings would be? It overwhelms me. I don't see any harm in kissing, though."

"Well, the trouble is if we let it escalate. That's why I'm careful. Don't ever believe I don't want to be as near to you as I can be, because I do." They held each other for a few moments. He sighed. "Go on in now, and I'll wait."

Ann squeezed him harder before she pulled back. She laid her hand against the side of his face. He turned his lips to her palm, kissed it, and murmured in a soft voice, "Goodnight."

He raised his eyes to hers, and she couldn't stop staring at him. His eyes were magnetic, their expression deep. Ann traced his mouth with her thumb. The painful, beautiful ache inside when she gazed at him entranced her.

"Ann." He stared back. Time turned fluid and endless while their gazes stayed locked, her hand on his face. He closed his eyes and leaned his head against her hand, then pulled her closer and pressed his forehead to hers. He whispered, "I love you. I know it."

"And I love you." Her voice broke as trembles flickered down her back.

A car pulled in near them and discharged a group of loud, boisterous passengers.

Tom released her as the people moved off. "Go in now, Ann. I'll call you tomorrow."

She ambled to the door, turned, waved, and floated inside. At the window she peeked out at his receding truck. Ann walked into her room, flopped onto the bed, and stared at the ceiling. She heard his words in her head, I love you. I know it.

She closed her eyes and pictured his face. His eyes met hers with the expression in them which made her weak. She rolled over and whispered to God. "I don't know what it means to be in love. I only know I am. What should I do? I might mess it up or do the wrong things. I need wisdom, Father. Teach me the way You taught Jesus. So I'll know how to be."

CHAPTER ELEVEN

THEIR DECLARATIONS OF love made everything before last night seem like a prologue. Now her real life began. Wherever she walked, he walked with her. Whenever she breathed, he breathed with her. The awareness and reality of him became part of her consciousness.

Her former reluctance at waking up evaporated. Today would be a day with him in it. Marvelous as love was, to be so focused on another person scared her at moments. Everything in her life accelerated like an internal roller coaster ride.

Tom dropped in at lunchtime, brought her a rose, and scooted around to kiss her as soon as Susan returned to the back.

"I love you," he whispered between kisses, and stopped at the sound of a car pulling into the parking lot.

"I love you," Ann answered. They broke apart and Tom strode over to the counter to sit down. Ann served the customer, her eyes traveling every few moments to meet Tom's gaze. After the client left, she stood across from him.

"You look nice," Ann smiled. "The shirt almost matches your eyes."

He reached to take her hands in his. They exchanged a lengthy gaze.

"So much for going slow." Tom laughed after minutes passed. "I didn't expect to be sure this soon. I mean, we haven't known one another long."

"Does it usually take longer?"

He grinned. "You're so cute. I don't know either, I guess."

"How much time went by with Judy before you were sure?"

"We'd been dating about four months and I knew. I thought it might be at least as long until I was sure this time. Especially since you're so shy. I figured it would take a while for us to get to know each other. Guess I was wrong."

They laughed. He stroked her palms with his thumbs.

"Your hands are wonderful," Ann told him. "They were the one of the first things about you I noticed. They're so strong."

"For me it was your eyes. I couldn't stop looking at them."

She stared at him and her cheeks grew warm. She wanted to gaze at him forever.

"Oh, sweetie," he breathed. After a few more minutes, he took a deep breath. "I have to go. I've got a lot of work the next couple of days, but I'll call you when I can, okay?"

She nodded, unable to speak. He kissed both her palms, stood, and strode to the door.

Susan popped out with fresh cakes for the showcase. "Bye, Tom."

He waved to them. Ann glanced at Susan, who remained next to her.

Susan studied her. "You're in love with him, aren't you?"

"Yes. He loves me, too. Can you believe it?"

[125]

"Well, it *is* quick. Still, I need to tell you something odd. The first time I saw you with Tom and Jesse, I had this weird feeling that you sort of fit together."

"Honestly?"

"Yep. The three of you seemed to be a unit."

"Wow. That's funny. I felt close to Jesse from the minute I met him. It took longer with Tom, but not much, I guess." Ann laughed. "Do you think it's too soon to be sure?"

"No. When you know something, you know it. I think most relationships take a while to develop, but plenty of times people meet and hit it off. Who knows why? Just don't get carried away. You've been lonely a long time, so these feelings must be pretty hard to manage."

Ann regarded Susan with wonder. "That's what Tom worries about, too."

"I'm glad. You deserve somebody who'll be sensitive to you. Have you told your family yet?"

"No, only you. It's happened so fast, I'm convinced they'll all think I'm nuts, since I'm as old as I am and never had a boyfriend. I'm not sure how to tell them."

Susan pondered for a minute. "Why not start by saying you're dating someone? Then as time goes on and they meet him, they won't think you're nuts."

"Aren't you the one who said my face is as readable as a clock? Once they see me with him, they'll figure it out, and they'll wonder how on earth I could be in love. They'll also be concerned because Tom has Jesse." She crossed her arms and sighed. "They'll say how hard it will be to have a relationship with someone who has a child, et cetera, et cetera. I can hear it all echoing in my mind." She shook her head.

"Well, let's not over-complicate everything. Maybe they'll surprise you and be fine with it and understand."

Ann raised her eyebrows and shrugged. "I guess anything's possible."

"There you go. It's better to be optimistic."

"I suppose...but you get your hopes up."

"Well, hope is good." Susan beamed. "Where there's life, there's hope. It's a lot better than fear."

Ann paused and studied Susan a moment. "You're absolutely right. It's not my usual style, but I'll try to remember it."

Susan grinned and left to check on the cake in the ovens. Ann folded boxes and stacked them on top of the showcase. Peace settled on her while she let her mind run free. It's what she liked about repetitive tasks and their comfortable rhythm. Her thoughts traveled wherever they wanted, and she still accomplished something useful.

Ann flicked a glance out the picture window. A wiry man stepped out of a car. She stiffened in fear. Oh, no. The guy from the porch. She turned fast and sprinted into the back before he spotted her. She crouched in the part of the room where she couldn't be seen from anywhere in the front. Ann remembered Tom's words about paying attention to warnings.

Susan studied her face and rushed over. "What's wrong?"

The bell sounded. "That guy scares me—I'm not sure why," Ann whispered. "Will you wait on him?"

Susan raised her eyebrows and shrugged. "Okay."

Ann listened to the sound of their voices as he made his purchase and left. Susan stepped into the backroom.

"He's gone."

Ann's shoulders relaxed. "I'm sorry. I've never hidden before. I felt like I had to."

Susan reached for a bowl of frosting and stirred. "It's okay. I know him...no, not really. I know who he is and a few things about his family. They're kind of rough folks. Some of them have been in prison, and I think he was, too, but I can't remember what for."

Susan furrowed her brow and glanced up for a moment before she continued. "One of his brothers had a conversion experience in jail, and I met him at Jim's when I visited last year. He told me his family doesn't want anything to do with him because of it. Still, he prays for them all the time." Susan shook her head. "Imagine...his being in prison is okay with them, but not his relationship with God."

"How weird." Ann puzzled on it for a moment. "So did he make you nervous?"

"Not much. He seemed polite." Susan frosted a cake with deft strokes.

"Did he ask you your name?" Ann took some butter out of the refrigerator to soften, and checked the order board.

"Nope. He asked if I was the owner, and said it was too bad I had to wait on the front and bake stuff, also. I didn't mention you because you were so worried. "

Ann stepped to pull a sheet cake from the oven. The bell dinged. Ann shot a nervous glance at Susan.

"It's all right." Susan smiled. "I'll go."

Congenial talk and laughter from Susan and another female voice calmed Ann's nerves.

Susan walked back through the archway, a big smile on her face. "It was Evelyn Cortland. She said thanks again for the cake, and she hopes we visit soon. I told her I planned on it."

"Good. Let's definitely go again." Ann turned away from the icing table and faced Susan. "I'm sorry about being scared. It's not right to make you wait on everyone. Even if he does come in, I'll be polite and careful. I'm not sure why he scares me, but it won't run my work life."

Susan nodded at her. "You should pay attention if you think you need to avoid him. Who knows why you feel that way, right?"

"Right."

Ann arrived home later, tired yet blissful, and thought about how wonderful it was to be in love. She did an inventory of the leftovers in the refrigerator. She diced fresh onion and garlic, sautéed it in a pan, and then chopped some leftover potatoes and roast beef. The warm, rich smell as it browned filled the apartment.

After dinner and clean-up, she contemplated the notes she'd jotted, and the questions she'd written. What is the kingdom of Heaven? Is it inside you? Is it a place? She hoped Tom or Susan could answer it. Jesus mentioned it many times. She began to read and became so engrossed, the ring of the phone startled her.

"Hi."

"Ann? Is this you?" Ann pictured her mother's intense blue eyes, her brow furrowed.

"Hi, Mom. Yes, it's me."

"You sounded different at first. Can you come over for Sunday dinner? Grandma D. is coming in and we'd love you to be here." Mom cleared her throat and her tone lowered. "Dear, I know how busy you are, but it just doesn't seem right that you're only fifteen miles away and we hardly ever see you."

Guilt thudded in Ann's middle while she worried she'd miss seeing Tom on Sunday. But she wanted to be with her family, too.

"Sure, Mom, what time?"

"Well, we'll probably eat around five, but can you come over earlier? Why don't you head over here after you wake up and spend the whole day? Grandma will be here Saturday night and all day Sunday."

Ann had never chosen between her family and someone else. She pressed her lips together. "Okay. Sometimes I sleep pretty late, though."

"That's fine, dear. I know you work hard. You need to get some extra rest now and then."

"Hey, Mom? I'm dating a wonderful man."

"Really? Who?" Silence which spanned a breath hung between them.

"Tom Tillman." Saying his name filled her with warmth. She closed her eyes for a moment, seeing his face.

"Tillman? I knew a Joe Tillman in high school. I was in choir with him. I remember he moved and went senior year at one of the smaller schools outside town. He was so nice, and funny."

Sounded like Tom. "Maybe they're related."

"Ask your friend if he knows Joe Tillman. I always wondered where Joe ended up. He had such a wonderful singing voice. He might be on Broadway now. Well, dear, you're probably tired, so I'll go now. See you early on Sunday."

"Right, Mom. Bye."

Ann let out a grateful breath, glad that Mom hadn't inundated her with the usual barrage of interrogation. How amazed would Mom be to learn Tom was much more than her friend? His declaration of love replayed in her mind, making her heartbeat rise. When she visited on Sunday, she'd need to guard against letting her expression give everything away, and not gush over his qualities too much. She sighed. Her mother and sisters were as skittish as unbroken colts. And just as unpredictable. The phone rang.

"Hello?"

"Hey, sweetie."

"Hi." Happiness surged through her.

"How's my serious girl?"

[130]

"Good. Actually, awesome now." She settled in a comfortable position. "So you think I'm a serious person?"

Tom laughed with delight. His tone sounded playful. "Didn't you know?"

"Well I'm much less serious around you and Jesse. Guess I must be a pretty grim character."

Someone should have told me.

"I'd hardly call you a grim character." He chuckled. "I think you take things to heart and consider them."

"Does it bother you? Would you prefer if I was always lighthearted and joking around?" She hoped he said no.

"I'd rather you be yourself, Ann. I love you the way you are. Of course I'd like you to be cheerful all the time, but it's not real life."

"No, it isn't." She relaxed at his sweet words.

"Were you serious as a child?"

"Yes, and bashful. I'd hide from people who stopped by our house. It drove my mom crazy. She's not shy at all." Ann laughed and fiddled with the tassel on her robe zipper. "I guess we're pretty opposite. She's more like Susan. High-energy...speedy, gets a lot done. Mom actually likes being rushed and having tons of things to do. After a while, that kind of thing wears me out. Hey, I've got a question from my reading."

"The first one. Fire away. I'm curious."

She glanced at her notepad. "Jesus keeps talking about the kingdom of Heaven, or the kingdom of God. I think they're the same thing, but is it inside you, or is it a place?"

"Quite a question." A short pause ensued. "Hold on, let me open the Bible."

Ann reached for hers and waited. Pages crinkled on his end of the line.

"You're right. Jesus does mention it a lot. My study Bible says it's mentioned thirty-one times in Matthew. From what I already know, when you become a believer in Jesus, a change begins on the inside. I've been taught that it's within you."

"I understand, but He keeps telling them about a kingdom. What it's like, and how it's at hand and which kind of people will be in it."

"Hold on a second. There's a commentary on it in here. It might help." She waited while he read it.

"Now, the commentary states that Bible scholars say Jesus talks about his ministry and teachings as a seed which continues to grow and spread until He returns to set up a peaceful kingdom on Earth that follows God's will."

Ann drank it in. "Wow... Thy Kingdom come, Thy will be done on Earth as it is in Heaven. In His prayer...is that the meaning? A kingdom here?"

"Here's what I'm thinking...the meek shall inherit the Earth...the government shall be upon His shoulder... Neither will they learn war anymore. It fits. I've got to study more about this. I wonder why I never paid attention to it before."

The excitement in his voice charmed her. "Maybe so we could learn together."

"You might be right. You've given me a lot to think about. And this is the first time you're reading it. That's pretty amazing."

"I'm just going by what it says. Since I wasn't sure, I wrote it down." She'd never have believed it if someone told her Bible study was exciting.

"I'm glad you asked. My mind is jumping all over it... I'll have to ask my folks and find out what they think."

She shifted in her chair. "Hey, speaking of family, Mom called me tonight to tell me my Grandma will be in town Sunday and she wants me to spend the day at their house."

"The whole day? I planned to spend time with you. My entire week is tied up with harvesting."

"Yes, I know." She sighed. They had so little time together. "I wanted to say I'd only come for dinner, but I do want to visit with everyone, and I haven't seen Grandma for a while."

"Maybe I can take you out to breakfast Sunday morning after you get up, before you go over. I can harvest later and still spend time with you."

"Great. I was afraid I wouldn't see you." She indulged in a lazy stretch. "It's funny, though. I kind of feel as though you're always with me. But it hurts to be apart."

"I know." His voice turned soft.

They were quiet. Ann listened to him breathe, and closed her eyes.

"I wish I had more time to be with you." The yearning in his tone made her breath catch.

She imagined him in the room with her. "I told Mom we were dating."

"What did she say?"

"She asked your name and when she heard it, she said she'd gone to high school and been in choir with Joe Tillman before he moved out of town."

"That's my Dad! My grandparents came out here and started the farm before Dad's senior year."

"Well, it is a small world. Mom said your dad had a beautiful singing voice. She thought he'd be on Broadway by now."

Tom let loose a hearty laugh. "Not likely. He loves to sing, but told me he always hated performing. He sings in the barn to the

[133]

animals when the radio's on and says it's the only audience he ever needs."

Ann laughed and Tom chuckled with her. "Your dad sounds cute."

"He sure is. He's an original. A while after I lost Judy he'd remind me of all the adorable or silly things she said or did. He told me, 'you should remember her alive, not dead.' He and Mom are amazing. I'd like for you to meet them soon. I know you met Mom, but I mean a real meeting with both of them at my place, for dinner."

"Oh, dear." Ann fidgeted in her chair. *Am I ready for this?*

"What's wrong?"

"Well, your Dad's not the only one with performance anxiety."

"It's not a performance, you goof. Trust me, it'll be fun. They're easy to talk to. Don't worry. I can wait until you're ready."

She sighed, stretched, and stifled a yawn. "Okay. I do want to get to know them. I wish I wasn't so shy with people."

"I'll help you. Now, you need to go to bed and sleep. I'm tired, too. I'll call tomorrow." His voice lowered to seriousness. "I love you."

His tone made her face warm. "I love you. So much."

"I want to drive over and kiss you goodnight... I'd have to wake Jesse, though. Or my folks."

Ann knew if she asked him to, he would. She wrestled with herself. "No, don't do it. You and Jesse need your rest. Not that I wouldn't love it."

"So would I." He sighed. "Good night."

"Good night."

After he hung up, she sat a while longer and held the phone. "I wish you and Jesse lived here," she whispered into it and hung up. She surveyed her apartment while she walked into the kitchen and viewed it all with new eyes. It seemed to lose its aura of permanence. Tom's red rose graced the table. She bent closer to inhale the sweet scent.

Guess I'm not such a recluse anymore.

CHAPTER TWELVE

THE NIGHT HAD been chilly, and it was still dark when Ann unlocked the bakery door and hung up her coat. She spread her arms out wide to welcome the heat and breathed in the warm, fragrant air. Susan wasn't in her usual spot at the ovens. The sound of water running in the sink issued from the bathroom. Ann began the morning measure of ingredients. She double-checked the order board on the wall. Susan emerged, walking at an uncharacteristic slow pace as her hand held a washcloth against her face. She eased herself onto a chair.

Ann opened her mouth to say good morning and halted in shock when Susan lowered the washcloth. Her bottom lip was swollen, one of her eyes looked blackened and rips showed in the arms of her shirt. Susan stared at the far wall.

Alarm filled Ann. "Did you get in an accident?"

Susan dabbed the cloth on her discolored, swollen cheek and winced. "No. I was attacked after I got out of my car this morning." Ann gasped in horror as Susan continued, in an odd, vacant tone. "I went to the all-night gas station after I woke up and dressed, because I forgot to fill the tank last night. I wanted to make sure I had fuel in case we needed to do any deliveries. I saw him getting gas, too, and said hello."

"Him who?" Fury rose in a sudden tide.

"The guy you were afraid to wait on yesterday." Susan took a deep breath.

The blood drained out of Ann's face and the energy out of her body as she wilted onto a chair next to Susan.

"Oh, no…oh, no…no." Ann covered her eyes with one hand, her other one resting on Susan's shoulder. Why? Why Susan? Ann managed to choke out words tight with anger and shock. "What did he do to you?"

Susan continued in a detached voice, as if she spoke about someone else. "He asked if the bakery was open yet and I told him no, because I wasn't there. I went in to pay and he was gone by the time I came back out. I drove here and when I walked around to grab a package off the floor in the back seat of my car, I straightened up and he was standing behind me." Susan shifted and winced. "I got nervous, and when he offered to help me carry stuff in, I said, 'It's okay, it's not much. I'll get it,' and before I knew it, he pushed me onto the back seat."

Ann rocked in her seat, eyes closed while she listened.

"Then he ripped my shirt and I screamed and he punched me three or four times and told me I'd better shut up. I was so scared all I could do was thrash around and try to escape. All of a sudden, I had this clear picture in my head of poking him hard in the eyes. I went limp for a minute like I'd fainted. He let go of my wrists and pulled at my clothes."

Ann stared at her, afraid to breathe.

"I jabbed him in the eyes as hard as I could. He yelled and hit the back of his head on the car frame and rubbed his eyes. I kicked

[137]

him in the stomach, and he went backwards enough for me to sit up and shut and lock the door. I jumped into the front seat, locked all the doors and pushed on the horn over and over." Susan took a careful breath and held her side. "I think someone turned on a light across the street. I'm not sure. He ran over to a car and drove away. After I thought it was safe, I came in here and locked up and went to wash my face."

"When did this happen?"

"About a half hour ago."

They were both quiet for a moment. Ann struggled for control. *I can't cry and lose it.* She had to be strong for Susan. Her voice wavered. "I shouldn't have hid from him yesterday when he came in here. Maybe if he'd seen you didn't work alone, this never would've happened."

Susan placed her hand on Ann's and spoke in a gentle voice, "Don't think that way. It's not your fault, and you only did what you thought you should do."

How could Susan be so calm? Ann unraveled every time she let her vision take in Susan's bruises. "Why aren't the police here yet?"

"I didn't call them. I've been wondering what to do. I'm not sure." She dabbed her face again.

Susan must be too rattled to think straight. Ann stood. "I'll call them for you."

"Wait." Susan held her hand up.

Ann stopped and stared at her friend. "Why?"

"Because I don't know what I'm supposed to do."

Did Susan have a concussion? Ann spoke in a slow, measured voice. "You're supposed to report it so they can catch him."

"Don't look at me like that, okay? I'm not crazy. My mind is perfectly fine."

[138]

"Good, but what else would you do other than call the police? This is a criminal act. They need to lock him in jail and keep him away from people." Every time her sight touched on the bruises and the sad expression in Susan's eyes, she wanted nothing more than to make sure the horrible man was punished as severely as possible. She imagined someone punching *him* over and over while satisfaction filled her at the mental picture. He deserved it.

"I don't know if you'll understand, but I want to do what's right by God. I sensed Him here with me through the whole thing. Maybe I'm supposed to do something different."

This couldn't be real. Ann sighed and sat back down. She stared at Susan. "Like what, forgive him?"

"Yes. This sounds nuts, but I was actually sorry for him when he ran to his car and drove away."

"You felt sorry for him?" Ann's mouth fell open and she shook her head.

"Yes. Only someone in some sort of desperate condition would do such a thing."

"Yeah, a crazy psycho. Don't you think a person like him needs to be penned up far away from potential innocent victims? He might have killed you. For all we know, that's what he went to jail for."

"It wasn't. After this happened, I remembered what his brother told me. If I'd thought of it before, I'd have been more cautious when I saw him at the gas station, and he wouldn't have been able to sneak up on me."

"What was he in for?" Dread flashed through Ann.

Susan paused and sighed. "Attempted rape."

Ann bolted up. "We need to call the police now. He might be attacking someone right now, or planning to because he didn't get what he wanted from you. Or maybe he's out in the dark waiting."

[139]

"I didn't think about it...you're right."

"I'm calling now." Ann rushed to the phone. *Please God, keep him away.*

After Ann hung up, Susan said, "I hope he hasn't tried to attack someone else. Ann, I still believe I'm supposed to find a way to forgive him. I realize he has to go to jail and not be able to hurt anyone. Maybe he'll consider what he did and turn to God like his brother. I hope so."

"I don't care about him or anything that happens to him." At Susan's disappointed expression, Ann's stomach ached. "Susan, I took a lot of psychology courses. Once a person derives pleasure from dominance and violence, they grow worse, and do more deviant things to people. They have to be stopped."

"I understand. Let me ask you something. Do you think they can't be helped, they can't change? I don't believe that. The Bible says in both testaments that if a person repents from evil, they can be forgiven."

"I know, but I don't see any evidence this guy is interested in turning from evil. It seems to me he's pretty taken over with it. So, he'll just get worse." She started to pace. "I do believe people can reform, but only if they accept how awful their actions are and they honestly want to change. Like it says in the Bible, repent and change direction. It's the only way they can be helped. They have to want to stop."

Susan grew quiet for a few moments. "That's true. What if I talked to him and told him there's hope he can change—"

"Susan, you should talk to someone like Jim or Evelyn before you ever consider it. Get some advice. Wouldn't you be scared to be in a room with him, even with bars between you?"

Susan reflected a moment. "I know it sounds weird, but no, I don't think so. He needs help—otherwise his life means nothing but pain and trouble. For him and everyone around him. For now, he's lost. He doesn't have to stay that way."

Ann stared at Susan and realized how little she understood her in some ways. Flashing lights reflected along the back wall. Ann rushed to answer the door at the sound of a loud knock.

An hour crawled by while they gave their statements. Afterwards, the police told them they'd need to identify the man in a lineup.

"Do you know who he is and where to find him?" Ann asked one of the officers, a tall, older man with gray hair and kind, brown eyes.

"We've got a good idea." Two policeman left with Susan to take her to the hospital for examination.

"I suggest you stay closed today. He may still be around," the tall officer told Ann, and added, "I'll escort you home after you lock up."

Ann studied the board and took down the phone numbers of people with orders for the day, then placed a sign on the door, "Closed Today." She hustled into her car. The policeman followed her home and walked her inside. He checked her apartment and told her to keep everything locked.

"We'll call you once he's in custody so you can come in and identify him."

"Thank you." Ann filled up with sincere appreciation and relief, glad he'd inspected the apartment. She hated the horrible unsettled sensation caused by mental pictures of him lurking nearby.

Ann phoned all the people with orders. She followed Susan's wishes, explained what happened, and apologized. The customers were all shocked and voiced their concerns for Susan. Ann thanked them for their understanding, sat in her chair, and waited for Susan to phone.

Anxiety lurked and pressed below the surface, yet she willed it away. She'd be no help to Susan if she gave into it. Ann reached for the phone more than once to call Tom. She pictured him in the barn with Jesse as they took care of the animals or in the fields with his father. If she called, the answering machine would take it. This wasn't the sort of thing people left messages about. Now she wished they'd gotten cellphones.

Her phone rang. "Hello?"

"It's me," Susan sounded normal. "I'm all done. The officers are taking me home in a little bit."

"*No.* You should come here. The officer who escorted me said he might still be around." Ann shivered at the thought.

"They told me he's in custody, and I said I'd call and tell you. We're supposed to be at the station in an hour for the lineup."

"Well, that was fast. Are you ready for all this?"

"Yes. I look worse than I feel. My face and the bruise on my side hurts, so I took some ibuprofen. No permanent damage, they said."

"Well, thank God. Don't you want to rest or something?"

"No, I'm fine, really. I've been lying around here, and I'm rested enough."

Susan's stamina amazed Ann. "I called everyone with orders for today and told them what happened. They were all kind and understanding and said to tell you how sorry they were."

"Oh." Susan sounded hesitant.

"What's wrong? I did what you asked."

"Nothing's wrong. Guess I'm nervous about people's reactions."

The sentiment puzzled her. "I told you how they reacted, though. What are you worried about?"

"I don't mean what they said today. Everyone's going to want me to be as harsh as possible in seeking punishment, especially after they see my face. I need to figure out how I'll handle it."

"You can understand those wishes, can't you? You might feel the same way too, if he acted as though what he did was no big deal and he doesn't care if you suffered."

"Well...anyway, I'll be home soon."

"I'll meet you there and we'll go to the lineup together."

"All right. Bye."

Ann hung up and wondered if she should call Tom and her family. It would be better after the line-up. If she waited, they'd be hearing some good news to go with the bad. She grabbed her coat and left. After she arrived at the bakery, Fred pulled in as she exited her car.

"What's going on?" Fred's brows furrowed and his eyes held concern. "I stopped by this morning and found everything locked up, and at work I heard something on the police scanner concerning the bakery. I couldn't make out much, but heard a comment about taking one of the girls to the hospital. I drove down as soon as I got a break to find out what's happening. Where's Susan?"

Ann told him what happened and his attitude changed from concerned shock to rage. How did Susan imagine anyone would hear such news and not react like Fred? Just as she finished, Susan and two officers arrived in a patrol car. Susan climbed out and leaned at the passenger window for a moment. She turned around and Fred took in her bruised features. His expression broke into a grimace of pain, then went pale, his eyes haunted. Ann's stomach twisted with empathy.

"Oh, Fred," Susan stepped to him and put her hand on his sleeve. "I don't look like it, but I'm fine."

"No, you're not," he squeezed his eyes shut and blinked them open, their surface glazed with unshed tears. "Who did this? Do you know?" He clenched his fists. "I'm going to do the same thing to his face."

"Fred, don't get yourself in trouble over this. Anyway, it wouldn't change what happened."

"It would show him the pain he put you through. How could he do something like this to such a gentle, kind—" his voice choked. He shook his head and swallowed hard. Ann found herself fighting tears as sympathy for Fred ached inside her.

Susan breathed in, her eyes taking on a pleading look. "Fred, if you really want to help me, you'll try to understand I don't need retaliation, all right?"

Fred's mouth fell open as his eyebrows drew down. "How can you expect me to agree with you? You girls are the same age as my daughter. Do you know what I'd do to someone if they did this to my girl?"

"Even if she asked you to try and understand she didn't want you to take revenge?" Susan's eyes were calm and steady.

Fred stared at her for a moment and clenched his jaw.

"I won't talk about this now." He turned and hurried into his car. Before he drove away, he glanced at her and told her in a tight voice, "I'm glad you're all right."

His tires squealed when he whipped out of the parking lot. Susan sighed as Fred whizzed away.

Ann swallowed. The anguish on Fred's face filled her mind's eye. "You shouldn't expect people not to be furious, especially all the men who know you. You're so slight and gentle and they're naturally going to feel protective like Fred does. You can't blame him for it."

"I don't. It's only...he might never understand where I'm coming from. If all people do is seek revenge, all the mess and trouble in this world won't change."

Ann remained quiet and scanned the beauty of the trees and the clear sky. How could it be such a pretty day? "Well, you've got a point, I'll give you that. However, it's not vengeful to want someone like him to be safely locked away from others."

"I agree, but I'm talking about seeing past it to the end result. If I, as a believer, won't do what I need to do to be able to honestly forgive him and pray for him, how can I ask Fred not to seek revenge?"

Ann shook her head. *I can't process this.* "How will you figure out exactly what to do? I mean, if it says to forgive, does it tell you how long it takes? It's got to be more than only saying the words, right?"

Susan gave a small smile. "All I know is, I cast my cares on Him, and become willing to do things His way, not mine. He says, 'Vengeance is mine. I will re-pay.' So I leave it to Him, and work out the rest in prayer."

Ann glanced down while emotions swirled in her. "I don't understand. It doesn't make sense to me." She took in a breath and brought her eyes back to Susan. It hurt so much to view her injured face. "Isn't it almost like letting him get away with this?"

"No. He'll still be forced to deal with the consequences of what he's done. I'm speaking of his future, anyone's future. It's not enough for me to declare my faith, or to say I'm a Christian. If I won't do as Jesus did, then I'm fooling myself, and I'm lost, too. He gave everything for me, for all of us." Susan's eyes filled with tears. "How can I not be willing to do this for Him?"

No response surfaced in Ann's mind. She offered a gentle pat to Susan's shoulder and stood in silence with her. After a minute, Susan wiped her eyes and gazed around. "Beautiful day...let's have some coffee before we go."

Ann walked to the bakery's back door with her. She was as confused as she'd ever been in her life. It drove her internal focus further inward, searching for answers.

CHAPTER THIRTEEN

ANN'S NERVES SPIKED when they walked into the police station, and she studied Susan's calm features. How did she manage it? One of the officers strode over to them.

"Are you up to this? We can re-schedule if you need to."

"I'm fine, thank you." Susan followed him, and he ushered her into the viewing room. He returned, and Ann asked him, "Don't we go in together?"

"No," he answered in a pleasant voice, sat at the desk, and jotted something on a sheet of paper.

"Oh." She fidgeted with her hands.

Susan walked out after only a few minutes. Ann was escorted in by an older officer who nodded at the policeman seated at a small table inside. The door closed. The large window across from her dominated the room. She stepped to it, scanned the men in the lineup, and picked him right away.

"Third guy from the left," she ground out through her clenched jaw. The seated officer wrote something. Her gaze returned to the attacker, and an unfamiliar sensation flooded her. She wished to grow tall and strong. She'd stomp in and punch him the way he'd done to Susan, or worse. He must realize Susan or someone stood behind the one-way window, but didn't appear at all ashamed. Ann couldn't fathom how Susan harbored any sympathy for someone like him. She averted her eyes and the anger dissipated. The intensity left her shaken and frightened.

The officer double-checked with her for confirmation and had her sign a paper. He opened the door for her. "Thank you, Miss Shaw."

"So that's all?" she asked.

"For now," he nodded. "You should both go home and rest. We'll make sure he's not going anywhere."

"Thank you for your kindness."

She stepped out. Susan was seated, engaged in convivial conversation with the young officer who'd left the desk and stood near her. He nodded to Ann, took Susan's hand to help her stand, and said in a gentle voice, "Take care."

"Which one did you pick?" Ann asked while they walked to the car.

"The third guy from the left." Susan's response was quiet.

"Me, too." Ann wanted to ask her what her emotions were when she viewed him, but decided not to. Susan might want to know hers, and she shied away from telling her about the murderous rage she'd experienced. It still shocked her.

Susan appeared tired and stayed quiet as Ann drove her back to the bakery. Ann asked, "Do you want to stay over at my place?"

"I'm fine, really." Susan smiled at her. "I want to pray about all this and then lie down. I'll see you in the morning."

"Bright and early." Ann delivered her usual answer and hugged Susan before she climbed out. Her friend walked to the door and turned to wave. Ann returned it and waited until the door closed. On the drive home, Ann said a silent prayer for Susan's quick healing from emotional or physical damage. Once at her apartment, fatigue weighed her down. She decided to take a nap.

Thoughts of Tom and her conversation with Susan ran through her mind and kept her from sleep. Ann sat up a few times. Would Tom be in the house yet? He'd have to stop work to eat, but maybe he and Jesse ate lunch at his parent's place. He'd said he had to harvest all week. She lay back down and closed her eyes.

Ann wanted Tom with her, but he had so much work to do. If she could just hold him, she'd be able to relax. She turned onto her side and sighed. The guy was in custody, and nothing else needed to be done. How would Susan learn to live with this?

Will either of us feel safe again, like before? Ann dozed off and on, only to wake and have the same thoughts run through her mind. She prayed, and the tears flooded out of her. She fell asleep in prayer.

Yikes. Five pm already. Ann stretched and sat up. She should call Tom now. No, he and Jesse would be in the barn with the animals. She shuffled into the kitchen and peered out the window over the sink. The clouds were high and moved in slow patterns in the blue-gray sky. Her mind focused on Susan. She walked to the phone, punched in the numbers and flopped down on her chair.

"Hello?" Susan's voice sounded normal.

"Just checking in on you. Are you all right?"

"Yes. I slept for a while after I called my parents. I'm about to make some dinner."

"Want to come over here? I can fix us something." Ann's stomach let out a slight rumble.

"It's okay. I've already got the water on for pasta."

"Susan...do you still plan to forgive that awful guy? I can't stop thinking about it."

Susan exhaled a small sigh. "Yes, Ann. I've prayed, and I know what I need to do."

"A tiny part of me can understand your view, but most of me is angry and partly at you."

"Me?" Astonishment filled her tone.

"Yes. It's like you're giving up, as though it doesn't matter what he did, and you're going to let him get away with it." Relief washed through Ann while she gave voice to her thoughts. "That can't be right."

Susan stayed silent for a short pause. "Ann, I don't expect you to agree. I do understand your feelings, though. You wonder if I have any anger or want to seek punishment. Part of me does. It's as though two paths are ahead of me, and both are acceptable. It's my choice to make. I want to choose the one which has the most potential for good. For everyone involved, even if it's painful to do."

Ann's eyes filled with tears. How could she comprehend this? Why should Susan have to go through any more pain or difficulty? She was innocent. This couldn't be the way. Frustration surged while she tried to analyze the turmoil inside. "Susan...I..."

"Ann, you don't have to agree with me. Just trust I'm fine and I'm sure about what I'm doing. I'm all right."

Now Susan was comforting *her*. Everything seemed upside down.

Is this really what You want for her? How can it be? How can I trust You if this is what You want her to do? I'm sorry, but it's not right.

Ann sighed. "Well, I'll let you get back to your dinner prep. Guess I should eat something, too."

"Thanks for checking on me, and I *am* fine. See you in the morning." Her voice held a smile.

"I'll be there bright and early. 'Bye."

Ann sat for a long while and stared at the phone. Her mind meandered from one thought to another, her body immobile as she tried to make sense of the conflicted emotions inside. She'd better not call her parents yet. Not until she calmed down.

Ann plodded into the kitchen and rummaged through the freezer. She removed a glass container of macaroni and cheese and green beans. She set it in the oven and slumped in a chair at the table. Next to her arm sat her Bible with some of her note papers on top of it. Part of her wanted to read, to try and receive guidance or comprehension. The rest of her feared this new road.

I don't think I can do it, if this is what it means.

She laid her head down on her arms. Where was the peace she'd had? Where were the answers she needed? Ann yearned for Tom. He'd be able to help. She ate part of her dinner and stared at the clock. Tom would call after he got Jesse to bed. She could wait. Better call Mom and Dad.

"Mom?"

"Hello, dear. You're still coming on Sunday, aren't you?"

"Yes, Mom. I called to tell you something."

"About your Tillman fellow?"

"No... Mom, Susan is all right, but she got attacked in the bakery parking lot this morning."

Mom gasped. "Oh, no." Her voice rose in pitch. "I don't believe it. I don't believe it. What happened? Do you know who did it? Where is she? What happened?"

"She's at her place, Mom, and she's okay except for some bruises. She fought him off and he drove away, but he's in custody now."

Mom's words poured out like floodwater. "How do you know he's not back out already? Were you inside when it happened? What if he's stalking you right now? You and Susan need to stay here where you'll be safe. We'll leave right away and come for you."

Ann closed her eyes. "Mom, please calm down. It happened before I got to work. I don't think he knows I even work there." No point in telling Mom the guy had seen her on the street. She sounded frantic enough already. "The policeman told Susan he wouldn't be getting back out because he's on parole and now he did this. He said not to worry."

"How can he be sure? People get out all the time on bail. I want you girls to come here."

"Mom, previous offenders on parole don't get released unless they're rich or something. But he's not. We're both fine. If I thought I needed to, I'd be there."

"Well...I'm not sure about this. I'm going to ask your father." Her mother relayed the details.

"Ann?"

"Hi, Dad." Thank goodness. He'd get Mom calmed down.

"Honey, I agree with Mom. I think you and Susan should be here."

Ann took a deep breath. "We're not in danger, Dad. I realize it would make you feel better, but honestly, we're both fine. We'll be at work tomorrow like usual, and I'll come over on Sunday." She gave a small laugh. "Believe it or not, Susan is calmer than me."

"I have a friend at the police station. If he tells me not to worry about this, then all right. Otherwise, I'll come and get both of you. No arguments."

"Okay, Dad."

"I'll call you back. Bye, honey."

"Bye, Dad."

Ann breathed in relief. Ten minutes later, the phone rang.

"Well, I guess you were right, Ann. He won't be out on bail, even though the judge hasn't said so yet. Don't tell anyone that except Susan. If either of you are the least frightened, the offer stands. We'd be only too glad to pick you up and have you here."

"Understood, Dad. And thanks. I'll be fine."

"We love you. Tell Susan how sorry we are this happened to her."

"I will. I love you guys, too. Bye, Dad."

"Bye, dear."

Call me, Tom.

Ann sat in her chair as her thoughts and emotions swirled like leaves in the wind. At seven-thirty, the phone rang.

"Hello?"

"Hi, sweetie." At the sound of his voice, something tight inside her came unraveled. "So what's up? Did you have a good day?"

Ann laughed, the last thing she expected to do. The laughter emptied out a measure of stress. After she stopped, he said with a knowing tone, "Either you had a really good day or a really bad one."

She took a deep breath and told him everything. He interrupted a few times to ask for clarification, his voice serious. Once she finished, he remained quiet. She waited a minute, and asked, "Is something wrong?"

"Yes. Two things. One, do you realize it easily might have been you? And two, why didn't you call me right after it happened?"

"I know it could've been me." She closed her eyes for a moment. "He came into the bakery yesterday afternoon. I was scared and hid from him in the back while Susan waited on him. I guess he figured she worked alone from what he asked her." She rubbed her forehead and sighed. "I felt guilty later when I thought about it. Maybe if I'd gotten to work earlier or hadn't hidden from him, it wouldn't have happened at all."

"You can't be sure of that. He might have tried to attack both of you if you'd been around. Now what about not calling me?"

"Well, I wanted to and almost did more than once, but I figured you'd be busy with Jesse and all the farm work. The police asked us to come to the station after Susan was checked at the hospital. I wasn't sure when I'd get home or where I'd be later."

She leaned back in her chair and stretched her neck and shoulders. "Then when I came home this afternoon, I was worn out and took a nap. By the time I got up, made dinner and cleaned up, I figured you'd call me soon, so I waited."

Silence again.

"Are you okay?" she asked, when he still hadn't responded.

He sighed. "I don't know. I'm pretty upset. I wish you'd called me right after it happened. I hate finding out about it like this. We need to get cell phones. I should have been with you, especially before you found out he'd been taken into custody. Didn't you want me with you?"

"Of course I did. But I didn't want you to think you were stuck with one of those hysterical types who can't calm down. My parents always taught us to cope on our own." Even though Mom doesn't. She grinned at the thought.

"All right, stop that." His voice held a firm edge. "I don't care how you were raised. I want you to call me any time of the night or day, no matter what. I should've been with you today, period."

"Well, you told me you had so much work to do," she protested.

"Didn't you hear what I said?" His angry tone surprised her.

"Sorry." Frustration surged. Why didn't he appreciate her consideration of the demands on his time? They were both quiet. Discomfort tensed her neck and shoulders. She remained still, not sure what to say.

"I'm sorry." Tom blew out a breath. "I haven't been this upset in a long time. I didn't mean to snap at you. I can't stand the thought you might've been harmed. Don't ever think my work is more important than you are."

"All right." She breathed in while her shoulders relaxed.

"Well. I guess we had our first fight." His voice was soft.

"Not much of a fight, really. More like a misunderstanding."

"That's how most fights start." He chuckled.

"True." She smiled and took a luxuriant stretch. "Guess we can't argue about that."

He laughed. "I'm coming over. I want to hold you and make sure you're okay. I'll ask Mom to stay here in case Jesse wakes up or needs something. I'll be there soon."

"All right. Bye."

She hung up, and hurried to make herself presentable. She waited by the window, and her heart raced when he came into sight, striding to her door, his expression solemn. How dear, how handsome. He was still a few steps away when she flung open the door. He swept in, shut it, and took her in his arms.

They stood in the hall, wrapped around each other while one of his hands pressed her head against his chest. They breathed together for many minutes. Ann listened to his heartbeat as if it were the most beautiful music in the world. Tom pulled away and scrutinized her.

After a few moments he gave her a gentle kiss and walked with her to the couch. She burrowed her face on him while he held her. They sat in peaceful closeness as the minutes eased by. His presence drew the anxiety and pressure out of her. She floated and twirled inside like a leaf on water.

He nuzzled her hair. "Thank God you're safe. Tell me how you are."

"Happy, now." Ann snuggled closer and let out a contented sigh. She wanted to stay next to him forever.

"Ann, I wish I'd been with you today. I could have—" She raised her face and drew him to her in a kiss.

Tom's caress started as gentle, yet she responded as though she wanted to melt into him. His fervency rose to match hers, but after a few intense minutes, he broke it off and breathed out, "Whoa."

She made a small, involuntary noise of frustration. He laughed and clasped her to him. "I think you're more upset than you realize."

"It's not that," she shook her head against his chest. "I want to keep kissing you and stay close. I love you."

He chuckled again. "I love you, too. But trust me?"

She sighed. "Okay, I will."

They gazed at each other. She caressed his face with her hands. His head dipped back to hers, and another kiss left her breathless. Tom rocked her in his arms for some minutes, as her respiration grew more even.

"Will you be all right? Not scared or anything?" He studied her.

"I'm fine. I'm not afraid now he's been caught. I wish you'd stay with me anyway. I'm happy around you."

"Ann, believe me, I'd love to stay. Or bring you home with me." She became lost in his eyes.

"I think I better go." His tone sounded blank as he continued his steady gaze. He cleared his throat, glanced away and then back

[156]

to her. "Keep your door double-locked from now on. Always check first before you open it."

"I will," she replied, mesmerized by his face.

He released her. "You should get some sleep." He traced the outline of her face with tender fingers. "I'll phone you tomorrow. Remember, you call me anytime if you need me. I'll be here."

Ann gave him a tremulous smile and nodded.

"It's so hard to leave you." Tom's voice broke with emotion. He sighed and stared at her before he stood and drew her up with him. They walked to the door and embraced as though trying to absorb each other. Finally, he gave her a quick, tender kiss and left. She locked both locks and ran to wave to him from the window, as a few tears trickled down her cheeks.

CHAPTER FOURTEEN

WHEN ANN PULLED in to work the next morning, a police car sat next to Susan's. A flash of alarm shot through her. She hurried to get inside, her eyes focused on the squad car as though she'd figure out the reason for its presence if she stared at it.

The bakery exuded its usual warm, inviting smell of coffee and cake. Susan's laughter from the front joined the aromas in the back room and dispelled Ann's fear. She hung up her coat, listening to two men's jovial tones.

At one of the tables past the end of the counter, Susan talked with the two officers who'd brought her back from the hospital. The attentive officer from the line-up sat next to her. Steaming cups of coffee were in front of all three.

Susan caught sight of Ann. "Here she is."

Susan's lip appeared much less swollen, but the dark purple bruises under her eye and on her cheekbone still showed, though Susan had applied some kind of concealing cream over them.

It struck Ann how animated Susan appeared. Quite a contrast with the sober, quiet person of the day before. "Ann, you remember Officer Jensen and Officer Mason from yesterday?"

Susan gestured to the policeman closest to her when she said the first name, so now Ann knew which officer matched each name. Officer Jensen had blond hair, dark eyebrows and sensitive blue-gray eyes. Officer Mason had a black crew-cut, intense hazel eyes, and strong, masculine features.

"Hi," Anne replied with a smile. What a comfort to have them there.

"Well, we're pleased to meet up with you again." Officer Mason gave Ann a big smile. "Have some coffee with us."

Ann's mouth fell slightly open. Susan never sat down and drank coffee this early.

"Sure." She poured herself a decaf and joined them.

"So guess what we just did." Officer Mason asked Ann.

"Stopped a bank robbery?" Ann teased.

The two men exchanged a grin.

Officer Mason chuckled. "Nope. Never did one of those. It's a pretty well-behaved town, even with all the college students."

An expression of slight shock flickered across Officer Jensen's face as he glanced over at Susan. Ann experienced a flash of nerves and wondered if Officer Mason realized how his statement might affect Susan. He didn't appear to notice.

Officer Mason continued, "We stopped to check out a traffic snarl on the main drag downtown. We had to get out and walk to find the source of the jam-up. You won't believe this, but some guy decided to teach his girlfriend how to drive a stick shift. On the busiest street, in the early morning. How dumb can you be?"

Ann chuckled when she pictured it. "So what happened?"

Officer Jensen answered. "They were in a pretty heated argument when we got to them. I talked the fellow into getting in the driver's seat and moving the car. The girl's face had turned all red from crying and her hands were shaking. Guess she thought we planned to arrest them or something. We managed to get them on their way, though."

"Too bad her boyfriend's a moron. But, all's well that ends well, right?" Officer Mason grinned.

"Guess he won't do that again." Susan smiled at Officer Jensen.

A few minutes later, Officer Mason drank the last of his coffee and glanced at his partner. "Ready?"

"You bet. Back to the streets." They nodded at the girls and the two trooped out the door.

Susan gazed through the picture window. "What fun. Aren't they something?"

"Quite a pair," Ann agreed. They cleared the table and got to work. Around eleven, the bell rang.

Officer Mason's voice sailed out, "Hey, girls, here we are."

Goodness, back already? Susan stepped out while Ann finished taking cakes out of the ovens. Susan usually expected Ann to go out front. Interesting. She heard Susan ask in a teasing tone, "Don't you fellows have work to do?"

They laughed, the hearty sound followed by the squeak of chairs being pulled out. Ann joined them after she placed the cakes on cooling racks and smoothed her apron.

"Here she is," proclaimed Officer Mason. Self-consciousness flashed inside when everyone's eyes fastened on her. Ann took a short breath and pushed the unwanted emotion away.

"I agree with Susan." Ann drew down her brows. "How come you're not out there fighting crime, officers?"

She cracked a smile at their wide eyed, surprised expressions.

"Good one," Officer Mason said. "Call us Jeff and Eric, all right? We had to stop fighting crime and refuel, so here we are with our sandwiches. Can you girls come sit with us?"

Ann and Susan shared a glance. Would Susan want to take another break? Things certainly were different today. Ann studied the glow in Susan's eyes.

"Sure we can." Susan agreed and nodded at Ann. "We've got some time."

They arranged themselves at the table and the two girls faced the men.

Eric unwrapped his lunch. The scent of warm roast beef and mushrooms rose upward. "Traffic was backed up, and Jeff threatened to use the siren so we'd get here faster. I'm never sure if he's joking or not."

Both men chuckled, and Jeff picked up his sandwich. "Hey, I feel bad eating in front of you girls."

Susan glanced at Ann and stood up.

"We might as well eat our lunch now, too. Ann, is yours on the top shelf?" Ann nodded and began to rise. Susan told her, "I'll get it."

Susan strode to the refrigerator in the back. Both men waited to start until the girls had their sandwiches.

"This is nice." Jeff announced and smiled at Ann. "Normally we wolf our food down in the squad car. I like this set-up a lot better."

"Sometimes we have to hurry so much, I forget what I ate for lunch." Eric leaned back in his chair to brush a crumb off his shirt and onto the open wrapper.

"Sounds like us, doesn't it?" Susan asked Ann.

After they'd finished, a sound from one of their radios interrupted the post-lunch conversation. The two men cleaned up the wrappers from the table, threw them away and bid the girls a quick thanks before they rushed out. In the squad car, Eric spoke into the radio while Jeff turned the car onto the road. The siren pealed.

"Hope it's nothing serious." Susan watched the car barrel down the street out of sight.

A few hours later, they were back again.

"We're about to go off-duty. We decided we need some cake to take home. What do you recommend?" Eric grinned at Susan.

Ann stood while Susan pointed out the various flavors, and when she glanced at Jeff, his eyes were on her. She gave him a friendly smile, which he returned. Ann handed Susan two small bags for their choices. It gladdened her that the officers came by so often. The wary sensation since the attack had lessened. Ann and Susan strolled into the back room.

"Goodness," Ann remarked, "Guess we've got some new regulars. It's a good thing it's slower now or we wouldn't have time for them."

"Mm-hmm," Susan agreed in a chirpy tone and frosted a cake. Ann studied her and smiled to herself. She'd never seen Susan happy when business slowed down. Almost every customer who stopped in that day expressed their sympathy to Susan and said how glad they were the man had been arrested. Susan listened without comment to angry descriptions of what should happen to him.

Ann arrived home earlier than usual and checked her new answering machine. Warmth spread through when Tom's voice issued from it. "Hey, sweetie. One of my cows started her first labor, so I might be in for a long night. If I don't get a chance to phone you, I'll be thinking of you, and I'll call tomorrow. I love you. Sleep well."

She sighed in disappointment. Her whole evening centered on talking with him. She shuffled into the kitchen and searched through the contents of the freezer before she decided to order a pizza. After the delivery, she changed into pajamas and settled in her chair to watch some news shows before starting a movie.

Ann only half-listened to the television while she thought about Tom and all the changes in her life. The movie failed to hold her interest. She stretched, yawned and found herself staring, unaware of the passage of time. Might as well go to bed. It wasn't likely Tom would call so late.

The next day when she got to the bakery, the police car was parked outside again. Ann waltzed in. In a replay of yesterday, Susan sat at the table with Jeff and Eric. Fred showed up and bantered with the officers. They all left around the same time and the girls got to work.

"Well, I'm glad Fred came back." Susan stirred a batch of cupcake batter. "When he didn't come in yesterday, I thought maybe he'd stay so upset with me he wouldn't return."

"Are you kidding?" Ann took some butter out of the refrigerator. "He can't go too long without a piece of our cake."

The two girls worked throughout the morning and sang along with the radio when a favorite song played. As they bit into their lunch sandwiches in the office, the front bell rang. Officer Mason called out in his loud confident voice, "Hey, girls, where are you?"

Susan's face lit up. "Back here. We'll be right out."

The men stayed for almost an hour this time, and Ann realized Jeff flirted with her. She'd have been uncomfortable with it weeks earlier, but now she enjoyed the ability to interact with a man and not be intimidated. She didn't want him to think she returned the flirts, yet it was fun to be comfortable enough to joke around like anyone else would. At long last, she'd become a normal person.

When the two stopped in after work, Jeff announced, "Time to buy our dessert."

They both studied the available choices. "You know," Jeff continued while Ann and Susan waited, "We should all go out to dinner together sometime."

Susan's expression brightened. She glanced over at Ann.

Ann replied in a polite tone, "Well, thank you, but I can't. I'm dating someone."

Jeff's features showed disappointment for a second, but after a quick recovery he offered, "It's only a friendly meal. Dinner doesn't mean anything. We've been having lunch together, right?"

Ann pondered a moment while she studied Susan's countenance. She couldn't say no. Susan's eyes were all lit up in her poor bruised face. Ann wondered if Tom would be upset if she agreed. He probably wouldn't mind her cultivating some new friends. After all, she *had* eaten lunch with them.

"Oh, I guess you're right. It's just a meal."

"Super." Jeff gave her a broad smile. Ann glanced at Eric as he smiled at Susan.

"So how about tonight then?" Jeff asked.

"We should be done by six thirty," Susan answered. "You can meet us here."

Ann didn't want to be late for Tom's call. They all watched her, making her nervous. She breathed in. "Okay."

Jeff nodded at her, they paid for their cake and left, calling out, "Catch you later."

After they were out the door, Ann asked Susan, "You don't think Tom will be upset, do you?"

"I doubt it. Jeff's a new acquaintance. Tom doesn't seem like the type who'd mind if you make friends." Susan went back to work and Ann realized she'd only mentioned Jeff as a friend, not Eric. Obviously, Susan already thought of Eric as more than that.

Tom might be glad they'd made friends with policemen after what happened to Susan. He'd probably be relieved to know they stopped in the bakery every day.

After finishing work, they each arranged their hair and washed their faces.

"Good thing we wear such big aprons." Susan smoothed and scanned her clothes for any traces of flour or sugar. She reapplied some concealing cream on her bruises. Ann tried to call Tom twice, but got a busy signal. If only he had call waiting. He was right. They needed to get cell phones. The two of them were practically back in the Stone Age.

The two officers showed up at six thirty, and it caused a mild shock for Ann to see them in street clothes. She'd expected them to be in uniform. Oh, dear. It seemed more like a date now. Discomfort prickled through her middle.

"Let's go in my car. I know a super steak place," Jeff said. Ann sat in the back with Susan and listened to Jeff and Eric chat during the short drive.

"Good news, Susan," Eric turned to look at her. "I called the station before we came over. Your attacker's been charged with assault and attempted rape. The judge refused bail because he's on parole for a previous offense. He said the guy is a public menace and shouldn't be free."

Ann breathed in a relieved sigh. Susan asked, "So he has to stay in jail until the trial verdict?"

Eric nodded. "Right. I'm sure he'll be found guilty, so don't worry."

"Thank you."

"Here we are," declared Jeff. He opened the door for the girls. Once inside, he sat next to Ann in the booth he picked out.

"Smells good, doesn't it?" Jeff bumped his shoulder against hers and gave her a once-over.

Uh oh.

"It sure does." Ann glanced away and focused on the interior of the restaurant. "Nice place."

"So, tell me about yourself," Jeff murmured and fixed her with an intent gaze.

She couldn't figure out the best way to deal with Jeff's obvious interest. How irritating. She told him she was dating someone, and he still tried to pursue her. She'd be friendly and ignore anything else. Ann shrugged and answered in a casual tone. "Not much to tell."

The waitress stopped by with the menus. They ordered iced teas with lemon and chatted while they studied the choices. Ann didn't let herself become drawn into any exclusive conversations with Jeff. She made sure she joined in on table conversation only. It proved to be a difficult balancing act for her. Part of her wanted to be polite and attentive to him, but she had to resist the pressure he tried to exert. Every time she glanced at him, his probing eyes were on her.

As the minutes passed, Ann delighted in the results of her ability to navigate the situation. Though she did enjoy the outing, she yearned inside for Tom. At eight, they'd finished dessert. Ann seized the opportunity. "I hate to be a party pooper, but I'm tired and need to go home."

Susan appeared disappointed and Jeff offered, "I'll drive you, and Susan and Eric can stay if they want to."

Ann darted a glance at Susan and tried to telegraph her discomfort. Susan said, "No, don't go to all the trouble. Ann needs to go back to the bakery anyway to get her car." She gave a warm smile to Eric. "We wake up early, so I probably should leave, too."

Jeff shrugged. "Fine, whatever you girls want."

The waitress brought the check, and Eric stretched his hand out. "I've got this one."

Susan and Ann spoke in unison, "Thank you."

If Jeff had offered, Ann would've said she liked to pay for herself, or proposed covering it all instead. She pondered at the strong instinctive resistance in her to take anything from Jeff. They chatted about the meal on the way to the bakery. The two men waved to them when they drove away.

"Well, how lovely." Susan's voice and face exuded contentment. She unlocked the door and said to Ann, "See you in the morning."

"Bright and early." Ann hurried into her car and drove home as fast as she dared. She sprinted in to call Tom. The sound of the phone ringing reached her ears as she opened the door. She slammed it behind her and sped to answer. "Hello?"

"Are you all right? I called on and off for the last hour. I called the bakery, too, and nobody picked up. I've been pretty worried."

She sat down and took a deep breath. "I'm fine. I just walked in."

"Where were you?"

"I went to grab something to eat with Susan and the two officers who brought her back from the hospital. They've been stopping in at work the last couple of days to check on us. Tonight they told us the attacker got charged, and the judge denied bail. What a big relief."

"That's good." He stayed quiet.

She wondered what his thoughts were. "Are you okay?"

"Well, to be honest, I'm upset you didn't call me and let me know you wouldn't be around until later."

"I'm sorry. I did try twice before we left, but all I got was a busy signal. I figured I'd be back earlier than this, and I'd call you as soon as I came home." She fidgeted in her chair. "I should be totally honest and tell you I didn't want to go to dinner with them. I'm pretty sure one of the officers is interested in Susan, which is fine, but the other one seems interested in me. I was afraid he might think of tonight as a date or something." She sighed. "I could tell Susan really wanted to go, so I went."

After a pause he asked, "Do you like this guy?"

"I enjoy having them both as friends, and I think Susan likes Eric Jensen a lot. They're fun to talk to. The other guy's name is Jeff Mason."

"Oh," Tom replied in a knowing tone.

"What?"

"I met both of them. They took my statement at the hospital after Judy was pronounced dead. The Mason guy acted suspicious about why we waited so long to bring her there. The questions he asked made it sound like he thought I'd waited until I figured she wouldn't survive."

Ann's heart fell, and icy shock thudded inside her. Tom paused and drew in a breath. "I know police officers are supposed to investigate all possible angles, but I sure didn't appreciate it. He's kind of full of himself, but the other officer seemed pretty decent."

She wished she hadn't said she wanted Jeff as a friend. Someone who'd been so unfeeling to Tom in the midst of a horrible tragedy? Sometimes she was such a dunce.

"You can be friends with him if you want," Tom assured her. "I forgave him a long time ago. He was trying to do his job, I guess, and he doesn't seem to be a sensitive or perceptive person anyway, so there's no point in expecting him to act differently than he did."

Jeff did give off an aggressive, take-over-the-room attitude, now that she thought about it. She realized part of the discomfort she had around him was because he didn't listen to people. He wanted to be listened *to*.

Tom cleared his throat. "I hope I didn't ruin your evening. You sound like you had a good time, and I don't mean to put a damper on it."

"You didn't. I'm embarrassed about saying I'd like him for a friend." She massaged her forehead and sighed. "I can't stand the thought of how he treated you." She shook her head. "I didn't want to go, and the whole time I had to resist his flirting and the way he tried to get me to talk only to him. I kept wishing you were with me instead. But the meal tasted really good," she added in an optimistic voice.

"So do you want to be friends with him? Like I said, it's okay with me."

"Susan really likes his partner. Jeff is perfectly fine to be around if you're small-talking, because he's pretty entertaining. He takes his job seriously and is close with Eric, who seems to be a good guy. But if he keeps flirting and trying for more, I guess I'll need to ignore him. I don't think having a talk with him would help."

"Probably not." Tom chuckled. "I'm glad you're home. I imagined all sorts of things until you answered the phone."

"Well, I won't be going to dinner with him again, that's for sure. So I won't miss any more calls."

"How did he persuade you to go?"

"Susan looked so excited, and he told us it would only be a friendly meal. They'd already eaten lunch at the bakery with us." She paused for a moment and continued, "I probably shouldn't have, because he's likely to believe my relationship with you isn't serious. It didn't occur to me at the time, but I can see it now."

"Well, as my Mom says, 'Live and learn.' There are lots of men like Mason, you know. There'll be other guys who try and flirt with you."

"I hope not. It was uncomfortable."

Tom laughed again. "I love you."

"I love you, too," Ann stretched in satisfied relaxation and asked, "So how is your cow?"

Tom provided details about the long labor and difficult birth and how tired he'd been all day. "But hearing your voice perked me right up. She and the little one are doing really well today."

"Well, I'm glad. I'll bet Jesse's excited about the calf."

"He is. She's got this cute pattern like a little mask on her face, and he said, 'Daddy, let's call her Batman.'" They shared a laugh. "I told him the name's kind of weird for a girl. But he said, 'She won't mind.' The calf wobbled over to him and licked his hand and he said, 'See? She likes it.' So, now we have a calf named Batman."

Ann chuckled and Tom said, "Jesse's like having a live-in comedian. He always makes me laugh."

"Me, too," Ann agreed. "I miss him."

"He misses you."

Tom yawned and Ann smiled. "It's time for you to get some sleep. You must be all-in."

"I am. Now I know you're home and safe, I can fall asleep. I'll come by in the morning to take you to breakfast. All right, sweetie?"

"You bet. Call me before you leave, and I'll be ready. Goodnight."

"Goodnight, Ann."

Oh, Tom, you're such a gem.

[170]

CHAPTER FIFTEEN

Tom CALLED HER at 7:00 and she hurried to get ready. The sunny fall morning hinted at warmth, but the chill hit when she opened her door to go outside and climb in the truck. Most of the leaves had changed into brilliant colors and the fallen ones swirled around the street while they drove by. Ann experienced a swell of happiness while she rode with Tom and Jesse. They traveled to a restaurant a few blocks away from her apartment, which offered a good breakfast menu.

"Boy, am I hungry," Tom declared when they parked.

Jesse bounced in his seat. "Me too, Daddy, me too."

"Me three." Ann fluffed Jesse's hair.

Tom and Ann ordered western omelets with cheese and toast, and Jesse wanted scrambled eggs and flapjacks from the children's menu. The plates were delivered promptly, delicious aromas issuing from the hot food.

"Oh, boy," Tom said as he dug in.

"Daddy makes good pancakes." Jesse licked some syrup off his thumb. "And sometimes Grandma gives us them for dessert and puts chocolate chips inside."

"Oooh, it sounds yummy." Ann grinned and marveled at Jesse's precision with his knife and fork.

"Mmm-hmm." Jesse nodded with vigor and took another bite.

Her bond with them both overwhelmed her, as though they were already a family somehow. When Tom dropped her off he gave her an intense, loving gaze before telling her he'd call her later. She answered him with a jolly smile, said goodbye to both of them and waved from her door before heading inside.

Ann decided to take a short nap before she left for her parents' house. She always relished extra sleep on her day off, and dozed for a while. She woke and stretched, immersed with a sense of thankfulness and gratitude. Ann glanced at the clock. 10:35. In a flash, she decided to go to services at Jim Cortland's, popped up, and rushed to dress and leave.

Ann arrived during the instrumental music. She slipped in the door, sat in the back and listened while her eyes scanned the assembled people. She recognized Susan a few rows up from her, and Eric Jensen sat next to her. How unexpected. Why hadn't Susan said she'd attend with Eric this morning?

She didn't have much time to ponder it, as the music stopped, and Jim started the prayer before the song service. Ann's eyes were closed on and off during the song service, but she glanced often at Susan and Eric, curious to view their interactions. They both joined in on the songs with obvious enthusiasm, and exchanged frequent smiles.

When the song service, Jim's teaching, and the Bible readings were over, Jim spoke to all of them concerning Susan's situation.

"Susan and I have talked about this a few times since the attack, and she's told me many people, including other believers, don't understand her decision to forgive her attacker. I sympathize with their reaction, but Susan wants to do what the word of God and her inner convictions teach her to do. We should pray for her, and also realize that no one can tell her which choices to make, no matter how angry they may be at this man's violent actions."

Guilt pressed down on Ann. She was one of the people he spoke about. Jim stopped and scanned everyone. "Susan is glad he's in jail and can't harm anyone else as he did her, but she feels it's important we reach out to him and try to show him a path away from where he is." He sighed and shook his head before he continued.

"All things are possible with God, and it's our job to let people know if they repent and turn away from wickedness and evil deeds, they can be forgiven. For many, it will be a hard road, and the consequences of their actions will follow behind. We need to offer them not only God's forgiveness, but the cleansing, transforming power provided through His Son, without which they cannot enter the kingdom."

Jim asked for anyone wanting prayer to please come up. Susan rose right away, and many people moved forward to pray. Eric stood behind Susan, his head down as the Cortlands and others prayed for her. Ann bowed her head at her seat, wanting to be part of the corporate prayers.

Please forgive me if I did wrong by discouraging Susan's intentions. She needs to listen to You, not me. Please guide her, heal and help her.

Numerous voices cried out while they prayed, and soon a dynamic rush of power swept through the room. Some people jumped and shouted as though in celebration while others gave thanks and raised their hands. This continued for long moments.

[173]

Ann cried, too, overwhelmed at the emotions she perceived. As the strong sensation of power melted into an even stronger sense of peace, Ann knew she'd been part of some kind of healing process she didn't comprehend. She sensed the reality of the experience, and that it had something to do with Susan's honest wish to follow the example of forgiveness set by Jesus.

A compelling curiosity and yearning to understand more about things like this filled her. What did it mean? Ann scanned the faces around her and discerned from their expressions how moved many of them were. Jim stood in front of them.

"Please continue in prayer for Susan and for all involved." He closed his eyes. "Father, guide us through the week and be with our hearts and minds, in the mighty name of Jesus." He looked up and smiled. "You're dismissed. God bless you all."

Eric helped Susan with her coat, and Ann waited for them to spot her.

"Ann." Susan chirped when they drew near.

"Hi." She beamed at both of them.

Eric asked, "Hey, Ann. Want to have lunch with us?"

"I'd love to, but I told my Mom I'd be over today once I got up and around. I decided to come here first, so I better get going." She smiled at them both, a peaceful sensation inside her. "I'm glad I came today."

"Me, too." Susan's voice sounded serene, and Eric nodded in agreement.

"Anyway, see you in the morning," Ann called to Susan as they walked toward their cars.

"Bright and early." They grinned at their little ritual.

Ann drove to her parents' house. Her older sister Margie and her husband Dane arrived when she did. Ann loved and enjoyed both of her brothers-in-law, especially Dane. He possessed a droll sense of humor and said things which made them all erupt in laughter. His father had been stationed in England during Dane's teen years and he often voiced his funny observations in an English accent.

"Hi-ho, Miss Annie." Dane greeted her with a boisterous hug. She loved his friendly, light brown eyes, their color almost the same as his hair. Dark eyebrows created a handsome contrast. Margie, though more reserved than her husband, followed suit with a quick embrace. Brown bangs framed her oval face and blue-gray eyes.

Glenda, Ann's second older sister met them at the door, her eyebrows raised. "You're finally here. Did you really sleep this late?"

Glenda would never understand her love of naps or sleeping in. Once Glenda woke up, she hit the ground running and didn't quit until nighttime. She needed a mere five or six hours of sleep and popped awake near dawn, ready to go.

"Actually, I got up at seven." Ann wondered what she'd think of that as she made her way to the living room and greeted everyone. "Where's Gram?"

"Hi, honey. She's on the phone." Dad waved, his tall build wedged into his easy chair. His dark hair had grayed and thinned, but his gentle expression wore a youthful aspect.

"Why weren't you here earlier?" Glenda demanded. Her unflappable husband Greg glanced up from the newspaper, his handsome face turned to study the interaction. He gave Ann a smile of welcome. Greg bore a quiet demeanor similar to their father, and Glenda took after their mother in both physical and emotional characteristics. Ann thought it comical how this dynamic played out in the next generation.

Guess I'm like Dad on the outside, and Mom on the inside. Funny.

[175]

Ann was accustomed to questions by her sisters about her sleep habits. She might as well jump right in. "Let's see. I went to breakfast with Tom and Jesse at eight and came home, took a quick nap, and attended church before I drove here."

She delighted at their widened eyes and surprised silence.

Margie's pert face turned to her and she furrowed her brow. "Who are Tom and Jesse?"

"Went to church?" Dane asked, with an incredulous look on his open features. He blinked his eyes at her.

Mom said, "I know who Tom is, but who's Jesse?"

"His son," Ann said. "He's four and the cutest little boy I've ever seen."

"Well, who's Tom?" Margie asked with obvious impatience, her hands on her hips. She resembled their mother, most of all when her blue eyes sparked with strong emotion.

"Tom Tillman. We're dating."

"I assume he's divorced. How does his ex feel about this?" Glenda folded her arms and tilted her head. Ann sighed. She figured they'd triple-team her.

"His wife died after she gave birth to Jesse," Ann answered in a calm tone.

"Oh." Glenda's voice lowered, and her cheeks turned pink.

"Did you meet him at church?" Dane prompted.

"Actually, no, he doesn't go to church. I met him at the bakery when he ordered Jesse's birthday cake."

Mom jumped in. "I used to sing in high school choir with his father, Joe. So is he on Broadway yet?" she asked Ann. She flashed her gaze around the room and commented, "I always told him he should be on Broadway with a voice like his."

[176]

"He's still a farmer." Ann smiled. "Tom says his Dad sings to the animals in the barn, and they're the only audience he wants or needs."

Everyone chuckled. Dane asked, "How did you end up going to church? Sorry I keep asking, but I seem to remember you saying you thought it was a big waste of time."

"I did say that, didn't I?" Ann remembered. She added, half to herself, "Well, I sure was wrong."

Dane's brows crinkled while he contemplated her. "Is it because of what happened to Susan?"

"No, Susan and I visited before the attack."

"Visited where?" Margie asked.

"At Jim Cortland's church," Ann answered.

"Oh." Mom's tone sounded like disappointment.

Ann's attention turned to her mother. "What?"

"Well, nothing really, dear. I've heard some odd things concerning them. The Cortlands are kind of old hippies and their services are overly emotional."

"I don't know about that," Ann defended Jim and Evelyn. "They're genuine, and I'm quite comfortable in their church. He's an excellent teacher, too."

"I hear they have electric guitars playing right in the church." Her mother scanned the room.

"Yes, they do," Ann agreed in a bright voice. "It's wonderful music." Though Mom meant it in a negative way, Ann decided rather than to try and argue with her about it, she'd respond as though Mom intended to be positive. Dane pursed his lips and suppressed a smile while his eyes danced at her. Ann's father studied her, a grin crinkling the laugh lines around his eyes.

Grandma stepped into the living room. Arthritis had slowed her gait, and white hair crowned her head, but her eyes were ageless. She made her way over to greet Ann, and clasped one of her hands in hers. "My, you look wonderful and happy, honey. So what's going on with you?"

"I *am* happy. Let's sit on the porch, and I'll tell you."

"You two go ahead while we finish getting lunch ready," Mom said.

The Shaws' home sported a glassed-in back porch with baseboard heat and lots of sunlight. Pots of herbs and flowers in pretty containers stood all around, adding to the beauty of Ann's favorite place in the house. They sat, and Ann told Grandma everything about her recent events. When she spoke at length about Tom and Jesse, her grandmother observed in a knowing voice, "You're in love, aren't you?"

"Yes, I am. I haven't dared tell anyone except you and Susan, and of course, Tom. Everyone will say things like, 'You've never had a boyfriend,' and 'He's got a child who isn't yours,' or, 'How can you be sure you're in love so soon?'"

Her grandmother studied her for a moment. "You know your own heart and mind. Stand up for yourself. It's your life."

"That's true, but I feel as though my life belongs to God, too, not only me." Ann described some of the experiences she'd received during prayer at home and at church since she'd met Jim Cortland. "All of this happened after he told me God loves me. My heart opened up. The world looks different to me now."

Grandma listened in silence while she spoke, and remained quiet for a minute before she gave Ann a bright smile. "Well, you've given me something to think about, old as I am."

Mom popped her head in the doorway. "Come on in to lunch now, ladies."

They rose and followed her, after Ann and Grandma exchanged a confidential glance. The aroma of minestrone laced the air as they assembled and sat at the table.

Mom steered the conversation, as always. She glanced around, passed the plate of sandwiches and announced, "The principal is considering expanding the media rooms."

Dane scowled and replied, "Not by cutting the music budget, I hope. We're already a bare-bones operation. In fact, bones may end up to be the only extra instruments we'll be providing in future."

"Ha, ha." Margie frowned at Dane. "That's nothing to joke about."

Dane saluted her and grinned. "Precisely, my love."

Dad smiled and added, "Humor is a useful coping tool. And Dane wouldn't be Dane without joking around."

Greg laughed, nodded, and spooned up some soup. Glenda informed everyone, "We'll just have to wait and see what the school board decides."

Dane added, "And if we don't agree, we'll organize one of those sixties-style protests, right?"

"Not likely," Greg pronounced after a chuckle. The conversation flowed in its usual pattern. Mom, Margie, Glenda and sometimes Greg contributed most of the talk with Dane's added comments and jokes. Ann preferred to listen anyway, but often wondered if Dad ever felt ignored or left out.

After lunch they spent all afternoon watching televised football games and engaging in lighthearted disputes over the performance of the players and coaches. Mom bustled back and forth between the kitchen and the living room. Luscious aromas seasoned the air. That evening after enjoying her grandmother's favorite dinner of corned beef, potatoes, carrots, and cabbage with homemade biscuits, they sat together in the living room.

Mom asked, "How is Susan doing?"

"Her face looks so much better, and she's been very calm about the whole thing. Also, she's seeing one of the policemen who took her to the hospital. Eric Jensen."

"Hey, I know him," Greg remarked, "He works as a mentor to troubled kids after school. He's a good guy."

"I think so, too." Ann nodded her head and grinned.

"How wonderful for Susan. A policeman." Mom murmured. "Such a sweet girl."

Mom didn't say it was wonderful when she told her about Tom, and hadn't said so in subsequent conversations, either. Did she disregard him because he farmed? The thought bothered her. Mom did hold kind of a bias and preferred associating with other professional people.

Ann drew in a breath and studied her mother. Instead of making assumptions about what Mom thought, she should ask her instead. No, it wouldn't be wise to do that during a family gathering. Mom tended to get volatile if questioned on her opinions.

By half past nine, Ann covered a yawn. "I better go. I have to wake up earlier than usual. We've got an extra college order again, and they always take a lot of time."

"You get up early enough as it is." Mom retrieved her coat from the closet.

Ann hugged everyone. When she embraced her grandmother, a gentle whisper sounded in her ear. "Remember, stand up for yourself."

Grandma kissed her cheek, and a tide of love warmed Ann inside. She waved good-bye at the door while the others chorused their farewells to her. Too bad she couldn't relate to Mom the way she did to Gram. Mom never seemed to have enough time to concentrate on listening.

At home, Ann perched in her chair while her mind traveled over the day. Tom wouldn't call her this late, so she settled for thinking about him. She jerked when the phone rang.

"It's me," Tom's voice sparked her smile. "I called earlier then figured I'd wait until tomorrow, but I feel like I can't go to sleep until I say good night to you. Hope you don't mind."

"Why on earth would I? I'm sitting here thinking about you. I'd rather be talking to you." She relaxed into the chair.

"You know, sometimes I worry Jesse and I have turned your schedule upside down, and you'll start to miss your old life."

Ann laughed so hard she grew short of breath.

Once her laughter ceased, he said, "Guess I was wrong, huh?"

They talked in cheerful contentment for a time. Ann told him about Eric coming to church with Susan, and what happened during prayer. Tom became so silent, she wondered if he'd fallen asleep.

"Still with me?"

"Yeah, I'm here." His voice sounded quiet and serious. "Does Susan honestly want to go visit him in jail?"

"Yes, she does. She said it right after the attack, and I told her she shouldn't forgive him or even talk to him. I figured she'd drop the idea."

They were both quiet.

"Wow." Tom whistled.

"I felt guilty about what I said after Jim talked to all of us today. I realized Susan has a deep relationship with God, and in all the time I've been her friend, I didn't realize the depth of it. You can't react like she did unless your perspective is different from most people, myself included."

"Well, a lot of times you don't see things right in front of you until you're looking for them."

"It's weird but true. Ever since Jim told me God loved me, it's like this whole other world came into focus. It's one I want to be part of, but sometimes it's kind of scary."

"You're right...well...better hit the hay. Long days tomorrow for both of us."

"True. I love you. Good night."

"And I love you. Good night."

She hung up and wished Tom had experienced the prayer at church. If he had, some of his obvious discomfort might be less. Someday, maybe.

THE NEXT MORNING she arrived early to spot an unfamiliar car next to Susan's. She wondered who it belonged to and raced in. Her shoulders and stomach relaxed at the sound of Susan's laughter out front. The aromas of chocolate and raspberry rose from the pans lined up to cool off.

"Good morning," Eric said when Ann walked through the archway.

"Good morning," echoed Susan.

"You're here early," Ann said to Eric in a playful tone.

"I thought I'd come say hello before work. After Saturday night, I'm not sure if Jeff will want to keep coming in for breaks."

"Why?" Ann asked.

"I think he got the message you're serious about the guy you're seeing. He's pretty used to attention from any girl he flirts with. Either he'll consider you worth the challenge, or he won't come around."

"He sounds like kind of a jerk." Ann wished she hadn't spoken. It sounded so petty. "Sorry."

"Don't be." Eric raised a hand. "I understand, and I know Jeff pretty well, too. For all his swagger, he's kind of insecure. That's how he covers it up." Eric took a sip of coffee, smiled at the two girls and continued. "I've been his friend since we were in junior high. Jeff had a rough home life, and he's done pretty well for himself despite it. He has a good heart, but he's convinced the way he acts is how a real man is supposed to act."

"*You* don't. Doesn't he think you're a real man?" Susan eyebrows rose.

"Yeah, but sort of a different kind," Eric admitted and chuckled. "I've been his friend so long he knows he can trust me, even if he doesn't understand me sometimes."

"I'm glad you told me," Ann said. "Sorry again about the rude comment."

"Don't worry... Well, I better shove off and let you get busy." He waved at the two of them and his warm gaze rested on Susan for a moment before he left.

"Isn't he awesome?" Susan stared out the window.

"Yes, he is. My brother-in-law said he mentors troubled kids at school after hours."

Susan grinned. "He does."

They rinsed their cups and stepped in the back.

Susan opened the refrigerator. "We've been on the phone every night since I got attacked. I used to be attracted to guys for dumb reasons, but he's a real person, a good guy. I like him a lot. I hope he feels the same way."

"He must. After all, he met you when you looked like Frankenstein," Ann teased. Susan chuckled while she assembled frosting ingredients.

Ann grinned, looped her apron over her head and tied it behind her back. "Hey, that made me remember something my mom told me when I was a teenager."

"What?" Susan mixed butter and sugar.

"You know how she would never tell my sisters or me anything too positive about our looks? Always telling us how unimportant appearances were. Well, one day, I guess I must have been around fifteen, all chubby and lumpy with braces and freckles, and I asked her, 'Mom, am I pretty?' She studied me for a moment and said, 'You have the kind of face people remember.' I said, "Thanks, Mom. So does Frankenstein."

The two girls laughed together. Ann turned her eyes to Susan and added, "I just realized something. Maybe Mom got so dismissive about looks because of me. I mean both my sisters are cute like Mom and didn't go through the fat, awkward, braces phase. I never thought of this before, but I actually think that's partly why. You know something? Maybe I don't understand Mom as well as I think I do." She shook her head. "Pretty sweet, really."

Susan gave Ann a fond, understanding smile before they both got too busy with work to converse. The hours sped by, and Ann pondered the absence of Jeff and Eric for their morning coffee break. She regretted that the regular visits were over. She enjoyed their personalities, stories and funny banter.

Just before noon, Ann glanced out the window as Eric and Jeff pulled up. She smiled when they walked in.

"Hey, girl," Jeff said, "where's your pal?"

"Hi, guys. In the office on the phone."

"I'll go tell her we're here." Eric headed to the back and Jeff parked onto a stool.

"So, how've you been?" His voice held a jovial note.

"Busy, busy, busy. You know." Ann lifted up the coffee pot and raised her eyebrows at him.

"Absolutely." She poured a cup and delivered it to him.

"Aren't you going to have your lunch?" He plunked down the sandwich he'd brought.

"We already ate. We had an earlier start today and finally hit a lull about a half hour ago. We wolfed down our lunch in case we got busy again."

Jeff took a bite, chewed and swallowed while he studied her. His voice turned nonchalant. "So, who's this fellow you're seeing, anyway?"

"Tom Tillman."

Jeff furrowed his brow and barked out a short, derisive sound. "That sap? The guy who let his wife die?"

Ann's mouth almost popped open as angry shock coursed through her.

Jeff scowled. "Oh, man, you don't want to get serious with him. He could hardly give me a straight answer, and when I pressed him, he looked like a hammered sheep or something. He should have done a better job taking care of his poor wife."

He kept eating and shook his head. Ann forced her anger down. She took a deep breath and compelled herself to remain outwardly calm.

"Tom was so devastated he couldn't think. He deeply loved Judy, and if he hadn't had Jesse to care for, he'd have given up. She insisted Jesse be born at home, and he wanted to make her happy. That's the reason he waited to bring her to the hospital. She bled so fast after delivery they couldn't get her there in time. It's not Tom's fault."

Jeff shrugged. "I didn't remember all that. I figured if he'd been a real man, he would have told her they were going to the hospital

[185]

no matter what she wanted. She'd still be here, and the little boy wouldn't be motherless."

He plowed his way through the sandwich, unaffected by anything she'd told him. How primitive he seemed, so cut and dried about everything, as though his opinion were the only one possible, and whoever didn't agree with him must be an idiot. His closed-mindedness enraged her, yet she found herself pitying him, too.

Susan and Eric appeared out front, their demeanors chipper. Eric sat down next to Jeff while Susan poured him some coffee, and he unwrapped his lunch.

"The girls ate already," Jeff informed him as he finished his own sandwich and gulped coffee down. Ann turned at the sound of the bell, and Tom breezed in, his boots muddy and his nose pink from the chilly wind.

"Decided I'd come say hello and get some hot coffee," he grinned at Ann. "The tractor needs a part again."

He sat at the counter and nodded at the two policemen. A quick flash of shock crossed his features when he looked at Susan. The bruises on her face and around her eye were light purple, showing up through the concealer. His expression changed to a fond smile. "Hey, Susan."

"Do you want the cup to go?" Ann reached for the coffee pot.

"No, I'll drink it here. Can I use your phone?"

"Sure, it's in the back. I'll show you." Ann set the steaming mug in front of him, and he rose to follow her.

As soon as they got in the office, he pulled her to him, and they shared a long kiss. Tom whispered, "Hello."

"Hello." Heart racing, Ann ran her hands along the sides of his face. They kissed again. When he straightened up, she asked, "Did you want to use the phone?"

Tom reached behind her, picked it up, pressed a few buttons, and hung it up.

"I used it." He grinned and shot her a mischievous smirk. She laughed, delighted. When she stopped, he drew her to him and gave her an intense kiss. "I really do have to hurry. I better go drink my coffee."

"Okay." Ann let him go with reluctance.

Never enough time together.

She followed him out. Jeff's expression held a slight scowl while he scrutinized the two of them. Susan and Eric talked and laughed while Eric finished his lunch. Ann stood across the counter from Tom and spoke with him in quiet tones as he drank his coffee. Tension from Jeff radiated in the room, and she knew he watched her.

Tom paid, stood up to leave and said to Ann, "Call you later," then waved to everyone. "Bye, all."

"Bye," Susan and Eric chimed and Jeff dispensed a tiny wave, his features stern. Once Tom drove away, Jeff relaxed and began to joke around. Ann hoped he realized there was no use to continue flirting with her. She didn't want to have to say it out loud to him.

Eric stretched his arms. "Well, we'd best get back to work, or as my Dad used to say, 'Back to the salt mines.'" The two girls laughed. "He's never been a miner, though."

"Guess we'd better get back to the salt mines, too," Susan added while Eric and Jeff paid for their coffee and waved to the girls as they left.

"Whew." Ann blew out a breath and they walked to the back.

"Tired?"

"No, Jeff said some cruel things about Tom when I told him who I was dating. It took a lot of energy not to let him see how angry it made me. I'm glad he's gone. I like Jeff, but it was so unpleasant to hear that side of him."

Susan shook her head then carefully measured powdered sugar. "That's disappointing. Try to remember the other sides to his personality. Eric's told me a lot of brave, selfless things Jeff's done over the years. And of course he'll be negative about Tom because you're seeing him and he's probably jealous."

Ann stirred a bowl of vanilla icing. "I think there's more to it. He met Tom right after Judy died and his opinion of him is based on the fact that he didn't force Judy to come to the hospital for the birth. I don't think he cared about what I told him, though. He thinks Tom's a sap who let his wife die."

"Well," Susan replied in a diplomatic tone, "it's because he doesn't know Tom. We do, and we know he's not a sap. If Jeff ever makes friends with him, he'll change his mind."

Ann sighed. *Anything's possible.* "I hope so."

They focused back on their work and the afternoon marched along. Eric stopped in around four thirty, and Ann told Susan, "You go out and sit down. I'll finish boxing up the last orders."

"Sure?"

"Yep. If he's still here when I'm done, I'll come out and say hello."

"Thanks." Susan smoothed her hands over her apron and breezed out to talk to Eric. By the time Ann finished, Eric had left.

Susan strolled in the back room. "Guess we're going to dinner later. I asked him to come here instead, and I'd fix us a meal. I'm concerned when people see him with me they might think he's the one who gave me the bruises. He laughed and said not to worry about it, and he didn't want me to cook after such a long day." Susan let out a joyful laugh. "I told him I do it all the time, and he said I wouldn't tonight. Isn't he sweet?"

Ann nodded. "He is. I wonder something. He's a policeman. How does he feel about you going to visit Doug Miller in prison?"

Susan grabbed the broom and swept around the worktables. "I think it's pretty interesting. He's worried it might be hard for me, but as a believer, he thinks it could be a good thing. He considers himself a peace officer and looks at his job as a way to help prevent trouble, or keep things from getting worse." She leaned down to sweep under the tables. "He says some of the guys he works with view it like that, and others see their job as a way to control and intimidate anyone who's thinking of doing wrong."

Ann pondered this while she ran hot water in the sink basin and added soap. She figured Jeff subscribed to the second line of thought. Tom told her he'd been intimidated by Jeff's attitude. It amazed her how Jeff and Eric were such a good team, as different as they were. Ann said out loud, "Maybe they sort of balance each other out."

Susan's expression turned puzzled, and Ann explained what she'd thought. Susan nodded. "I think also you'd need both approaches in a situation. Some people respond to reason, others to force. It all depends on the person, I guess."

Ann shook her head in wonder. "You're really something."

"Everyone is." Susan stopped sweeping and beamed at her.

Ann enjoyed a warm laugh and wished all people were like Susan. What a civilized world it would be.

AFTER HER DINNER Ann sat and waited for Tom's call, too full of thoughts to read. Should she tell her family she was in love? Or would it make them overly critical when they met him? She knew they'd all adore Jesse, though. Everybody loved Jesse.

Ann's phone rang. "Hello?"

"It's me. Guess what? The harvest is in and the fall planting is finished. Hurray!" He chuckled. "Now I can see you more. Will you come out here for dinner? My parents keep asking to meet you."

Her heart thudded within her and her pulse increased. She took a slow, deep breath. *Courage.* "I'm nervous. But yes, I will. How much did you tell them about me?"

Tom paused a moment. "A lot, really. We're pretty close."

"Do they know you love me?"

"Yes."

"Oh, dear." Why couldn't she be brave like Tom?

"What?"

"Well, I haven't told that to anyone but my grandmother. Susan figured it out by herself. Everyone in my family is going to pepper me with questions and objections about my judgment and how fast this happened, et cetera."

"So? Just explain things to them. They're your family. They'll listen."

Ann guffawed. "My dad will, and my brothers-in-law, but you don't know my mom and my sisters. They're pretty high-strung and not the best listeners. They react right away."

"Do you want me to be with you when you tell them? It might help to tone things down."

"You'd be willing?" She pictured his calm presence in the face of her mother's and sister's possible over-reactions. She almost giggled at the picture.

"Sure, why not?"

"So you're up for walking into a hornet's nest?"

"I'd walk through fire for you. I can handle a hornet's nest."

She melted inside and closed her eyes. "You're sweet."

"Hey, will you come for dinner tomorrow?"

The turmoil rose again. *I need more time,* part of her clamored. She ignored it and tried to remember if they had any special orders. "I think I can be done by around six."

"How about if I pick you up at the bakery at six thirty?"

"Fine. I'll bring a change of clothes to work. Should I wear a dress?"

"Wear what you're comfortable in. I want you to be relaxed, not nervous like on our first date," he teased.

"I was so jittery I could hardly talk. I figured you'd think I was the most boring person on earth. Until I made myself relax, I couldn't think of anything to say." She smiled at the memory. "But you were great, and after a while I realized I didn't need to be afraid of you."

"What were you scared of?"

"I'm not quite sure. I worked so hard at being wary around boys and men, it became a habit. But once I reminded myself you didn't ask me out so you could pick on me, I relaxed."

A pause stretched out. Tom's voice dropped down. "Ann, why did you need to protect yourself? Did someone hurt you?"

"Only the usual teenage stuff." Ann made her tone sound light despite a surge of unease. She didn't want to talk about it. Why press down on a bruise? Besides, everyone had pain to live with. "I'm overly sensitive anyway." She let out a small, nervous chuckle. "I used to hide under the bleachers when my family went to the fireworks, because the noise scared me."

"I don't think you should make it sound as though something's wrong with being sensitive. I love that about you."

Ann's face grew warm. She found his tender sincerity comforting.

"Can I ask you a question?" Tom's voice sounded tentative.

Curiosity arose at his uncharacteristic caution. "Sure."

"Well, I've been thinking. Maybe it's me being insecure, but I need to ask." Ann never pictured him as harboring any insecurity. Was this about the dinner with Jeff?

Tom continued, "Part of me has wondered if any bit of the reason you love me is because you still think you're plain and boring, and you don't figure anyone else would love you. Okay, I said it." He took a breath and added, "Don't believe that I mistrust your feelings for me, because I don't. The thought crossed my mind and kept bothering me, so I had to ask."

Ann's heart overflowed with happy amazement at his honesty and how much he cared. "I have to admit I was surprised you liked me and wanted to keep seeing me. It's not something I'm used to, but no, I love you because of you. I think you're wonderful and admirable and I still can't believe sometimes you love me."

"I feel the same way." He chuckled. "Well, I'm glad I asked. It's bothered me ever since you told me you thought you were plain and boring. Do you still believe that?"

"Not much anymore. Sometimes I'll feel the old, sad disappointment about myself. I guess because it's familiar. But then I remember the wonderful things in my life, and that it's all right to trust in happiness."

"Good for you. The Scriptures tell us to keep our thoughts fixed on positive things. I'm curious. What made did you think of yourself in such a negative way?"

Ann thought fast at how to give a truthful reason. Without many details. "Well, all I ever heard from boys were negative comments about me...fat, shy, braces...you name it. I knew my family loved me, but most of their encouragement had to do with always working hard. I think I've been on autopilot for the last ten years. After the first meeting with Jesse, I felt different about myself. He thought I was wonderful, and it really touched me."

"Jesse's got that gift, doesn't he? He looks right into you and embraces you. My parents do, too."

"So do you." Ann snuggled into her chair and yearned to be cuddling next to him instead.

They spoke a while longer before saying goodnight. She anticipated the next evening and the prospect of time with Jesse. Ann missed his face, and even her shyness at meeting Tom's parents didn't dampen her joy at the thought of him.

CHAPTER SIXTEEN

"Relax," Tom soothed after she climbed in the truck, and he clasped her to him. "Your face and shoulders are tight," he teased, and kissed her. She relaxed into the embrace and laced her arms up around him. He pulled away after a few hypnotic moments. "Okay. You look better now."

They laughed, and he put the engine in gear and started out. Tom did a good job of keeping her mood light the entire drive. He regaled her with funny stories and diverted her nerves. The streetlights of town gave way to quiet rolling hills and farmhouses, the terrain lit by moon and starlight. When he pulled in a driveway, her nerves clenched up again. She studied the house with its outside lights shining clear into the cold night. Through the sheer curtains, she spotted people moving around.

"This is my house." Tom pointed up the road. "And my parents' place is across the street and up a short way with the bright outdoor floodlight. Dad loves that thing. He says it helps him spot any raccoons trying to pry the lids off his trash cans." Tom grinned. "Jesse heard the truck. See him peeking at us?"

He pointed at the parted curtain to the right of the door. The sight of Jesse's little silhouette delighted her. Tom settled his warm hand on the back of her neck and massaged. "They're going to love you. Let me know when you're ready."

She gazed at him, full of gratitude, so glad of his kind patience with her fears. "Thanks. We can go now."

Ann took a deep breath and let it out slowly while he strode around to open her door. Jesse jumped up and down at the window as they advanced up the stone walkway. Ann laughed at his exuberance.

"Annie," Jesse exclaimed with delight when they entered, and he ran to her.

"Hold up, Jess. Let me get Ann's coat and then you can give her a big hug." Tom helped Ann take off her jacket while Jesse waited. Once it was off, Jesse raised his arms to her and she picked him up. Tom's parents approached.

"Mom, Dad." Tom put his hand on her shoulder. "This is Ann."

"Yeah, this is Ann," Jesse echoed, and kissed her on the cheek before he turned his eyes to his grandparents. They walked forward, broad smiles on their faces. Jesse exuded such joy, Ann couldn't help but begin to relax and enjoy the playful sensation she always experienced around him. She squeezed Jesse before setting him down.

Tom's parents looked thrilled to see her.

"Pleased to see you again, Mrs. Tillman." Ann shook her hand.

"Call me Kathy." Tom's eyes were so much like his mother's.

"And this is my dad, Joe." Now she knew where Tom got his height and strong build.

Ann extended her hand. "The one with the wonderful voice."

Joe's smile grew broader when he returned her handshake. "A pleasure to meet you, Ann."

"For me, too." Their easy manner lessened her tension.

"Let's go sit down and have a visit before dinner." Kathy motioned to a large room off the hallway.

Ann took Jesse's hand and followed them into a cozy, light green room with a white ceiling. It held numerous comfortable chairs and a couch with a fluffy cat asleep on it. A fireplace in the far wall emitted gentle heat. Ann sat next to the cat and admired him.

"He's my kitty, Abner," Jesse announced and climbed up onto Ann's lap. He reached over to pet him, and the cat stirred slightly, stretched and yawned. Ann stroked his gray fur and shared a delighted grin with Jesse when Abner purred and licked her hand.

Tom asked, "Want some tea? I've got lots of different kinds."

"Peppermint?"

He nodded and turned to leave. Tension gripped her when he left the room, but Kathy gave her a sunny look and said, "Tom's told us a lot about you. Do you like working such long hours?"

"Well, when the weather gets colder, it's comforting to work in a warm place, and the hours aren't as long then, either. But I don't care for the summer as much." She made a small grimace, and patted Jesse's head.

"We do so many weddings, graduations and anniversaries I hardly have a chance to go outside and enjoy it. Plus, it's pretty hot inside with the ovens all going, even though we have a good ceiling fan system. Now with seeing Tom and Jesse," she added, giving Jesse a squeeze, "I wish I had more time off."

Jesse stopped petting the cat, smiled, and turned to hug her back. Joe and Kathy exchanged a grin. Tom stepped in with two cups of tea and a small cup with a cover for Jesse. Her nerves receded.

"Brought you some juice, pal." He set everything down on the low table in front of them, and asked his parents if they wanted tea.

"I'll get ours, honey." Kathy left for the kitchen.

"Come here, son." Tom held his hands out. "Sit next to both of us and we can all have a drink."

Joe asked, "So how's your mother, Ann? She constantly encouraged me to sing as a career. I always said I liked farming, but she didn't believe I wouldn't want to go onstage if I could." Joe chuckled. "Your mom was something. I've never met anyone with more energy. I told her she ought to be one of those people in the circus who spins plates, or juggles ten different items at once."

They laughed as Kathy brought two cups in. They spent a congenial half hour in cheerful conversation. Joe and Kathy teased Tom and told Ann some of the funny things he said and did while growing up. The aromas from the food grew stronger, and Joe declared, "Mmmm. Smells ready."

"Everything should be by now." Kathy stood while Tom gathered up the empty cups and followed Kathy into the kitchen. This time she sensed no tension after he left. Amazing.

Joe said, "Tom's gotten to be a decent cook. We taught him a few things when he was a teenager. Since Judy's parents were busy and didn't cook much, Judy never learned. Tom fixed most of the meals after they were married. He used to tease Judy about the taste of her cooking. She was a good sport with it, though."

"If they didn't cook, what did they eat?" Ann asked with curiosity, as Jesse climbed off the couch and headed toward some toys.

"Packaged meals and fast food, usually," Joe replied. "Tom prefers home-cooking, so his mother and I taught him what we knew. He also likes to watch cooking shows in the winter when he has more time. He made everything tonight except the rolls and the pie."

"He didn't tell me." Ann marveled at his abilities.

"Soup's on," Tom called out and Joe and Ann stood up.

"C'mon, Jesse boy." Joe stretched his hand out. They walked into the adjoining dining room, and Joe lifted Jesse onto his booster chair.

"Sit here, sweetie." Tom pointed at the chair on one side of Jesse after he set a casserole down on a ceramic tile in the middle of the big round table. A large bowl of salad sat next to a container of cottage cheese, a plate of rolls, a carved, roasted chicken on a platter, some glazed carrots, and a dish of green beans with mushrooms. Tom took the lid off the casserole and announced, "Old rotten potatoes."

Ann's expression must have telegraphed her shock. Tom chuckled. "Au gratin potatoes," he explained. "It's how Jesse used to pronounce it."

Ann laughed. "I love those."

"We do, too, don't we, pal? We eat them a lot." Jesse nodded and his eyes traveled over the loaded table. Tom dished up Jesse's plate for him while they passed the various dishes around. Tom asked, "Want to say grace tonight, Jess?"

"Yes, Daddy." Jesse bowed his little head. Ann lowered hers, interested to hear his words. "Thank you, God, for the food and Daddy and Grandma and Grandpa and Abner and Batman. Thank you, God, for Annie. Amen."

Touched at his simple sweet little prayer, Ann's throat tightened when she glanced at Tom's face.

"Amen," Tom said, his eyes soft on his son. Ann couldn't believe she sat here at this table, a part of their life.

"Let's eat," Tom proclaimed with a smile, and they dug in.

"This is wonderful," Ann told Tom after she'd tasted some of everything. "Your dad told me you made it all except the rolls." She nodded at Kathy. "Which, by the way, are also wonderful."

"Thank you, Ann. Tom said for me not to tell you he fixed most of the meal in case it didn't come out well." They laughed, and Kathy added in a playful voice, "That way you would have only thought *I* was a bad cook."

"Mom, you're tattling on me," Tom teased back.

Joe said, "Too late. I already spilled the beans before we came in."

Kathy grinned at Joe. "It's a parent's privilege to tell on their children." She brandished a silly face at Tom which made them all laugh again. Kathy told Ann, "It's mostly home-grown, too, except the mushrooms and the wheat for the rolls."

"Really?" Ann studied the food. "No wonder it's so tasty."

Tom glanced at Jesse. "Is yours good, pal?"

"Yum, Daddy," he chirped and speared a piece of carrot. Tom grinned at Ann. She returned it and kept eating. To her pleased surprise, she found herself able to join in the dinner conversation with ease.

Jesse finished his plate, and Tom asked, "Do you have room for some of Grandma's pie?"

"Yes, yes, pie." Jesse offered a vigorous nod.

Tom stood up and cleared the dishes. Ann rose. "Can I help you? I haven't helped at all yet."

"Sure."

She followed him to the kitchen. He gave her a quick kiss after they set the plates in the sink.

She placed her hands on his shoulders. "Should I wash them?"

"Nope." He smooched her again, and steered her back to the dining room, carrying an apple pie. Jesse cooed when he caught sight of it.

After they'd finished their dessert and chatted over cups of tea, Jesse yawned. "I'm tired, Daddy."

"I can see." Tom gazed around the table and joked, "Guess the pie kicked in."

He began to rise, and Kathy offered, "I'll take him to brush his teeth and get his jammies on. You sit and finish your tea."

"Thanks, Mom. I'll be up in a bit, son."

Tom asked Ann, "Want to come up with me when I read his story? He's tired, so it will probably be a really short one."

Ann nodded, her eyes bright.

"If he's exhausted, he's out before you reach page three," Joe added with a smile. "But he loves to be read to even if he's all worn out."

JESSE'S ROOM HAD light blue walls, and the comforter on his bed sported pictures of Batman. Ann grinned and thought of his little calf. A full bookshelf stood next to the bedstead, and a toy chest in the corner held stuffed toys and trucks. A small wooden house and barn were assembled on a low table, with toy horses and cows next to them. Family pictures were mounted on the wall, along with some original paintings of farms and landscapes.

Jesse's tired eyes widened with delight when he spotted Ann in the doorway with his dad. He asked in a croaky little voice, "Are you both reading my night-night story?"

Kathy and Ann giggled together. Kathy gave her grandson a cuddle and kiss before she left. Ann sat at the end of the bed while Tom read to Jesse. She studied both of their expressions and the way they looked at each other. Jesse fell asleep after five pages. Tom stroked back Jesse's hair and bestowed a light kiss on his forehead. They tiptoed out, and Tom closed the door half-way.

"Now that he's sleeping in his own room in a big-boy bed, he likes me to leave his door open so he can see my bed, even though my room's dark. I keep this hall light on in case he wakes up in the night. He hardly ever does, anymore." They walked past Tom's bedroom.

Ann stole a curious glance inside. She could just make out his bed and a small table next to it with a clock. A strong momentary impulse to go in and absorb what it felt like inside his room rushed through her. Glad he walked ahead of her and didn't notice her blush, she followed him down the stairs to the living room.

Tom told them, "I need to get this girl home. She's had a long day and has another one tomorrow."

He brought their coats. Tom helped her on with hers and Ann said, "I had such a wonderful time tonight. Thank you all so much."

His parents stood and Kathy hugged Ann. "You're a delightful girl. Tonight's been special for us, too. It's good to see Tommy happy."

Joe embraced her. "Come over again soon, and don't work so hard."

As they rode back to the bakery, Ann said, "I hope you have as much fun when you meet my family. I'm not sure you will, though. They're kind of nervous and serious."

And they nearly always disapproved of her choices. No point in worrying him about that now.

"I know it'll be fine." Tom took her hand and gave it a warm squeeze. He remained quiet, and Ann leaned her head against his shoulder while the scenery drifted by. What wonderful parents Tom had. They'd been so easy to interact with.

They were both funny, like Tom. Her sides were sore from all the laughter. How had they managed to make her feel secure and accepted in only one visit? Too soon, Tom parked at the bakery.

She unbuckled and snuggled against him. He hugged her to him with one arm and kissed the top of her head. After a few lazy minutes passed, he sighed and said, "I'll start your car so it'll get warm, and I'll come back here and sit for a bit until I follow you home."

When he returned, he studied her with a serious air. Ann tilted her head at him. "You were so quiet all the way back. Everything okay?"

"So I'm usually a blabbermouth?" He cracked a smile.

She rolled her eyes at him. "No, silly. You seemed deep in thought, or tired."

"I'm curious."

"About what?"

"I wondered what your impressions were concerning the farm and the house and everything. I mean if you liked it out there. You've always lived in cities and I just hoped...you were comfortable."

She cuddled up next to him. "Of course I was. My grandparents grew up on farms, and my parents always took us camping on vacations. Sometimes we went to our relatives who have a farm in the Catskills. I loved hanging around in their big barn and petting the animals. Must be partly my Scottish farmer genes." Her voice softened. "And because it's your house."

He tilted her head up to him and kissed her. "My sweetie," he murmured before he caressed her again. "I wish you had more free time now like I do."

She stroked the side of his face. "We've been finishing up lately by six most nights. The days before Thanksgiving, we get lots of dessert orders, but it should be slower until then."

His eyes widened as his brow rose. His delighted expression reminded her of Jesse. "Can you come out to my place for dinner at night after work? I hate only seeing you a day or two a week. Would you be too tired?"

"No, but I wouldn't want you to go to all the trouble." Plus, what if Tom grew weary of her company?

"What trouble?" He squeezed her tighter. "I cook every night for Jess and me anyway, unless I'm at Mom and Dad's. C'mon. Say yes."

"All right, but you have to let me help with the meal and clean up. And I'll drive out so you don't have to come and get me."

"Deal," he grinned and embraced her. "I'll see you tomorrow night."

CHAPTER SEVENTEEN

THE NEXT MORNING Fred, Jeff and Eric had left.

Ann turned toward Susan. "I'll be driving out to Tom's after closing from now on. I want you to know I won't leave you holding the bag if we get unexpected late orders. I'll stay and finish."

Susan stopped work for a moment and gazed at her with an attitude of pleased surprise. "You want to know something funny? I've been thinking, now that we've landed so many standing orders from restaurants and the colleges, we should close the retail end down at noon. Then we can finish up the regular orders and any call-ins. We don't get a lot of walk-in business after lunch anyway."

Ann grinned at her in delight. "Why didn't you say anything to me about this?"

"Well actually, it came from your idea. Remember around two years ago you mentioned it would be a good plan to expand the wholesale orders? That way, we'd get a better idea of how much to make every day and end up with less waste."

"Oh, yeah... It didn't seem like you wanted to, so I kind of forgot."

"Well, it's crossed my mind on and off, but until the wholesale part really took off this past year, I figured it wouldn't work. But since we're both seeing someone, it'd be nice to have extra time to ourselves for a change."

Ann rushed to Susan and gave her an exuberant squeeze, then stepped back and studied her. "I thought you'd be upset with me, or concerned."

"Well, I'm not." Susan grinned at her. "And I figured you'd stew over this if I mentioned it before I went through the books and made sure it would work. So we were both worried for nothing."

"Hey, what about the regulars?"

"They always come before noon anyway. Our other customers will get used to the new hours and schedule call-in orders if need be. It'll work out." Susan shot her a big smile.

Ann couldn't wait to tell Tom. She imagined the three of them together in late afternoon preparing dinner. After sharing the meal, she and Tom would play with Jesse, and read him his story at bedtime. Then they'd cuddle on the couch in front of the fire and talk. She sighed with happiness at the picture.

THAT EVENING WHILE she was at Tom's, a knock sounded after dinner. Tom left the room to answer it.

"Hey." Tom's voice sounded pleased. "C'mon in."

A little boy close to Jesse's size ran in and stopped when he caught sight of Ann.

"Jason," Jesse crowed, sped over and gave him a hug. "Look, Jason," Jesse pointed at her, "It's my friend Annie."

Ann smiled at Jason and glanced over when Tom re-entered the room. A man almost as tall as Tom with his same hair color and friendly grin stood beside him. Next to the man, a slender blonde woman with a shy smile held his hand.

"Tim, Sharon, this is Ann." Tom gestured toward her and grinned at the two boys. "And this is Jason."

Jason stared at her like a little owl. Ann sympathized with his shyness. "Hi, Jason."

She rose from the couch and stepped over to shake hands with Tim and Sharon. They exuded the same comfortable ease as the rest of Tom's family. What a warm group they were. Ann's reserve soon melted as she engaged in the jovial conversation. Her glance flicked often to the two boys, engrossed and quiet as they built a structure with small blocks. Another knock sounded.

"Grand Central Station," Tim yelled. They laughed and Tom answered the door.

"It's Mom and Dad," he called out.

Joe and Kathy walked in, their cheeks pink from the cold. Joe said, "Hi, all. We were driving back from the store and spotted everyone's cars. Thought we'd crash the party."

They settled in chairs and Tom asked, "Anyone want anything?"

"Nope. We just ate." Tim patted Sharon's knee.

"Us, too." Kathy smiled. "Sit back down, son."

Tom parked next to Ann and took her hand. His thumb stroked it while he talked. The room grew full of banter and congenial laughter. Ann's heart swelled and tears almost fell while she scanned the room and listened to their good-natured conversation.

The obvious love they shared warmed her. She so wanted to fit in with all of them and be part of their circle. After everyone left, they sat on the couch with Jesse between them. Jesse told them about the game he'd played with his cousin and acted out the different parts for them as they listened and laughed.

Jesse asked, "Are you going to stay here tonight, Annie?"

"I'd love to, but I need to get home so I can wake up early and go to work."

"Well, we get up early, too. Daddy and me'll wake you up." He gazed up at her and snuggled next to her.

A surge of yearning swept through her, and she wished never to leave. Ann clasped him to her before she raised her head. Tom stared at her with an expression she couldn't read. He appeared as though something hurt him.

"She can't stay, Jess. So, why don't you say goodnight now, and Ann can go home? She's pretty tired, pal. We don't want her to be sorry she came, right?"

Jesse said in a resigned tone, "Okay, Daddy." He gave Ann a smile. "I can get your coat for you."

He ran over to the rack and jumped up to unhook it.

"Yay, you did it." Ann exclaimed, raising her arms.

"Are you coming tomorrow, too?" he asked.

Tom answered, "Remember I told you I'm going to meet Ann's family? That's why you'll be at Grandma and Grandpa's."

"Oh yeah, I forgot."

Tom patted Jesse's head. "Give Ann a hug and kiss and put on your PJ's. I'll be right up after I say bye to Ann."

"Okay," Jesse gave Ann an enthusiastic squeeze and a peck. He turned to wave at her one more time before he raced up the stairs.

Ann couldn't help laughing in delight.

Tom's serious expression and pensive silence confused her. "Everything all right?"

"Of course," he replied in a hearty tone and helped her with her coat. He gave her a quick kiss. "I better get up there. Don't want him to fall asleep without his story."

"I love you," she said while he walked her to the door.

[207]

"And I love you. See you tomorrow."

She waved after she got in her car. Ann wondered if concern about meeting her family caused his different, almost sad expressions.

THE NEXT EVENING, Tom picked her up at her apartment. "It's funny," he said while he drove. "I'm not nervous, but I can tell you are." He kissed her hand. "You're such a sensitive little thing."

"I want them to like you, but they're hard to talk to sometimes. I'm worried their attitude might hurt your feelings."

Tom laughed. "I don't get offended easily. I figure anything they might say is out of concern for you, and I won't take it personally."

Ann smiled at his optimism and calmed herself for his sake. She realized no matter what anyone thought or said, Tom was the man for her. Nothing would change that.

Mom met them at the door and flashed them a bright smile as she shook hands with Tom then embraced Ann.

"Come in, come in," she encouraged them. Tom helped Ann take off her coat, and Mom pointed to the pegs on the wall. "You can hang them there."

She led the way into the living room and announced, "Here they are."

Everyone stood up to shake hands with Tom while Ann announced each name.

Mom and her sisters seemed to size Tom up with approval. He shook Greg's hand, and Greg said, "We have a mutual acquaintance. I know Eric Jensen."

Tom nodded. "Good guy. He dates Susan now."

Greg returned the smile. "Annie told us. I'm glad Susan found someone like him."

Mom said, "Both of you grab a seat. Would you like any coffee or tea before dinner?"

"Water, please, if you don't mind, ma'am." Tom sat on the couch next to Ann.

"Goodness, call me Rita. Want anything, Ann?"

"Nothing for me, Mom, thanks."

Mom left to get the water while Dad smiled at Tom. "How is your farm doing?"

"Fine. We've got a new member of the family. A baby calf. She's got a pattern like a mask on her face, so Jesse named her Batman."

Laughter traversed the room, and Ann's tight nerves unraveled a bit. Tom took her hand and gave it a slight squeeze. She glanced at him and caught his smile.

Mom strolled in with his water, and Dane relayed the Batman tale to her. She laughed and sat down. "So, Tom," she began, "give us the scoop on your farm."

Mom loved to hear any details about work. While Tom outlined some of the changes they'd implemented to make the farm more profitable, Ann glanced around at her family's expressions. They appeared to find Tom likable.

Tom paused and drank some water.

Mom asked, "How do you manage to work and raise your son, too? I'd think it would be hard with him not in school yet."

"My parents live across the road, and we run things together. My mother helps out with Jesse, and since he's bigger now, I bring him with me a lot while I work. He's a good helper," Tom added, with a big grin. "I'd have brought him tonight, but figured you'd better meet me first. Jesse's pretty much the center of attention wherever he goes, isn't he, Ann?"

She darted him a knowing smile and nodded. Tom regaled them with a string of cute Jesse stories. Her family added a few funny anecdotes about Ann when she was little, which delighted Tom and made Ann blush while she laughed with everyone. How wonderful that Mom and her sisters weren't grilling Tom as she'd feared they would. Like they always did to her.

Mom cleared her throat and said, "Well, girls, let's get dinner on the table, please."

Tom offered, "I can help out. I do lots of kitchen work at home."

Mom smiled at him. "Then you could help clear up afterwards."

"It's a deal."

Glenda followed Ann into the kitchen, and elbowed her in the side. She whispered, "Lucky you."

Greg had a notoriously non-domestic reputation, one of the few things about her husband which caused Glenda irritation.

"He cooks, too," Ann told her and added, "really well."

"Wow," Glenda responded as they fell into their familiar kitchen rhythm and got the food onto the table. Mom always prepared leg of lamb for special occasions, with scalloped potatoes and onions, green bean casserole, biscuits, and cake.

"Yum. Leg of lamb," Tom proclaimed when he spied the platter.

As they passed the scalloped potatoes around, Ann asked, "You know what Jesse calls au gratin potatoes? Old rotten potatoes."

They all chuckled and Dane said, "Good one. I'll remember it."

"I'm sure you will." Margie rolled her eyes at him as she handed him the biscuits.

Don't be so serious," Dane teased her. "Humor never hurt anyone."

Tom nodded at Dane and grinned as he passed the jar of mint sauce to him.

"So when do we meet the remarkable Jesse?" Dad asked, and gave Mom the platter of carved lamb.

"Whenever you like," Tom answered. "I finished all my fall planting, so now I've got more free time."

Glenda's eyebrows rose. "What do you plant in the fall?"

"Garlic, onions, hardy greens and root vegetables. Most of what I plant now is for our own family use, since the bulk of our fields go for animal pasture. "

"I see." Glenda nodded while she buttered her biscuit.

Mom asked, "How about if we plan on you coming over some weekend for lunch and bringing Jesse?"

"Sure," Tom speared a few pieces of lamb and passed the plate.

Mom smiled. "Ann and I will put our heads together and pick out a good time for everyone."

After they'd distributed all the plates around and began to eat, Ann observed Tom's quiet pause. She realized he'd said a silent prayer of thanks. She remembered Jesse's sweet grace and knew her family would be captivated by him.

After the meal, Tom, Greg and Dane cleared the table. Glenda flashed wide eyes and a popped-open mouth at Ann.

"Maybe Tom will teach Greg to cook," Glenda whispered and they giggled. They sat in the living room afterward and discussed school matters.

The subject of challenges at the high school came up, and Tom interjected, "I've considered home-schooling Jesse. What do you think about parents who choose to do that?"

Ann scanned the various expressions in the room. Uh-oh. She remembered the negative comments Mom had expressed on the topic. This might end badly. Why did he ask something controversial?

Mom answered, "Well, I used to be very much against it years ago. Since then, I've met quite a few children who were home-schooled. They changed my mind."

"Can I ask why you were against it?" Tom's demeanor was open and curious. Ann wondered if her mother would react as though he'd challenged her.

To Ann's surprise, Mom gave him a smile. "I thought a regular parent wouldn't be able to do the job of a teacher, and I still think some of them can't. But I've come to see how many of the parents who make the decision do take it seriously. And most of the children I've met who were home-schooled are thoughtful and well-spoken."

Dane added, "I concur. A number of my music students were home-schoolers for a time, and some of them are more mature than the other kids. I'm not sure why it is, but it'd be interesting to find out."

"Maybe there's too much socializing going on at school, so the students don't learn to be quiet and concentrate," Dad offered. "The ones I tutor get distracted all the time by their phones. So I made a rule. Phones not allowed in the tutor room. It's helped a lot, though they got pretty steamed about it at first."

"Don't get me started on the subject of phones." Glenda presented a grimace of frustration, and the others nodded or shook their heads and chuckled. A variety of cell-phone classroom stories ensued. It amused Ann how her mother and sisters curbed their combative sides. They must like Tom. The evening proceeded, and it gratified Ann how relaxed and comfortable everyone was with him. They showed genuine interest in his opinions.

Ann marveled while Tom drove her home. "If I'd known it would be this easy, I wouldn't have spent so much time worrying about it." She grinned. "The Shaw females were wonderfully well-behaved tonight."

Tom let out a hearty laugh. After he parked, she snuggled against his chest. She loved the sensation of his arm around her and the slight smell of aftershave on the warm skin of his throat.

He kissed the top of her head. "I told you it would be okay. They all love you very much. You just had to show them how sure you were."

Ann grinned at him. "I guess so, but I think it helps a lot that you're such a wonderful guy."

"Well, that goes without saying." She poked him in the side and Tom laughed. He returned the poke and asked, "Are you ticklish?"

"No," she answered in a warning tone.

"Liar," he teased and tickled her under her chin. She squealed and tried to stop his hand.

"Stop, stop," she gasped.

"Say please."

"Please, please." She tried to catch her breath when he stopped. He waited while her laughter slowed down.

"I love you." His eyes were dark and fixed on hers. She pulled him to her and they kissed gently.

"I love you, too," she replied when he broke the kiss off and clasped her hard against him.

"Better go in now." His voice held a slight break.

"I know." Ann sighed and climbed out of the truck. She blew him a kiss while in her doorway, and he waved before he drove away.

He always makes me happy.

Ann closed the door, leaned against it, and shouted out a whoop of joy at how well the evening had gone. She'd cleared a giant hurdle tonight, and her heart basked in the contented afterglow. The unopened Bible next to her chair caught her eye. She'd distanced her mind from God after the attack. Maybe instead, she should draw closer. Like Susan did.

CHAPTER EIGHTEEN

"I CAN'T BELIEVE how well things went at my parent's house." Ann stirred a batch of frosting.

"I knew they'd like him right away. He's a personable guy." Susan wiped some flour off her hands. "I was nervous about my parents meeting Eric. They're such dedicated pacifists, I thought maybe they wouldn't like me dating a policeman, but they're fine with it. We went over last week and had a fun time."

Ann started frosting a line of cakes. "What do they think of you visiting the jail?"

Susan stopped measuring flour and focused on Ann. "My father doesn't want me to, and my mother is afraid it will hurt me, though she did say she admires me for even wanting to."

"When are you going?"

Susan took a big breath and let it out. "On a Sunday afternoon in a week or so. Pastor Jim and Eric will be with me."

Ann thought for a moment and surprised herself. "I might decide to go with you, if you want me to."

"Honestly? You were dead set against forgiving him."

"Well I was, because I love you. It was such a brutal thing for him to do to you. But I keep thinking of the Scripture Jim quoted which says if I don't forgive other people, I can't expect God to forgive me. If you can find a way to do that, I have to try to do the same. I've asked God to help me."

Susan nodded at her. "If you think seeing Doug Miller won't upset you too much, I'd like you to come. I'm nervous, because I'm afraid it will be especially hard for Eric."

Ann stopped frosting for a minute. "Because he might be mean to you?"

"Yes. Jim told Eric it could be quite unpleasant and difficult, but he insists on going with me. You should speak with Jim, too, before you decide for sure. He's already been to visit once, so he'll have good advice." The two girls finished frosting the cakes in silence.

Ann drove out to Tom's after work, singing with the radio. She gazed with delight at the light snowfall. The temperature hovered above freezing, and the flakes melted soon after they landed. While in the air, they swirled downward in lazy patterns, giving her the sensation of driving inside a snow globe. She pulled into Tom's driveway and watched Jesse jump at the window while she approached the house.

"Annie, Annie," he sang when he hugged her and brushed the snowflakes off her shoulders. "Daddy made spaghetti and meatballs."

"Oh, boy." She hung up her coat. "It sure smells yummy."

"And garlic bread, too, and green beans. I helped with the green beans."

"You did?" She reached for the bag she'd set by the door when she picked Jesse up. "I brought some cake for dessert."

"Daddy," Jesse announced as he ran to the kitchen, "Annie has cake."

Tom turned away from one of the steaming pots on the stove when Ann walked in. He clasped her to him and gave her an enthusiastic yet short kiss before he glanced over at Jesse. Tom whispered in her ear. "Our little chaperone."

Ann helped him finish the meal while they both spoke with Jesse. Every time she caught Tom watching her, his features held a solemn expression. Since their evening with her family, she'd been so grateful and free. Why wasn't he as lighthearted as usual, now that they had no obstacles to worry about? After dinner, he asked her if she'd stay later once they put Jesse to bed.

They took turns reading Jesse his story until he fell asleep. Ann turned at the door for one more glimpse of him. His precious sleeping face touched and warmed her. Tom stood behind her, and settled his hand on her shoulder. They descended the stairs, and Tom sat on the couch then patted the seat next to him.

Ann snuggled up, and they lounged in silence for a few moments. She sensed his tension. "Tired?"

Tom remained quiet while she studied him. He stared at her a moment, kissed her, broke it off and bolted upright. He stepped to the fireplace, added more wood to the fire and stood in front of it. She waited, watching his back.

"Tom? Is everything all right?" Prickles of discomfort began in her stomach.

The flames hissed and crackled. His shoulders tightened when he slid his hands into his pockets. She heard him sigh. "I'm sorry, Ann. I'm really sorry."

"For what?" Concern spiked inside.

He turned and glanced down, his expression full of obvious discomfort. He spoke in a low, serious voice. "Ann, I've been thinking...a lot."

"Maybe this isn't fair to you," he added in a worried tone and stopped again. A stab of fear sliced through her, and twisted her middle. He walked to her and touched her cheek. "It's nothing bad," he assured her, then spoke almost to himself, "at least I hope not."

Cold panic rose in her. *He's already tired of me.*

Maybe he wanted to break off the relationship. How could he say it's nothing bad? Despair shortened her breath while images of life without him and Jesse raced in her mind.

Ann managed to speak through her tightened throat. "Tom, you're scaring me." She dreaded his next words.

"I'm sorry, I don't mean to." He stared down at her. The tension in the air intensified. Ann thought she'd be swallowed into the silence.

"I meant to do this differently, but I can't help it. I just can't—."

She stared up at him and waited. Her breathing stopped while alarm engulfed her. He knelt in front of her and leaned his face close to hers, his eyes wide.

"Will you marry me?"

Ann's tense body released while she covered her face and cried with happiness before she managed to say, "Yes, yes, oh yes."

After a pause, his gentle tone sounded in her ears. "Ann, look at me."

She wiped her cheeks and gazed at him. He reached in his pocket and held out a ring. It had a small diamond set in the middle of a circle of tiny rubies on a slender gold band. He slid it on her finger while she blinked away the last tears.

"It fits," he said with a quick grin. He sat next to her, and cuddled her to him. The last of her tension melted. He cracked his wonderful smile when her eyes met his.

His arms relaxed and she laughed. "You're so funny. Why did you think it might be bad or unfair to ask me to marry you?"

"Well, it would've been awful if you said no, and I thought it might be unfair of me to ask so soon. You're the sort of person who doesn't act on impulse and likes to have a chance to think things over. I figured you'd want more time."

She studied him. "You seem the same way."

"I usually am. Sometimes I can't believe how quickly I became sure about all this, but, well, I am. And here we are." He nuzzled her hair. "I never dared hope I'd be so blessed again."

"And I didn't imagine I'd *ever* be."

Tom pulled back to gaze at her. "People always say life is the greatest gift, but I think love is."

She smiled at him with her heart in her eyes as he bent to caress her with such tenderness it made her ache. His mouth traveled to kiss her forehead, cheeks and the tip of her nose before returning to her lips. He stopped and held the side of her head against his chest with a gentle hand.

"Is this why you've been so quiet the last few days?" she asked.

"Yes. I went and got the ring but thought I should wait longer. I was afraid I'd scare you off and ruin everything, but I felt like I had to ask. I want us to be together all the time. I couldn't think about anything else for days and it's been eating me up."

Ann sighed and closed her eyes. She chuckled and said, "I can't believe I'm not scared at all. I'm totally ecstatic."

Tom gave her a squeeze.

"My family is going to freak out." Ann grinned as she imagined their shocked responses.

"You think so? I bet they'll be thrilled once they get used to the idea. My parents have already dropped some hints to me about you, so I'm guessing they won't be too amazed when we tell them. I can't wait until we tell Jesse. Then we can tell everyone else in our family."

Ann smiled up at him. "Jesse will be so excited, but my family...yikes. I'm not looking forward to it at all."

"Want me to come with you to tell them?"

"Yes. That would be grand. At least for me. Are you sure you don't mind? They might get confrontational or overbearing."

"If they do, it's because they love you, so I won't let them bother me."

"Tom, you're so...wonderful...beautiful..."

He kissed her with a tender intensity. It tore her in half when the caress ended.

He said, "I wish we could get married now."

"My thoughts exactly." They gazed at each other and broke into simultaneous grins.

"For once, I can read your mind," she said.

"Well, you know what they say, 'Two great minds with but a single thought.' Too bad we can't elope."

"Wouldn't it be wonderful?" She let herself imagine it for a moment, but forced her thoughts back to the present with reluctance. "I'd better drive home. It's funny, though. Since I've been out here every night after work, my place doesn't seem like home anymore."

"Does it feel that way here?" His eyes were soft.

"Yes." She kissed him. "Yes, it does."

He stood up, walked with her to the door and waved when she drove away. Ann prayed with fervor and voiced her concerns about her family's reaction. She asked for help to be a good wife and mother. Now as she visualized such big changes, a twinge of fear entered. What if she wasn't good at being a mom or a wife? With God's help, she could do this. Confidence surged and the fear receded.

Thanks, Lord.

THE NEXT MORNING Ann said, "Susan, last night Tom asked me to marry him, and I told him yes."

Susan's eyes widened and a broad smile lit her face. "Why, what wonderful news!"

Susan rushed to her and threw her arms around her.

Ann laughed and returned the embrace. "I thought you might be concerned."

"Well, I'm not." Susan's eyes fixed on her ring. "Ooh, how lovely." The two discussed the changes they'd planned, and rearranged a few dates. It proved challenging to brainstorm while they filled orders, but they got everything finished on time.

Tom stopped in around eleven thirty and Susan offered him instant congratulations. "You're getting a wonderful woman here."

Susan embraced both of them. "I'm so excited for you two. And for Jesse."

Tom grinned. "I'm waiting to tell him until we're with him tonight. I wouldn't want Ann to miss his reaction. Can I steal her for a bit? I'd like to take her for a drive."

"Sure." Susan beamed, her eyes wide. "Go right ahead. It's slow now, and Eric will be here soon to have lunch with me."

Ann hesitated and shook her head. "I don't like to leave you by yourself."

Susan gave Ann a fond smile followed by a meaningful look. "I'm never alone. You go on ahead."

The certainty in her voice struck Ann. Even though Susan wasn't worried, Ann relaxed with relief when Eric drove up as they exited the parking lot.

Tom held her hand and steered with the other. "Would you ever consider stopping work altogether someday?"

She caught her breath. They'd never spoken about the subject. He gazed at her with serious eyes and continued, watching the road.

"I'm wondering. I realize I jump ahead with things, but I need to ask you this." He parked the truck and studied her. "Has it crossed your mind...having a child with me?"

"Tom...this is all pretty fast." She took his hand, her eyes fixed on his. "You're the man I want to be with, and I do want to have children. I've thought about that, too."

His shoulders relaxed while she continued. "I've always made my living since I left home, and it seems weird not to. I've been taught women should have their own career and be able to take care of themselves. I never pictured anything else for myself." She regarded his intent expression, and added, "But I remember how sad I was when my mother went back to work, and I started school. Nobody was home when we came in from the bus, and it didn't seem like the same place anymore."

Tom's expression turned soft. "Did you ever tell your mother?"

"No. At least I don't think so. I was only five." Ann shook her head. "Anyway, we didn't complain about things. We did whatever we were supposed to do."

Tom squeezed her hand. "What do you *want* to do?"

She regarded the sky for a few moments, closed her eyes, took a big breath, and let it out. "To be with you and Jesse. And any more children we're blessed with. Forever."

She looked at Tom and noticed tears in his eyes. The sight caused hers to fill up. He reached for her and drew her into an embrace. They held each other for long moments before they kissed.

Tom's lips traveled down the side of her neck and sent an electric, shivery sensation through her, followed by intense warmth. She made an involuntary sound in her throat when Tom slid his mouth back to hers for a fervent caress. He stopped and pressed his forehead against hers.

"I'm having trouble concentrating on my work," he confessed. He leaned backward to gaze at her.

Ann's vision traveled to his jaw, his hair, and returned to his soulful eyes. They pulled her in like a magnet. She couldn't speak, and laid her hand against the side of his face. His eyes closed as he turned to kiss her palm. The tingling sensation surged through her again. Tom clasped her to him, and she let out a small gasp as her head fell back.

I need air.

"Ann? Are you okay?" She opened her eyes, his concerned face hovering above her.

"I think I almost fainted. I never have, but I thought I might."

"Are you sick?" He stroked her cheek.

"No. It happened while we kissed."

He nodded his head and a slow grin spread across his face. "Guess I better be more careful with you."

He chuckled and pressed her against him. He didn't seem at all worried, so she snuggled into his embrace and wondered at this new reaction. What were the limits to what she'd feel? It was wonderful, but kind of scary.

Ann returned to the bakery to find Susan and Eric seated at a table, holding hands. Eric smiled and said in a jovial tone, "I hear congratulations are in order."

[223]

Susan added, "I hope you don't mind. He won't say anything." Eric patted Susan's hand while she continued, "I know you haven't told anyone else yet. It's because we were talking about some of the changes you and I discussed earlier. It made sense to tell him since it's part of the reason for the schedule change."

Ann smiled. "It's okay. Don't worry. Most people will figure it out anyway when they spot this."

She held up her left hand and Susan said, "Come here so Eric can see it."

Ann strolled over and stretched her fingers near Eric.

"It's beautiful, Ann." Eric smiled at her. "My congratulations to both of you. Please tell Tom I wish him every happiness. I'm glad for him." He shook his head. "Years ago at the hospital, he looked devastated. He's so cheerful now that he looks like a different person."

"Thanks, Eric. I appreciate it." Ann stepped into the back, still floating in the dreamy afterglow caused by Tom's touch. She hadn't realized love contained so many layers, or how powerful they were.

CHAPTER NINETEEN

TOM STOLE NUMEROUS quick kisses from Ann while they finished dinner preparations, and Jesse petted Abner under the dining room table. During their meal, she and Tom exchanged glances of anticipation at Jesse's reaction to their news. The dishes finished, Tom and Ann joined Jesse in the living room, where he played with his toy tractors. Tom gave her a nod. "Jesse?"

"What, Daddy?"

"Come here, son."

They sat down together on the couch with Jesse between them. Tom beamed at his son's little upturned face. "Ann will marry me soon. She's going to live here with us and be your mommy."

Jesse's eyes widened, and he stared at Ann with rising excitement on his features. "You'll be here all the time? Even at nighttime and the morning, too?"

Ann laughed and nodded. "All the time."

Jesse climbed onto her lap and embraced her, then studied her intently. "You'll be my mommy all the time?"

Ann's throat tightened with emotion at the sight of his sweet, innocent expression. "Every day, and every night, no matter what."

Jesse planted an enthusiastic kiss on her cheek and bounced off the couch. "Daddy, can I tell Batman?"

Ann grinned and Tom chuckled. "Sure, pal, we'll all go."

They bundled into their coats, and Tom grabbed a big flashlight before they stepped outside. Jesse held both of their hands and scurried along. The night was clear, and the icy wind gusts made her breath catch. Ann ducked her head farther into her hood. The barn exuded warmth and quiet and smelled like hay. Tom flipped the light on, and the animals blinked their sleepy eyes while watching from their stalls.

The small calf walked over to Jesse when he stood next to her stall. He plucked a piece of turnip from a basket, and while she munched it he told her, "Batman, Annie's going to be our mommy. She'll even be here when we sleep. And she makes good cake, but you can't eat cake, I guess."

He patted the calf's head as though in gentle consolation. Tom and Ann exchanged amused glances. Jesse offered Batman another piece of turnip and stroked her forehead while she chewed it.

After she finished, Tom tousled Jesse's hair. "Let's let her get back to bed now."

They bustled to the house, shrugged out of their coats, and hurried into the warm living room.

"It's so cozy," Ann said as Jesse climbed on her lap.

"Can you be married now and stay here? You can watch me feed Batman in the morning."

Tom laughed and reached over to tickle Jesse. "Not quite yet, son. We have to wait a while longer and plan things out."

Ann and Tom took turns making Jesse giggle while he struggled to return the attack. Jesse yelled, "Let's get Daddy."

Ann and Jesse tickled Tom until he held up both hands and said breathlessly, "Okay, okay, you guys win."

Jesse jumped on Tom and crowed, "We got you, Daddy, we got you."

Tom squeezed Jesse and wiggled him back and forth. A knock sounded on the door, and Tom shot her a mischievous grin when she glanced at him in surprise. He stood up and left to answer it. Tom's parents along with his brother, sister-in-law and nephew paraded in. Everyone shared enthusiastic greetings as Jason and Jesse milled around in their midst.

Once all were seated, Tom grabbed Ann's hand and gave it a squeeze. "I wanted you to stop in so I could tell you something wonderful. I asked Ann to marry me, and she said yes."

"Joe, you were right," Kathy exclaimed and beamed at her husband. "I'm so thrilled for both of you."

Everyone stood and took turns sharing hugs. Tim and Sharon waited behind Joe and Kathy. After the two brothers embraced, Tim patted Tom on the shoulder and teased, "I never figured you for such a speedy worker."

Jesse piped up, "Daddy's fast in the barn. He feeds all the cows while I feed Batman." He gave his uncle an emphatic nod. Laughs echoed around the room. Tom left for the kitchen and returned with a tray of glasses and some sparkling cider.

The cups were filled and distributed, including two small mugs for the little boys. Joe lifted his glass. With a broad smile, he proclaimed, "To Tom and Ann." He took a glimpse of Jesse's rapt face and added, "And Jesse. May God richly bless your lives together and guide you every day."

Jesse gave a solemn nod. "Amen, Grandpa."

Glasses were clinked, mingled with chuckles, while they took a sip of cider and sat down again.

"I remember when I asked your mother to marry me." Joe shared a glance and a grin with Kathy. "I came to her house to surprise her. She was taking a nap on the couch, and her parents were in the kitchen. I knelt down beside her and jiggled her shoulder to wake her."

Kathy took over. "I'd read a scary book before I fell asleep. I was having a dream where this man chased me through a dark store. So when your father shook me, I screamed."

She laughed and Joe continued, "I jumped up just as her mother and father ran in. They yelled, 'What did you do to her, Joe?' Her mother held on to her and stared at me like I was Jack the Ripper or something." Joe chuckled and shook his head. "I finally got the chance to explain what had happened, but I didn't say why I was there."

Kathy added, "I calmed down faster than my parents, I'll tell you. After they went back to the kitchen, Joe knelt and proposed." She took Joe's hand and their expressions were soft as they shared a smile. Ann rested her head on Tom's shoulder. Maybe this would be them someday, telling their children and grandchildren stories about their courtship.

A few more family anecdotes later, Tim said with a grin. "Guess we better call it a night. The little guys are tired." Jesse and Jason were stretched out on the rug in front of the fireplace, staring at the flames with vacant eyes.

Everyone rose to don their coats and gathered around the door to exchange good-byes. Tom, Ann and Jesse stood at the window and waved. After they drove away, Tom turned to Jesse. "C'mon, pal, story and bed."

Jesse raced up the stairs. Tom drew Ann to him and nuzzled her neck which made her giggle and melt at the same time. After

Jesse fell asleep and they were back downstairs on the couch, Ann asked, "Why didn't you tell me everyone would stop in tonight?"

Tom squeezed her. "You get more nervous when you know things ahead of time. I figured it'd be better this way." He kissed her forehead. "You didn't have a chance to stew about it."

Ann snuggled her face against his chest. His shirt smelled faintly of wood smoke.

Tom asked, "So how soon do you want to be married?"

"How soon do I *want* to, or how soon do I think we can?"

"Not the same answer, eh?"

"No, and you already know that," she teased, and raised her head to grin at him.

He kissed her playfully. "All right then, when do you think we could?"

"Susan and I decided we would make the business hour changes the first week of November. It'll give people time to get used to it before the Thanksgiving dessert orders start to come in."

"So, we'll be married right afterward? I don't see any point in waiting. We're both sure about what we want, aren't we? We'd go on our honeymoon and be back in plenty of time for Thanksgiving. Can Susan handle the shop by herself for a week?"

Delight filled her. Seven whole days with Tom. Ann thought for a moment. "Her mom can come in and help. She did once when I caught the flu, and it worked out. I'll ask her."

"I've been thinking..."

"Uh-oh," Ann grinned up at him, and stroked his cheek.

"I know, I know. I tend to put a lot on your plate, don't I?"

"Mmhmm," she murmured as he kissed her.

"What I thought—"

"More," Ann interrupted. He grinned and smooched her again.

"As I've attempted to say, my dear, I think we should go to your parents' house without Jesse, so we can tell them the news. If we bring him, he'll likely blurt it out first. Also, they might be uncomfortable and want to voice their concerns, but wouldn't do it with him listening. Or, they'd speak up and it would confuse him."

How sensible and thoughtful of both Jesse and her family. "You are so..." She gave him an enthusiastic embrace.

"So...what?"

"Considerate. Sensitive. You always think about me or Jesse or our families. You're wonderful."

Tom glanced away as a shy, embarrassed grin flickered across his features. "I do have faults, Ann. I think sometimes I move way too fast for you, and it worries me. Though you seem to hold up pretty well."

She traced down the bridge of his nose. "I'm doing fine at catching up."

He walked her to the door and kissed her goodbye. She hated to drive away. The biggest part of her stayed with him, and only a shell remained. Was that normal?

Ann arrived home, unsettled at the sight of a strange car parked in her driveway. Unease twisted through her when she spotted a lone man sitting in it. Her headlights lit up his face when she drove in, and the man's head turned. Jeff Mason. A sigh of relief escaped her. Why would he be here, though? He popped out of his car, and strode over to hers.

"Hope I didn't scare you," he said and stepped back while she climbed out.

"You did, until I recognized you." Ann smiled. "How did you know where I live?"

"It's on the report. Okay if I come in for a bit? I'd like to speak to you."

Ann shrugged. Must be about Susan's case. "All right."

She unlocked the door and flipped the light on. Ann hung her coat, and he followed her into the living room, still wearing a jacket over his street clothes.

"Have a seat." She motioned to the couch and sat in her chair.

"What's up?" Ann waited. Jeff looked nervous. Something was going on.

Jeff breathed in and said, "I'll get right to the point. I assume the ring means you're engaged. If I'm going to say anything, it'll have to be now."

Ann's mouth fell open. She closed it and paused a moment. "What do you mean?"

"I think you should reconsider your decision. Tom didn't protect his first wife, and you deserve better than that. I'd keep you safe. I'm good at it, and I'd take care of you. You wouldn't have to work all the time like you do." He leaned forward and as he spoke, his intense hazel eyes bore into hers.

He cleared his throat. "This is a surprise. I can tell by your face. Tom's a decent guy, but you'd be better off with me. You don't want to be stuck out on a farm for the rest of your life. You'd end up disappointed with him and unhappy. I've seen it before. Plus, I'm familiar with the kind of world we live in, and I can handle it. You're a gentle girl. I wouldn't let anything harm you. I love you, Ann."

He loves me?

Ann's breath caught in her throat. His expression appeared open and vulnerable, so unlike his usual attitude of command. What could she say without hurting him? She took a deep breath and glanced away. "I don't know what to say."

"Don't say anything right now. Just think about it."

"Jeff—"

He stood and held his hand up. "No, really. Don't say anything yet."

He started to leave, backtracked, kissed the top of her head and left. Ann sat in stunned silence.

CHAPTER TWENTY

WHAT IS GOING on?

Thoughts swirled through her mind. Jeff loved her? He'd sounded so sincere. Jeff said he'd protect her, keep her safe. She'd finally learned to stop racing toward safety, and now Jeff brought the subject up. He thought Tom would disappoint her. What did he mean by that? Did he want her to doubt Tom, so she'd consider him? And what on earth is wrong with living on a farm?

Ann rose and began to pace her apartment. She shouldn't tell anyone. It would make Jeff seem pathetic if others knew what he'd offered. If she told Tom, he might be angry, or hurt. Would he wonder if she'd somehow encouraged Jeff's attention? What a confusing situation.

She stopped at the sink and poured a glass of water. *Think.* Half the water downed, she set the glass on the counter and resumed pacing. It was too late to call Susan. She got up even earlier than Ann. A man's advice would be the most useful. Dad, Dane or Greg? She shook her head. No, too problematic. They didn't even know about her engagement yet. Jim Cortland. He counseled people.

Wonder if he'd mind a call this late? She sat down and looked up his number. Drawing a deep breath, she punched it in.

"Hello?"

"Mr. Cortland? This is Ann Shaw. I didn't wake you up, did I?"

"Oh, no. I'm a night owl. I like the quiet. Best time to think, pray or study. So what can I do for you Ann?"

Her shoulders tensed. "I've got a problem. I just became engaged to Tom Tillman. That's not the trouble, though. Tonight a friend came over and told me I shouldn't marry Tom. He said he loves me, and I'd be better off with him. I don't know how to handle this."

"Were you aware of his feelings before this?" Jim's voice held gentle concern.

"No. He flirted with me and didn't think much of Tom, but I never thought he cared for me. I'm pretty shocked." Ann took a breath.

"What sort of fellow is this man?"

"Well, he's a policeman. Sure of himself, kind of a take-charge person." No point in mentioning the things he'd said about Tom. Now she understood why he'd been so negative.

"Did you tell him your thoughts on what he told you?"

"I started to, but he told me to think about it before I said anything. Then he left." Ann waited and wondered what he thought.

"Hmm." Silence. "Has this made you question your relationship with Tom?"

"No. But I'm worried if I tell him, he might think I somehow encouraged Jeff. Perhaps I did by being friendly with him and enjoying his conversation. I don't know. I'm not smart about these things." Ann frowned, remembering the dinner date and how he'd flirted with her since.

Jim chuckled. "Not a lot of people can read another person's heart. So, you haven't told Tom. I believe you should, right away. For a good relationship and marriage, it's important to be honest with each other. By the way, congratulations on your engagement."

"Thanks. I'm thrilled about it. So, you think I should tell Tom before I say anything to Jeff? And how should I handle Jeff?"

"I think it would be wise to call Tom. As far as how to speak to Jeff, let him know you're honored by his offer, but your heart is fixed already. I'd be sure to mention that you appreciate his feelings, and want to stay his friend."

"I don't know how well it'll go over. With either of them." She kneaded her forehead, eyes closed. "I'm kind of nervous. I'm not good at things like this."

"We've got tonight to pray about it. You come up for prayer at church tomorrow. We'll talk afterward and see what we've each been thinking. Don't be afraid. 'Cast all your cares upon Him, because He cares for you.' Remember that."

"Thanks, Mr. Cortland. I'm calmer now. See you tomorrow."

"God bless you."

Ann sat for a while in thought. What honest words could she say to Jeff? Was she honored by his affection? Yes, along with flattered and worried. Jeff was such a strong person. It unnerved her to picture him yearning for her. His eyes had shone with longing when he'd told her he loved her. It hurt to remember.

He might be one of those people who fell in and out of attraction and considered it to be love. That would make this less worrisome. Her spirits lifted for a second at the thought. What if he wasn't? Oh, dear.

I need to call Tom.

"Hello?" Tom's voice sounded groggy.

"I woke you, didn't I?" Ann's tense stomach tightened.

"It's okay. Hi, sweetie. What's up?"

Ann swallowed. Might as well jump right in. "Tom...when I got home tonight, Jeff Mason was here. I thought it must be something about Susan's case, so I asked him in. He said I shouldn't marry you, and he loved me, and I should be with him." There. She said it. Ann waited with dread while the line stayed silent. Her stomach churned like a whirlpool.

Talk to me, Tom.

"So what did you say?" Tom's voice was unreadable.

"I started to answer, but he told me to think about it and not say anything. And he left."

More silence. "You let him leave with the idea you were thinking about it? Are you?"

"Of course not."

"Then why didn't you tell him?"

"He said not to talk."

"Good grief, Ann. Wow. Now he'll figure you're considering it. I can't help thinking part of you is, or you'd automatically have said something."

Her brow drew down as her dread spiked into anger. She clenched her jaw. What an unfair reaction. "I was so shocked by all the things he said. I tried to figure out something to say without hurting him, and he left so fast. Why are you blaming me?"

"I'm not. I'm saying you should've told him right away. What else did he say that made you speechless, and why are you so worried about hurting him? If you were, you ought to have been honest with him."

Honest? Should she tell him everything Jeff said? Good heavens. All this mess from trying to spare everyone. Ann breathed a heavy sigh as tears pricked her eyes, and the anger remained. "Fine. You want honesty? He says he'd protect me, and he knows

[236]

how the world is. He'd be able to keep me safe, and you wouldn't. He told me I shouldn't be stuck on a farm, and I'll end up disappointed with you. He says you're a decent guy, but I'd be better off with him."

She closed her eyes. The silence stretched like a rubber band about to break.

"I guess you've got a pretty clear choice. He put a lot of thought into it, and he may be right. I might disappoint you, and you'd regret being with me. I can't say I won't ever let you down. I'm sure I will. In light of that, you should think about it."

What? Her thoughts spun and tumbled. "Tom, are you crazy? I don't understand you."

"Listen to me. I'm telling you to think things over. Do you believe I'd want you to be with me if you have any doubts? Marriage is enough of a challenge without reservations hanging over it."

He thinks of marrying me as a challenge? "I don't wish to think about it—"

"Why? Does it worry you? It shouldn't. He's offered some valid points. I'm glad he said what he did."

She slumped. Anger, dread, confusion, all of it leaked out of her, leaving her as broken and hollowed out as an empty eggshell. His reactions, his words were beyond comprehension. She had no armor, no retort, and no defense to offer which would fix this. She swallowed hard as tears threatened to overwhelm her. "What am I supposed to say? I love you, Tom. I can't understand why you're saying these things to me."

"*Because* I love you. I don't want you to make a mistake. You need to be sure."

"I am," she reasoned. "I didn't ask for any of this. It's as much a shock to me as it is to you."

"Well, life is full of shocks. How you handle them is what matters."

Ann sighed. "I wish I understood this."

"So do I."

Incredible weariness weighed on her. She should have prayed before calling him. She'd made a hash of the whole thing. Now she had no idea what to do.

"Ann, I'm not mad at you. I honestly wish you'd think about what happened and what's been said. It'll help you be sure."

"I already am."

"Then thinking it over won't hurt anything. I'll call you tomorrow and we'll discuss this some more. I love you. Goodbye." He hung up. She stared at the phone.

His words, his reactions, propelled her into a fierce internal hurricane. Everything had been so clear before. Why did Tom react so strangely? Why would he even want her to think over Jeff's offer? Ann hung up the phone and trudged toward the bedroom, her head jumbled and confused.

God, please help me. Sort me out. Speak to me.

She flopped on her bed. Ann stared at the light fixture on the ceiling and examined the thoughts surfacing through the confusion. Tom hadn't been angry with her. His voice sounded serious and sad. He didn't sound mad at Jeff, either. Though he did seem jealous. Why didn't he fight for them, say how ridiculous Jeff's words were? She closed her eyes and tried to figure it out.

Mental images of her on the farm with Tom and Jesse sparked her smile. Of course difficult times would come. They might both let each other down. Pictures of her with Jeff surfaced, larking around town with Susan and Eric. It felt like a betrayal to Tom even thinking those things. But he said he wanted her to.

[238]

Could it be he'd become unsure about *her*? After all, she had no experience at relationships, at life. Working hard was her only true strength. Tom had been married, become a father, lost a wife and understood what he wanted.

She rubbed her forehead. With Jeff, she wouldn't step into expectations. He only wanted her to be with him. She'd have no role to fill, to mess up or cause disappointment. But she didn't love Jeff, and she often found his controlling personality distasteful.

Besides that, how would she ever stand not marrying Tom? Running into him and Jesse somewhere years later and not being part of their lives? The thought jolted her and brought agony and cold terror with it. Unthinkable.

Why would he want her to consider a man she didn't love? It didn't make sense. Did he believe her heart to be so changeable that if someone else offered her a different life, she'd be drawn to it? Another thing. Jeff never said anything about God or faith. His confidence lay in his own strength and abilities. Tom wanted her to consider taking on someone who didn't acknowledge God? What a bleak life it would be. She remembered all too well.

Realization struck, and she sat upright. Now she understood why Tom asked her to think about it. He'd mentioned his concern, how perhaps part of her love for him might be because she'd thought of herself as plain and boring, and never figured anyone would care for her. Now someone else did. A man he knew she liked.

Tom disclosed his deep feelings and traumas to her. She hid hurts she hadn't told him about, even after he'd asked. Why did she find it so hard to open up, to trust? No wonder he wanted her to be sure. If she were Tom, she'd feel the same way. He was right. She should have told Jeff right away. And she should have trusted Tom enough to tell him the things she'd been hurt by.

Ann lay back down and wondered what to do. She rarely opened up to anyone. Confiding wasn't something her family did, so Susan had been the only person she'd learned to rely on. But Susan's faith had presented a large barrier to Ann, until recently. Now she wanted to share the same hope, even though at times the level of commitment frightened her. The confusion receded. She had choices in front of her. It was time to make decisions.

CHAPTER TWENTY-ONE

SUSAN AND ERIC were seated toward the front of the church, and the music service had already begun. Ann chose a seat near the back and let her eyes adjust from the brilliant sunshine to the softer indoor light. The room gave off its familiar aura of peace, mixed with the scents of pine and furniture polish. She focused her mind on the worship service. Afterward, her mouth almost fell open when Jim said he would teach on trust. Wow. Exactly what she'd pondered last night.

More a study than a sermon, the words helped Ann's mind settle itself into clear directions. Trust meant to have confidence, reliance, to be convinced, something to rest in and hope. She almost laughed with joy. When the invitation for prayer arrived, Ann didn't hesitate.

She stood a few people behind Susan. While she waited her turn, a calm sensation spread through her. Susan noticed Ann after she'd received prayers, and stopped next to her.

"I'll go up and pray with you," she whispered. "Everything all right?"

"Yes," Ann murmured. "I want to be a Christian. I want to be baptized."

Tears sprang from Susan's eyes. She placed a gentle hand on Ann's shoulder while they shared smiles full of delight. When Ann's turn came, Susan stepped forward with her, and Ann declared to Jim and Evelyn, "I've decided to become a Christian and be baptized."

"Well, praise God." Jim's broad smile shone as he raised his hands and looked as though he wanted to jump. "We'll pray with you now, and afterwards, I'd like to speak with you before the baptism."

"All right." Ann bent her head as waves of prayer washed over her. She spoke her confession of faith in the atoning sacrifice of Jesus, and asked Him to accept her and dwell in her.

Please abide with me. Teach me. I love you.

When the prayer ended, Jim said in a quiet voice, "I know you're shy. Would you mind if those who want to stay can be here for your baptism? It's a joyful time for us."

Ann's blissful excitement drove out any shyness. "No, I don't mind at all."

"Evelyn, I'm going to take Ann to the office. I'll leave you to get things ready."

"I'll help," Susan piped up and shot Ann an excited grin.

Ann strolled behind him as quiet confidence rose inside. Jim smiled at her after they were seated.

"I can see how happy you are. Your face is shining. I figured we'd be praying and talking about last night's dilemma. I didn't expect this."

Ann laughed. "Me, either. I got all jumbled up after I talked with Tom. He thought I should consider the offer, so I'd be sure about my choice."

"There's wisdom in that. Jesus tells us the same thing, to weigh our decisions carefully. Not to put our hand to the plow and look back."

Ann nodded. "I understand. While I sorted my thoughts out, I realized the most important thing would be for me to move towards God. My whole life, I've been unsure. Of myself, what I should do, pretty much everything."

Jim studied her. "And what are you sure of now?"

"I want to be a child of God and follow the example of Jesus. And marry Tom."

"It will be difficult at times. Ann, I'll be honest with you. You're stepping into a new way of living, with both of those choices. You'll be tested in many ways, but you'll also have joy and growth. It's a commitment for life. Are you prepared for it, and you're sure it's what you want?" His features were intent.

Her eyes filled up. "Yes. I am. These are my choices. And please, always be truthful with me. I need to grow up."

"You'll definitely do that, my dear." Jim chuckled. "Now, I know you're familiar with hearing the invitation, and the Scriptures I've taught on about baptism. You haven't seen a baptism yet, so I'll tell you we follow the pattern the apostles used in Acts 2:38." He quoted from memory, "Repent and be baptized every one of you in the name of Jesus Christ for the remission of sins, and you shall receive the gift of the Holy Spirit." He nodded at her and asked, "Any questions?"

Ann shook her head. The transition inside her had already begun. "I'm ready."

Jim stood. "We'll go get your robe, and make sure the tank is uncovered. You can change in the rest room." He grinned and took a big breath. "Let's go."

Ann rose and followed him out. The sure, calm sensation remained while she walked through the door. Many of the church people were in attendance. Some prayed while others spoke in quiet tones and waited near the uncovered tank. Awareness of the gravity of her decision filled her with a mix of anticipation and clear, intense focus.

Evelyn stepped up to her, a garment cradled in her arms. Susan stood right behind her, eyes shining. Evelyn smiled. "The water's warm, in case you wondered."

Evelyn handed the robe to Ann and enveloped her in a hug. Susan embraced her next and stepped to stand by Eric, who beamed at Ann. Susan said, "I'll be here by the tank."

"Be right back." Ann entered the rest room.

After she changed into the floor length robe, she scrutinized her face in the mirror, the same way she had after Fred's words jolted her and helped begin her journey to God. Ann smiled and drew in a deep breath.

Well, goodbye, old Ann. Your life's about to change.

The seriousness of the moment consumed her. She closed her eyes. "Lord, here I come."

She straightened her shoulders, opened her eyes and strode out the door. Anticipation rose as she approached the tank. Jim stood next to it and held his hand out to help her climb in. Her reflection shimmered in the calm water. Jim motioned for her to sit on the low, built-in seat. "I'm going to pray first, and when I baptize you, I'll lean you back so the water fully covers you. Okay?"

She smiled up at him and nodded, too overcome with happiness to speak. She closed her eyes and listened to his gentle voice.

"Father, we come before you to baptize Ann into her new life. She has accepted the atoning work of Your Son. She has repented and is ready to receive remission of sins, and the gift of Your Spirit. Thank you, Father, in Jesus' name."

Ann held her breath as Jim leaned her backward. "I baptize you in the mighty name of Jesus Christ."

The water covered her, and Jim lifted her back up. Many voices around her were lifted in praise, creating an atmosphere which shimmered with energy. She kept her eyes closed.

I feel lighter than a piece of cork.

Overwhelming joy and awe flooded her. A golden light filled her inner vision and moved towards her. She could barely speak, but managed to say, "Hallelujah...Hallel...Halle." After some unintelligible syllables, her voice failed her. The light, which had been around her, was now within her. Shouts of praise and joyful cries echoed around her. She released all of herself into the light while peace unlike anything she'd ever experienced spread through her.

When she finally opened her eyes, the air had a barely discernible shine in it, as though she perceived the molecules of oxygen. She blinked a few times and gazed around as her eyes returned to normal. Jim held his hand out to help her stand. Faces wreathed in delight greeted her while she stepped out. Hands patted her back. Greetings of "Welcome, sister," sounded from more than one voice. Susan gave her an enthusiastic squeeze, and giggled as she glanced down at her damp sweater.

"Oops." Ann grinned.

"Who cares?" Susan lifted her hands, a huge smile on her face. "Now we're truly sisters."

Both sets of eyes held joyful tears.

"You go get changed now," Susan said.

"I just did," Ann joked, as she made her way to the rest room through the cheerful throng. Once inside the room, she stood still

[245]

and tried to process what had happened. She possessed no words to even begin to describe the change in her internal landscape.

I can't believe You did this for me. I feel so different. Are You sure You want to give me a gift like this?

A Scripture she'd studied a few days before popped into her awareness. "What God has cleansed, you will not call common." Ann's mouth dropped open. She closed it and bowed her head, eyes shut.

Thank you. I'll keep that in my heart.

AT HOME IN the afternoon, Ann sat in her living room chair while her mind danced with fresh ideas. So this is what it meant to walk in newness of life. Scriptures she'd read and heard in the last weeks correlated in her thoughts.

She let her gaze sweep around the room. It didn't look or feel the same. The existence she'd built and clung to in this place receded like a toy boat riding down a stream. A new, unknown world stretched before her, vital and full of learning. Jim had said it would be difficult, but also yield joy and growth. She smiled while a few tears of happiness rolled down her cheeks. She never understood faith until now. Susan tried to tell her so many times. Guess she wasn't ready yet.

Ann closed her eyes and gratitude filled her. The situation with Tom and Jeff still loomed, yet her heart stayed calm while she prayed for help to navigate everything with wisdom. The hardest part was telling Jeff. Tom would understand right away. He'd call soon. She rose and fixed herself a grilled cheese sandwich and a cup of ginger tea. The doorbell rang while she finished. She gulped down the last of her tea before she stood and walked to the door.

Ann glimpsed through the peephole. Jeff. A stab of unease pierced her serenity.

I thought I'd have more time.

She took a deep breath, blew it out, and opened the door.

"Hi." Jeff's mouth held a smile, but his eyes appeared guarded, not vulnerable as they were yesterday. Maybe he already guessed the answer.

"Hi. Come on in." Ann walked ahead of him to the living room and kept her emotions steady. *God, please. I don't want to hurt him. Help me do this, please.*

She gestured at the couch as she sat down in her chair.

He perched on the edge of the couch and leaned forward, resting his elbows on his knees. "I know I haven't given you a lot of time, but I'm sure you've thought about it as much as I have. I couldn't wait any longer." His eyes were intense and steady. She met his gaze and didn't glance away.

Here goes. "Jeff, I'm flattered by your affection. I value you, and I appreciate you. You're a good man." She drew in a breath. "I gave my heart to Tom, and it won't change." His features tightened. "It's painful to me if this hurts you. I consider you my friend. I enjoy your company. I'm hoping you'll stay friends with me. Please?"

Ann caught a flash of pain in his eyes before he looked down. Tears threatened and she swallowed them down. When his gaze returned, all vulnerability had been quenched. He stared at her with an unreadable expression.

"So this is it? You've decided on a life you'll regret? I wonder what you'll say to me ten years from now. Probably that you wished you'd listened to me." He took in a sharp breath, and let out a sound like a derisive, short laugh. He shook his head. "I don't think you realize what you're doing, but I'm a man. I accept it."

"Jeff, I'm not the right one for you. There's a woman somewhere who'll be thrilled to be with you. You deserve to be loved. You wouldn't want me to choose you and have my heart be with someone else, would you? It's not fair to you, or to me."

"I'm not concerned about *fair* right now." Jeff appeared angry and clenched his jaw. "You'd be safe and happy with me. I know it. It's too bad you don't. Tom is weak."

"I realize you believe that, but according to God's word, strength isn't what you think it is. I want to learn different ways."

"Are you turning into some sort of Bible-thumper? Pacifist, turn the other cheek stuff?" He shook his head at her. "How could I fit pacifism in with being a policeman? Guys like the creep who hurt Susan would love it if everyone let them run wild. Man, how deluded can you be? This world is a battleground."

Ann experienced a flash of insight. She didn't expect he'd understand what had occurred to her. "You're right. It *is* a battlefield."

"Well, I'm glad you've got enough sense to see it." He fixed her with a piercing stare. "Is your answer still the same? You're choosing Tom?"

She nodded. "Yes, Jeff. We're right for each other."

He stood and appraised her. "I hope for your sake it's true. I still think this is a big mistake."

Ann rose and held her hand out. "Friends?"

His tiny smile appeared reluctant. He shook her hand. "Friends."

Jeff waited a moment longer, turned and left the apartment. Ann sank back into her chair, relieved yet somber. It was hard to see such a confident person become deflated and realize she was the cause. She wondered if he'd stop visiting the bakery. She'd miss his jokes and high energy.

Oh, Jeff. I hope you find someone.

Silence reigned for a time until the doorbell buzzed. Tom?

She peered through the peephole. Ann opened the door wide to allow Susan and Eric to enter. "Hi."

Susan handed her some flowers and grinned. "Happy new start. We're not coming in, but we had to bring you a gift."

"Yeah," Eric agreed. "We can't stay. We're due at my folks' house. We wanted to give you something. It's an important day."

"You guys are sweet." Ann studied the flowers. "Beautiful. Thanks, you two."

They waved and left. Ann arranged the blooms in a vase and sat in the kitchen observing the intricate shading and delicate colors. If God put so much attention into a flower...where was the Scripture about how He clothed the grass of the field? She reached for her Bible and thumbed to the index. The phone rang.

She ran to the living room and plopped down into her easy chair as anticipation rose. He must have finished chores early. "Hello?"

"Is this you, Ann?" It sounded like Tom's mother.

"Yes."

"It's Kathy. Tom wanted me to tell you he's not sure when he'll get a chance to call you. The goats got through the fence in the back part of the property and are in the woods somewhere. Joe and Tom are searching for them."

Disappointment settled on her. She peered out the living room window. "Well, at least it's a nice day."

"For a while anyway. A cold front is coming soon. I hope they find them before dark."

"Will you call me when they're back?"

Kathy's voice sounded warm. "Of course."

"Thanks so much. Bye."

"Bye, dear."

Ann hung up and pictured Tom and Joe in her mind as they searched the woods. She thought of the Scripture about the lost sheep. *Please help them find the goats. Guide them where they need to go, Father. And thank you for helping me with Jeff. Comfort him, even though he won't ask You to.*

Should she drive out to Tom's and wait with Kathy, or go help Tom and Joe? Maybe it'd be a bad idea since she and Tom hadn't talked over what happened with Jeff yet. It would be better to stay put. She fetched her Bible and got comfortable in the chair. With a pad and paper handy, the enjoyment of study captured her attention.

She must have dozed off. Ann blinked her eyes repeatedly before realizing the room was growing dark. With the lamp flipped on, she glanced at the clock. Almost six. A quick step to the window showed snow as it swirled near the streetlight and tree branches struggling in the wind. The glass was cold to the touch. Were they still out in this? She called Tom's house. No answer. Jesse must be with Kathy at her place, so Ann looked it up and dialed their number.

"Hello?" Kathy answered.

"It's Ann. Have you heard anything?"

"They came back before dark to do the milking, grab flashlights, and warm up before they went out again. They brought three with them, but the rest are still in the woods."

"Are there any dangerous animals out this time of year?"

"Not usually. Foxes and sometimes a black bear, but they aren't normally aggressive to people or goats. They took the shotgun in case."

Ann's stomach clenched when she visualized a bear. "Oh, dear."

"Don't fret. I've lived in this area all my life, and I've only seen a bear once. It ran away as soon as it saw me."

"Do you mind if I drive out? I don't want to sit here and wait."

"What a good idea. We can keep each other company and Jesse will be thrilled. I've got supper waiting for them, and we've got plenty if you'd like to eat with us."

"Thanks, Kathy. That would be wonderful. I'll leave now. Bye."

"See you soon."

Ann hurried to don a sweater, followed by her coat. When she stepped outside, a strong gust hit her and she gasped. Yikes. A sprint to the car, and she waited until the defroster cleared the windshield. Thankfully the snowfall remained light and not much had fallen. The wind whistled outside the car as she drove, praying while the miles rolled by.

Ann parked, hurried to the door and pressed the bell. She gazed up at the swirling snow dancing around the outside light. Kathy opened the door, Jesse right behind her.

"Annie," he announced with a big grin, "It's snowing. Daddy and Grandpa are in the woods."

"Here, let me take your coat." Kathy closed the door and shook the snow off Ann's coat before hanging it. "Goodness, what weather. Come on in by the fireplace."

Ann picked up Jesse and followed Kathy. The aroma of stew and the pine smell of the fire filled the air. The large room had panels of knotty pine. A long, puffy black couch stood against one wall. A few dark blue easy chairs and a matching love seat with a colorful throw were across from it. There were some end tables with various knick-knacks on them and a large fireplace with a brick mantle and many family pictures on it and on the walls.

"What a pretty room." Ann sat on the love seat in front of the fire. Jesse snuggled against her.

[251]

Kathy remained standing. "Thank you. It's comfortable. Did you want something to eat?"

"I'll wait until Tom and Joe are back, if it's okay."

Kathy smiled and perched in one of the easy chairs. "We'll wait, too. I don't imagine they'll be too much longer. The goats will want to be in out of this storm, I would think."

"Do goats mind the weather?" Ann glanced out the nearest window, light falling flakes visible in it.

"Not much. They're pretty hardy, but they'll want their feed and their beds by now. Just like people, I guess." She chuckled. "So how was your day, dear?"

Ann left out anything about Jeff. No need for her to hear it. "Well, I was baptized today at the Cortland's church."

Kathy's features lit up. "You were? My, how wonderful. I wish I'd been there. Tommy got baptized when he was sixteen. Joe and I were baptized...let me think," Kathy glanced up for a moment. "Thirty-two years ago. We were about your age. Time goes by so fast. Shoots right along. How do you feel?"

"Different...and peaceful, as if I'm part of everything and I fit in. I don't remember ever feeling like this. It's beautiful."

Kathy's eyes were soft, and she nodded. "Yes, it is. There aren't words for it. Like the Word says, peace which passes understanding. I know...I know."

They shared a smile. Jesse lifted his head from Ann's shoulder. "I see flashlights outside."

Kathy stepped to the window. "They're headed to the barn. Looks like they got the rest of them. Well, good. They'll be milking them before they come in. I'll go check on the food." She turned from the window. "You and Jesse stay here and surprise Tom."

Kathy grinned and strode to the kitchen.

"We can hide and jump out." Jesse threw up his hands and yelled, "Surprise."

Ann chuckled and squeezed him. "We don't want to startle him. He's had a long day. How about if we sit here and watch his face when he walks in?"

"Okay."

Ann reached for a storybook on the end table. "Let's read 'til they get here."

A few pages into the second book, they heard the door open and feet stomping. Voices full of animation followed. The door sounded again. Did they go back out?

Kathy walked in. "They left to go treat some cuts on one of the goats. The neighbor on the other end of the woods has a barbed wire fence and it cut into Gracie's shoulder and flank."

"Gracie?" Jesse exclaimed. "Is she okay?"

"She'll be fine, Jess. Daddy and Grandpa are fixing her up. Lord, how I hate barbed wire. If it doesn't hurt the livestock, it hurts the wild things." She headed back to the kitchen, shaking her head.

"Gracie's so nice." Jesse gazed up at Ann. "She follows Daddy and me, and she likes squash. Last spring she made two babies."

Ann stroked Jesse's hair. "Grandma said she'll be all right. Want me to finish the story?"

"Yep." Jesse cuddled against her while she picked up the book.

When they'd finished and looked over the next book to read, the door opened again. Ann and Jesse shared a grin. After a few moments, footsteps sounded toward the living room and Tom appeared. Ann's pulse quickened.

"Daddy." Jesse jumped off the loveseat and ran to Tom. "Surprise."

Tom lifted him up into an embrace while his eyes locked on Ann.

"Surprise," he repeated and grinned at Jesse, then Ann.

"Daddy, is Gracie okay?"

"You bet. The cuts weren't as bad as we thought. She's all fixed up and warm in the barn." Tom walked over with Jesse and sat next to Ann, exuding the scent of pine needles and snow.

Jesse hopped off Tom's lap. "I'm getting a drink, Daddy."

"All right," Tom replied, his eyes still intent on Ann as Jesse darted toward the kitchen. Tom clasped her to him and into a kiss. Her head leaned back against his shoulder as the caress intensified and she melted into him. She stroked his face, and he broke off the kiss and clasped her tighter.

His warm breath tickled her ear as he whispered, "Did you decide?"

He pulled back and studied her.

"You, of course." She drew him into another kiss. At the sound of running feet, they broke apart.

"Daddy, Grandma says to come and eat. It's beef stew."

"We're coming, pal." Tom stood up and held his hand out to Ann.

BACK AT TOM'S after dinner, they put Jesse to bed and settled on the couch. Warmth radiated from the fireplace.

"You didn't finish telling me how Jeff reacted." Tom's arm cradled her and she laid her head on his chest.

"I think he took it pretty well. He said he still thought I'm making a mistake, but before he left, we shook hands and agreed to stay friends. I told him he'd find someone who would love him." She sighed. "I hope he finds his way to God someday. He's pretty negative right now. Guess we need to pray for him."

"Why didn't you tell me you'd be baptized today? I'd have wanted to be there. My parents would've loved it, too." Tom's voice sounded disappointed.

Ann stared into the fire. "I decided this morning before church. I've been thinking a lot about it, and I was sure. It's not that I didn't want you or your folks to come. It never occurred to me to think of baptism like an occasion where you tell everybody. I decided it was what I needed to do. Do you understand?"

Tom shifted. "I guess. Am I in the 'everybody' category? Why are you still so private, even with me? Don't you want us to share things?"

"Of course I do. You've told me so much about what you've gone through and I appreciate it—"

"Then why won't you confide in me?"

Ann's peace disrupted as tension prickled inside her, and she searched for how to answer him. What was wrong with her?

His tone softened. "Ann, don't you trust me?"

"Oh, Tom." Her voice broke as her throat tightened and tears gathered. His arm clasped around her, and his other hand stroked her hair.

"What's made you so scared?" His voice turned low and gentle. "You can tell me."

"I'm not supposed to bother people." She sobbed into his shirt and clenched her hands in it. "I'm supposed to be strong."

"You're not bothering me, and I'm not a 'people.' I'm going to be your husband." His voice held such tenderness.

"It hurts...to say it." Ann cried harder as the resistance cracked within her. "When I was thirteen," she began and had to stop and calm her sobs, trying to take a deep breath. Moments passed. Shame pierced her. "When I was thirteen, I had a crush on this boy, Dale. I didn't know one of my friends did, too, until he made fun of her.

[255]

Sally looked heartbroken and ran from the lunchroom crying. She'd always been a strong girl. I'd never seen her so upset. I got furious and told him what a mean, conceited person he was."

Ann took a few shuddery breaths and continued, the side of her face pressed hard against Tom's chest. "The whole lunchroom watched me, and I couldn't believe how I said all the stuff I did. I was too mad to be scared. When I finished, he gave me this look, and smiled and said something to his friend. I left and his friend followed me. He told me Dale thought I was cool and wanted to meet me after school behind the outdoor bleachers."

Her crying nearly stopped. "I was scared and excited, too. I didn't tell Sally. I figured she'd be hurt and mad at me since she liked him. I was flattered and couldn't wait until after school to see what he'd say. He was waiting with two of his friends. When I got there, the other boys moved away. Dale came up to me and said, 'I didn't know you had so much fight in you.' He gave me a look that made me think he liked me. I looked down. He moved closer, and I thought maybe he wanted to kiss me."

Ann stopped and remembered. She didn't want to go on. But she couldn't stop now. Tom held her and remained silent. "I didn't move. All of a sudden, he ripped my shirt open and the buttons flew off. My chest had begun to develop, but I didn't wear a bra yet. I screamed, and he held my arms back and turned me toward his friends." She squeezed her eyes shut at the memory.

"I tried to get away from him, and he yelled, 'How do you like it? How do you like it? How much fight have you got now?' His friends laughed and ran up to me. Dale told them to hold my arms. I shrieked and he grabbed my chest, and laughed at me while I cried. Then he told them to let me go and shoved me down. He said, 'Don't ever make fun of me again. And keep your mouth shut or you'll get something worse.' She breathed out and opened her eyes.

"After that, they left. I lay on the ground until they were gone. I couldn't feel anything. I didn't even cry about it again. I was just empty. My grandmother died the next week, and the grief mixed in with the shame and fear. Every time I noticed a boy, those feelings would hit me. I put on weight and got taunted for it, and then for my braces. The only safety was to forget all about ever having a boyfriend."

The relief of disclosing it spread through her while the release of long buried fear and shame made her weak. She went limp against Tom and drew strength from his solid warm embrace. She let out a deep, shaky sigh and shut her eyes. He stroked her hair. The hypnotic steadiness of it caused her to drift as though she floated on water. Tom cleared his throat and her focus returned to the present.

"You never told anyone this?" His voice sounded husky.

"Just Susan, because I knew she wouldn't tell. I thought if my family found out, they'd get him punished, and he and his friends would come after me. I was scared all the time. Especially at school. Dale and his friends spread gossip about me, and said I tried to get their attention by showing them my chest. All the kids except Susan believed them. My family heard the rumors, and I told them they were lies. I'm pretty sure I convinced them."

"I'm sorry. I wish I'd known you then. Teaching him a lesson would've been satisfying."

Ann gazed up at him. His eyes were forlorn and glossy with unshed tears. She kissed his cheek. "It doesn't matter anymore. It's gone and dead. Washed away." Realization hit her, and a slow smile grew. "You want to hear something? It's not only the things I've done which got cleansed, but whatever's been done to me, too. Isn't it amazing?"

The sadness left his eyes, and he pulled her to him into a tender caress.

"No more holding back. Agreed?" Tom's intent gaze riveted her for long moments.

"Agreed." Ann kissed the tip of his nose, and his cheek, laying her hand on his other one. He clasped her to him, and after long, ardent kisses he pressed his forehead against hers. "I love you. So much."

"And I love you." She snuggled her head on him for sweet minutes before announcing with reluctance, "I better go home."

Tom took a breath and let it out. "First I want to check the road." He peered through the front window. "The road's clear. Most of the snow on the ground melted already. Drive slowly, though."

Tom helped her with her coat and they shared a goodbye smooch. Ann sat in the car for a few minutes as the windshield cleared, watching Tom's silhouette at the window, his hand raised when she drove away. She'd thought life should be carefully planned and contained, fenced in and controlled. All her gates were open now.

CHAPTER TWENTY-TWO

ANN DIDN'T EXPECT Jeff to show up with Eric the next morning, yet there he sat when she stepped out to the counter. A slight twinge of nerves prickled through her. Would interactions be strained around him now?

"Hi, guys," she turned to pour their coffees.

"Where's Susan?" Jeff's voice sounded normal.

"On the phone taking down an order." Ann set the cups in front of them.

Eric yawned, and grinned at Ann. "Guess I need this coffee."

She glanced into Jeff's eyes, surprised at her lack of discomfort. His expression appeared open and calm. What a relief. It was as though the last two days hadn't happened.

Thank you, Father.

Worries which had hounded her about Jeff's ongoing reaction receded, and peace filled in the space. It was good to see his normal attitude. He seemed comfortable and friendly with her, as before. His emotions couldn't have been that deep in the first place. The thought relieved her. She hadn't wanted to be the source of ongoing pain for him.

She asked, "Do either of you want any cake?"

"You bet," Jeff smiled at her. "How about getting me a piece of chocolate almond?"

Ann returned his smile. "Eric?"

"Carrot cake for me."

She served their pieces. "So what have you guys been up to this morning?"

"Nothing much. Traffic stops mostly, and one fender-bender down near the lake." Jeff took a bite of cake and a sip of coffee. "Seems like most of the traffic problems lately are foreign students who aren't used to the rules here. They pass on the right and don't come to a full stop at the lights. Last week we ticketed someone who passed on the right and drove over the sidewalk."

Eric chuckled, "He told us he saw it in an American movie and thought it would be okay."

"I think he said it to try and get out of the ticket, but it didn't work." Jeff grinned at Eric. Susan walked out, and the timer buzzed in the back.

Ann told her, "I'll go."

"WHAT TIME WILL Tom pick you up?" Susan closed the office door and stood at the entrance leading up to her apartment.

"He's coming to my place at six thirty, so I better skedaddle." Ann sighed and regarded Susan. "I'm nervous. You know how my Mom and sisters can be."

"Tom will be with you. I'm sure they'll curb themselves."

"Wish I was sure." Ann rolled her eyes at Susan before she waved and left.

On the drive home, she imagined her family's reactions. Dad would be quiet and contemplative while Dane could be counted on to make a joke. After listening, Greg probably wouldn't say anything. She expected eruptions of questions from Mom and Glenda, followed by Margie chiming in. She hoped Tom could keep from being offended if things got negative.

Ann arrived home and spotted Tom already waiting in the truck. She climbed in next to him.

"Nervous?" He looped his arm around her.

"Not too bad," she replied as he chuckled.

"Did you tell them we weren't bringing Jesse?"

"Yes. I said something came up, but we'd bring him next time. Mom seemed fine with it."

They soon rolled into her parent's driveway. Tom eased the ring off her finger and slid it in his pocket. "No point in confusing them. I'll put it back on afterwards."

"Okay." She sighed. "Let's go."

Mom had prepared a lavish salad, potato soup with cheddar and broccoli, and grilled roast beef and Swiss cheese sandwiches. They chatted and enjoyed their meal. Ann said, "Mom, I want this soup recipe. It's scrumptious."

Tom nodded. "It sure is. We'll make it for Jesse. He loves potato anything."

"So have you always liked to cook?" Glenda asked him.

"Not until I was a teenager. Mom and Dad both like to, and they showed me some techniques. I still can't do bread and rolls or pie as well as Mom, but I'll get there. Who doesn't love those things?"

"Annie's quite a baker." Dane shot her a grin.

"Thanks, but I've never done much in the way of pie or pastry or bread. Just cakes and cookies and such." Ann replied.

Tom patted her hand. "And they're all excellent. Especially the designs she puts on the cakes. Jesse liked his so much we had to take pictures of it before he would let us cut it. I guess you might say Ann's baking and decorating skills brought us together."

Tom's eyes grew soft while they grinned at each other. Ann's glimpse caught Margie and Glenda sharing a knowing look. After dinner while they lounged in the living room talking, Tom grabbed Ann's hand and squeezed it before scanning the group.

"I'm sure this will seem too fast since you hardly know me, but Ann and I are engaged." He gave Ann a nod of encouragement as she smiled at him. He took the ring out, slid it back on her finger, and kissed her forehead. Ann glanced around at her family and waited.

The room remained silent while the family studied the two of them with various degrees of shock and surprise.

"My, how sudden," Dane offered in a light tone. His comment didn't ease the obvious tension in the air.

Margie flashed Dane an irritated scowl before she turned her attention back to Ann and Tom. "Excuse me, but what on earth is the rush? Marriage is serious, and you should know each other better before you get engaged. Ann, you've never even had a boyfriend before."

"And you never had a husband before you had one, did you? But you knew what you wanted. I know what I want." Ann spoke in a calm, firm tone. She let her eyes travel the room, as though to welcome their objections. Tom gave her hand another squeeze.

Mom appeared shell-shocked, her cheeks pale. "I'm not sure what to say."

Glenda piped up, "Well, I am. I agree with Margie. This is way too fast. Remember the old saying, 'Marry in haste, repent at leisure?' You should continue to date for a much longer time before you even consider marriage. You're treating it with the same seriousness as deciding what movie to go to. It's ludicrous."

Ann took in a short breath. "Glenda, I realize you think you're right. Maybe you're sure this is what we need to hear, and you'll jolt us to our senses. However, you're as wrong as you can be. We both take this with extreme seriousness, and it's unfair of you to assume we don't. Since when do I make rash decisions?"

"How about starting a bakery with Susan and not continuing towards a teaching degree? That seemed pretty impulsive." She nodded and glanced at the others.

"I only studied to be a teacher because you all encouraged me to. I never wanted it. And I started in the bakery because it's what Susan wanted, and I needed to work. This engagement is a decision based on what *I* want." She gazed a moment at Tom. "Like my choice yesterday to be baptized."

"Baptized?" Mom's mouth dropped open.

"Wow," Dane said and stared at Ann as though seeing her for the first time.

Greg's eyes widened. "My, my."

Glenda threw her hands up, "See what I'm talking about? You're making all these...crazy decisions."

Tom held a hand up. "With all due respect, let's calm down here. It's not crazy to be baptized or get engaged. It doesn't help toward understanding another person to characterize them with a word like crazy."

"Well, I've known Ann a lot longer than you, so I think my opinion is valid," Glenda huffed.

Dad fixed Glenda with a sober gaze. "I think you should listen to Tom."

Margie rolled her eyes. "Ann, you don't truly know yourself. You always said church was a waste of time, you'd never be in a

[263]

relationship, and you were going to be a teacher or guidance counselor. I don't think you said any of it because of us. And now none of it is true. How do you expect us to react?"

"Rationally and reasonably, *if* you're able." Ann's voice stayed steady.

"Ouch," Dane said.

"You're not helping, Dane." Margie glared at him.

"That's what you're doing? Helping?" Dane asked, as his eyebrows rose.

"Yes," Margie exclaimed. "She doesn't know *what* she wants. She said herself she decides things because of what other people want. Then she expects us to believe all of a sudden she makes mature decisions."

Ann let out a sigh. "Why do you talk as though everyone agrees with what you're saying? How would you understand what goes on inside of me? Do you ever ask? Even if you did, would you listen if I answered in words you didn't agree with?"

Glenda jumped in. "You're not fair, Ann. Margie listens and cares as much as all of us. You never ask us how we're doing."

"I don't need to. You both mention it without being asked. I'm aware of what goes on in your lives and your minds because you tell me. I'm not like you. It's not easy for me. I always figured you weren't interested, or you'd ask."

Tears sprang into Glenda's eyes. "Of course I'm interested. So is Margie. How can you even say that?"

"I'm being honest. The two of you were always close, and more alike than me. I never felt listened to by either of you." *I can't believe I'm saying this. And I'm calm.*

Mom spoke up. "Girls, please don't hash over the past. No one can change it."

"No," Dad replied, "but it doesn't need to be repeated in the present. Why don't we try and listen to each other better?"

Silence filled the room and the tension level receded.

"All right, Dad." Margie nodded at Glenda, whose expression softened. Her gaze traveled to Ann. Margie's voice trembled a little. "Do you really think I don't care?"

Ann gave her a gentle look. "I'm sure you do, both of you. I said I didn't think you were interested in what I thought because honestly, you hardly ever asked me. I guess you figured I agreed with everything, or I'd speak up if I had something important to say."

"Well, you're certainly making up for it now." Dane grinned at Ann. "You're full of surprises."

Ann beamed back at him. "I am, aren't I? I'm sorry for upsetting you, Margie and Glenda. It's a lot to take in all at once. I'm finally deciding things for myself now, and God is teaching me how to live a different life. So is Tom."

Tom and Ann shared a smile.

"Well, I for one will be interested to hear about what you learn." Dad nodded at Ann and Tom. "I'll ask you questions, too. Now, even though this engagement is rather fast, I can tell you're both sure of your decision."

He stood and walked over to Tom, shook his hand and kissed Ann on the cheek before heading back to his chair. He glanced around with a pleased expression. Tom smiled at Ann. Dane got up, strode to stand in front of them and saluted the two of them with a grin on his face before he offered them both a vigorous handshake.

Mom rubbed her forehead and sighed. "I don't object to it. I...well, it's so unexpected and quick for me. Baptism, engagement, goodness...my head is spinning."

Tom laughed. "We didn't expect it either. But it's real."

Greg ambled over, shook Tom's hand and kissed Ann's cheek. "God bless you both."

Glenda crossed her arms as she asked Tom in a serious tone, "What about your little boy and your family?"

Tom assured her, "They know, and they're all very thrilled. And Jesse's loved Ann since he met her. He's ecstatic."

Mom observed Margie and Glenda, then rose and stepped over to Ann and Tom. She opened her arms to them as they stood up to hug her. Mom's eyes were filled with tears after she embraced them. Her lips trembled when her gaze rested on Ann. "My baby. I've always worried about you. You're so sensitive."

"Oh, Mom." Ann's own eyes teared up as she clasped her mother to her again. Mom held her in a tight embrace. After they let each other go, Margie and Glenda stood near, eyes soft while they waited to hug Ann. They were more reserved than their mother and shook Tom's hand instead of hugging him, though they offered him warm smiles when they did.

Everyone sat down, and Mom and Ann wiped their eyes. Dane asked Tom, "Still want to marry her?"

Tom chuckled with the rest of them. "You bet I do. She's wonderful."

Ann blushed and smiled at Tom and at her father, grateful for his quick, gracious acceptance.

Dad grinned back at her. "Now you need to tell Grandma D."

"She's the first one I told about being in love with Tom. No, wait, Susan knew first because she asked me. I told Gram last time she visited, and she said I should stand up for myself. So I am." She grinned at their surprised expressions and told them, "We plan to marry as soon as we can work out the details. We thought we'd come over soon and bring Jesse."

[266]

"That'll be fine," Dad answered. Ann was amazed at the lack of opposition from her mother and sisters at the idea the marriage was imminent. Ann had them laughing at the story of Tom's proposal, and her sisters added their own tales. The evening ended on a harmonious note.

Ann pondered while she and Tom climbed in the truck and started toward her apartment. Maybe she should have stood up for herself before now.

"See?" Tom said. "It wasn't bad at all. They just needed to realize we were serious."

"They *do* respect decisiveness. I tend to second-guess myself and maybe they think that means I'm unsure. I wonder sometimes if I'm able to handle people or situations well, but it doesn't mean I'm not convinced about what to do. It's funny how people in the same family can be so different."

In her driveway, they held each other and gazed at the clear, starry sky.

Pretty soon I won't live here anymore.

In the back room the next morning, Susan said, "The prison visit is this Sunday."

Ann widened her eyes and took a breath before she asked, "Nervous?"

"Nope. I'm fine with it. You don't need to go if you're worried about it. In fact, if you are, you shouldn't come with me. Jim's talked to me, and he's visited at the prison twice already."

Ann stopped mixing frosting. "How did it go?"

"He didn't tell me much, other than he doesn't see signs of remorse, just defiance and defensiveness." Susan finished filling a line of cake pans and slid them in the ovens.

"So Jim still thinks it's okay for you to go?" Ann covered the bowl of frosting and set it on the icing table.

"Yes. I told him it doesn't matter to me if he's repentant or not. I'm praying he will be someday and he'll turn to God. This is the only way for me to be free of it, if you understand my meaning. Once I offer my forgiveness, I've done everything I can do, and it's over for me."

"But you'll still need to testify at his trial, so it's not over." Ann tested a cake on the cooling rack to see if it was ready to frost.

"That's true. I'm talking in terms of releasing the burden, the weight of it. The emotions, I guess is what I mean. Offering forgiveness frees me from the whole thing." Susan assembled fresh ingredients for the next batch of cake batter.

Ann stopped work and stared at Susan, digesting her words. "I think I understand. I'm not sure if I'll go or not. It's not really clear to me yet."

"Pray about it. If you decide to come, Jim will want to discuss it with you first." The bell rang and Susan stepped to the front.

Ann closed her eyes. Well, Father, I'm going to need some help with this one.

All week as she worked and spent her evenings with Tom and Jesse, Ann thought often about the prison visit. It loomed ahead of her, weighted with an importance she didn't comprehend. Why did it matter so much? It hadn't before.

Tom would voice questions and concerns if she decided to accompany Susan. Until her mind became sure, she'd have no good answers to offer. By Friday afternoon she'd made up her mind after daily prayers and pondering. She needed to go, as much for Susan as for herself. Possibly even for Doug Miller, though she wasn't sure if anything would result in a positive impact on him. She had to begin learning to practice forgiveness. That's what mattered.

[268]

Ann turned from the icing table and faced Susan. "I've decided. I'm going with you."

Susan glanced up from a large bowl of batter, her expression serious. "All right. If you're sure."

"As soon as we get a lull, I'll call Jim."

ANN SAT AT the desk in the office, phone in hand. She stared at the fall landscape scene on the computer monitor. So beautiful. Taking a breath, she tapped in the numbers.

"Jim? It's Ann Shaw. I want to go to the prison with Susan and Eric this Sunday. Susan told me to talk with you first."

"So you've been in prayer about this?"

"Yes, all week long. I made my mind up today."

"Are you prepared for the fact we'll not be received well? He's not repentant and is belligerent also. I imagine he'll be even worse to Susan than he is to me. Can you deal with it and stay calm?"

Ann imagined an ugly scene directed at Susan. She closed her eyes and exhaled. "I can remain outwardly calm. I can't promise I won't be upset inside, but I'll control it."

"It's not necessary for you to be there, Ann. This is important to Susan, as I'm sure you realize. If you're at all unsure, I'd suggest you not go. It'll be difficult."

"I understand. I've thought about all of it. Something keeps running through my mind. If I'm to learn new ways, I need to practice them. I have to work to change my thoughts, so my behavior will be different. Isn't it a big part of being a believer?"

"Absolutely. Every thought must be brought into obedience to Jesus. This is a long process, one to take up daily. I'm glad you comprehend the challenge. The mind is our foremost battleground."

Ann exclaimed, "Funny you should use that word. The other day, someone told me this world is a battleground. As soon as I heard it, I realized the battle is spiritual."

Jim let out a quick, delighted laugh. "I'm so proud of you. You're digging in to your new life, aren't you?"

Ann's cheeks warmed. "You told me I'm a co-laborer with Jesus. I'm just trying to do my part, is all."

"Well, you're obviously applying yourself and studying. It's wonderful to hear. All right, Ann, if you're sure. I think you've got the right mindset. Continue in prayer for guidance and strength. I'll see you Sunday. Perhaps one of these days Tom will come with you."

"I've been praying about it." Ann's heart rose at the thought of Tom next to her at church.

"I'll add him to our prayer list."

"Thanks, Jim. See you Sunday at church."

They received a short-notice anniversary cake for early pick-up Saturday morning and she wasn't able to go to Tom's on Friday evening. She slumped in her chair when she finally got home and regarded her apartment with disappointment.

Wish I was at Tom's.

Her stomach rumbled. She should eat something. A glance at the clock showed almost ten. She'd call Tom first.

After they spoke about their days, Ann informed Tom of her decision. Silence. She waited a few moments. "Are you okay?"

He stayed quiet a moment longer before he answered in a tone she'd never heard before. "No. I'm not."

Ann paused, puzzled and concerned at the sound of his voice. After he said nothing else, she asked, "Will you tell me why?"

He heaved out a sigh. "I thought you weren't going to hold things back from me anymore. You never even told me this might be a possibility. Why do you want to do this? It's totally unnecessary, and to be honest I think it's stupid." His voice grew louder and more agitated. "The guy could have raped you if you'd been around. Are you and Susan going to start picking up rattlesnakes now? What are you trying to prove anyway?"

He'd never spoken to her like this. Shock filled her in a cold wave and no reply came to mind.

"Well?" he demanded.

"I don't know how to talk to you when you sound this way," Ann replied with honesty and forced down rising tension with a deep breath.

He retorted, "How about giving me a straight answer? What are the two of you trying to prove by doing this? How did you get talked into it anyway? I thought you were against it."

She shot back, "I was. And nobody *talked* me into this. I'm not some sort of mindless puppet. And we aren't attempting to prove anything. We want to do things the way we think God wants us to."

"Wow, that's priceless." Tom's voice dripped with uncharacteristic sarcasm. "You believe God needs you to go speak to some guy who doesn't give a hoot about Him or either of you. Now I've heard everything."

"I can't talk to you if you won't be reasonable." Frustration and fear of her strong reaction to his words filled her. What on earth was going on here?

"Fine," Tom barked and hung up. The phone emitted a loud clattering sound.

Ann held the receiver out and stared at it, her mouth open in shock. Tom had always been so kind and even-tempered. She scarcely believed it had been him on the phone. Her mind entered overdrive while she tried to figure out what just happened. Should she call him back, or wait? What words would reach him while he was so upset? Incredible heaviness engulfed her.

She positioned the phone on her ear, thinking she'd call him back, and realized he hadn't hung up, but had thrown the telephone instead. Sounds of pacing and muttering came through. Ann wrestled with herself about whether to listen or not, but strained to hear, desperate to understand him. He mentioned Jim Cortland's influence in a furious voice, then something about brainwashing.

"Why are you taking Ann away now? Why? Wasn't Judy enough?" Harsh sobs burst out of him and the sound of his desperate pain broke her heart. She had to get in the car and drive out to his house. She was about to, or call out to him and find out if he could hear her when he said, "Maybe I'm not good enough to have anyone, is that it? Maybe it's not fair to Jesse to try to be with Ann. He's already used to not having a mother. But I told him...I told him."

He sobbed again and the forlorn sound made her close her eyes as she cried along with him. After a few minutes passed, he cried out, "She won't want me now anyway, will she? I won't go in the same direction she is. I can't. If I make her choose, she'll pick You. And I can't. I can't choose You." Another sob followed, and Tom yelled, "I don't trust You."

Muffled crying sounded, as though he'd covered his face. The vehemence of his anger and despair stunned her. The frantic desire to go to him overwhelmed her, but something held her back. She didn't want to hang up the phone. It was a lifeline, her last chance to reach him. After hearing nothing but silence for over ten minutes, she finally hung up. Ann walked in a daze to her room. She fell on the bed with a sob and cried out prayers for him until exhausted sleep swallowed her.

ALL DAY AT the bakery, Ann grasped at the desperate hope he'd stop in for a talk. She tried her hardest to act happy. He'd call later like always and they'd work it out. Maybe she should phone him and leave a message. What if he was still upset and not ready to talk?

She wracked her brain and tried to imagine words to say that might help. In her mind she perceived the message to wait more than once. It got her attention but proved to be the most agonizing thing she'd ever done. Susan seemed preoccupied, and they were so busy they couldn't speak much anyway. Ann didn't want her to know about Tom's reaction. Susan failed to notice anything amiss in Ann's demeanor, so at least she had that to be thankful for.

How should she handle tomorrow's lunch with her family? What if he didn't call her tonight? She fretted all the way home after work, thinking about her family. They already thought she and Tom moved too fast. She couldn't tell them they had a fight, and it was the reason they wouldn't show up, but she didn't want to lie, either.

She sat in her chair at home, jumpy and unable to eat, while she waited for his call. The minutes crawled on, heavy with tension. She bolted up and paced until she had to sit again. Pace. Sit. Fret. Pray. By nine thirty, she accepted the realization that he wouldn't call.

Ann picked up the phone and dialed. "Mom? I'm going to the jail with Susan tomorrow. I'm sorry to let you know so late, but can we do the lunch another time? I decided I wanted to be with her when she went."

"All right dear, we'll reschedule the lunch. Are you positive you want to do this? Your voice sounds awfully worried. I don't even think Susan should go, and I know her father agrees with me."

"I'm sure, Mom. Other people will be with us. We both believe this is something we need to do. Don't worry," she added in as cheerful a tone as she could manufacture.

[273]

Mom's reply sounded unconvinced. "I wish both of you would reconsider this." Ann remained silent and her mother sighed. "Well, let me know how it goes, dear."

"I will, Mom."

Ann hung up and finally gave in to tears. "Maybe he's not going to call me ever again," she said out loud to God. "He might not want to marry me anymore."

Her gaze dropped to the ring he'd given her, and she remembered how jubilant they'd been. Head in her hands, she cried until she wore herself out. She woke in her chair to blink and stare at the clock. She'd been asleep for over two hours. Her heavy gaze turned to the phone before she shuffled to bed.

Ann stared up at the dark ceiling as the stress built again. What were Tom's thoughts? Did he still want to be with her? At the thought that maybe he didn't, sobs erupted. She couldn't believe she had any tears left in her as she turned on her side and let them soak into the pillow. Ann prayed for God to help her and Tom somehow, while she cried herself to sleep again.

CHAPTER TWENTY-THREE

For the second morning in a row, Ann held a cold washcloth over her eyes. Maybe it would help relieve the swelling. It was nine, and she should eat breakfast before church. She hadn't consumed much food the last two days. Ann stared at the phone more than once and wrestled with herself.

I want to call Tom. Tell him I love him. He'll expect me to say I won't go with Susan. I can't. I said I would.

Ann sighed as she set down the washcloth and trudged to the kitchen. She waited to leave until 10:55. Arriving late meant not having to greet anyone. If someone spoke to her, she'd collapse into desperate tears and frighten them.

The pulse of music reached her ears before she entered the building. Her eyes closed when she slipped into a seat. The melody and the sense of peace it generated calmed the turbulence inside her.

Help me, Father. I need to find stability.

After the Scripture reading, Jim taught about the strength it took to truly forgive, especially if the person who wronged you

[275]

wasn't sorry. Jim glanced around with a solemn expression. "When I raised children, I thought it must be the hardest, most rewarding job I'd ever do."

He paused, gave a slight shake of his head and smiled. "Confronting my own selfishness, stubbornness, anger, and shortcomings proved to be much harder and not at all fun. It was only the first step, to face the things in me I didn't want to see. Then I had to be willing to let go of my ways and thoughts and embrace His. And I had to forgive myself."

Many heads nodded. She wished Tom understood the changes happening inside her. Maybe he wouldn't wish to be with this new Ann, whose mind and heart grew in unaccustomed directions.

I'm still me, Father, and I love him so. I don't want to go through my life without him and Jesse. Please help us.

She bowed her head and listened to Jim.

"I've spoken with so many folks who say it's not hard to live a decent life, and who think anyone who turns to God is weak and needs some sort of crutch or excuse. It used to be painful for me to hear it because the words hurt my pride. I had to let go of that, too. You see, I want to be weak in the ways I once thought were strength, the things the world teaches you a strong person is. The person I was before wasn't fit for the kingdom of God. It's that simple."

He looked around, his demeanor serious, his eyes kind. "If anyone wants prayer, please come up."

Ann had listened intently while he spoke, at first with a few tears, then with a gradual sense of hope. The tentative internal steps she'd taken in this different way of life became firmer and more deliberate. It wasn't clear what would happen with her and Tom, but she held solid faith they'd manage to work things out. She knew her course was set, and nothing could deflect her. As she stood in the prayer line, a sense of strong resolve rested inside her heart, along with hope.

"I'd like prayers for guidance," she requested when her turn came. Jim and Evelyn nodded and laid their hands on her shoulders, as did others. Ann received again the beautiful love and care from the people around her. The rest of her heaviness and worry lifted while she prayed in silence for God to guide her life and show her the right path.

And please be patient with me. I probably won't get it right at first. But I am trying.

Ann lifted her head, wiped her eyes, and said a grateful thank you to everyone. As she walked to her seat, a shock jolted her. Tom sat in the back row, bent over, his head in his hands. She couldn't see his face at all, but his posture looked so sorrowful her heart flooded with compassion for him. Ann rushed to slip in next to him, not afraid of his temper anymore. He gazed over at her, an agonized expression on his features, tears in his eyes.

"Oh, honey." Ann clasped her arms around him. His chest shook with a few silent sobs while he pressed her to him and held her tight. The world seemed to stop and contain only the two of them as they relaxed in the embrace.

"I'm so sorry," he whispered in a broken voice, "so sorry. I wasn't mad at you. I was angry at God. I didn't even know it until I blew up at you."

He pulled back and studied her. He placed his hand on her cheek, and asked, "Will you forgive me?"

"I already did." She smiled as tears of happiness rolled down her cheeks. Tom wiped them away one by one and kissed her forehead. She laid her head on his chest while they sat together in healing fellowship. Prayer time ended, and Jim dismissed everyone.

Tom asked, "Do you think I could have a talk with him?"

"Jim?"

"Yeah."

"Of course." Ann beamed. "I'm sure he'd like it."

"Hi, Tom," Susan said in a bright voice.

"Hey, Susan, Eric." Tom smiled and stood up with Ann.

Ann said, "We're going over to speak with Jim. I'll meet you back here at three-thirty, okay?"

Susan nodded. "Okay."

Tom and Ann made their way over to Jim. As soon as he was free, Ann said, "Jim, this is my fiancé, Tom Tillman. He wondered if he could speak with you."

Jim shook his hand. "Pleased to see you, Tom. I've heard great things about you and Jesse."

Tom grinned at him. "I've heard the same about you and your wife. I want to thank you for your teaching today. I felt like you were speaking right to me."

"It's funny how often that happens. God will lead me to speak in a direction I didn't plan on, and a lot of folks come up and tell me afterwards what you just did. It never ceases to amaze me." Jim asked, "Would you like to step into my office, Tom?"

"Sure."

"I'll wait out here." Ann perched on a chair. She could tell by Tom's face he'd gone through a lot the last two days, but they were past it now. She breathed out a happy sigh.

Thank You. Thank You.

After many minutes passed, Ann stood and meandered around the room. She read some of the printouts on the back table and after a while sat down again and closed her eyes. A gentle aura seemed to radiate from the walls, as though they somehow absorbed the energy from the songs and prayers. Jim opened his office door soon after.

"Come on in now, Ann."

She settled in the chair next to Tom. His features appeared relaxed and content when he took her hand in his.

Jim said, "Ann, Tom would like me to pray with both of you for God to bless and guide your relationship. He'd like to go with you to the jail later and wants to pray about that as well."

Ann gazed at Tom and smiled in delighted wonder. She bowed her head while Jim prayed out loud for them. A wave of healing peace washed through her. After the prayers were over, Tom and Ann grinned at each other before they thanked Jim.

"Don't thank me. I'm glad to do whatever I can. You're a charming couple." He stood up. "I'll go eat some lunch now. Would you like to join Evelyn and me next door?"

Tom glanced at Ann. "Thanks for the offer, but I think Ann and I want to talk together, if you don't mind."

"Not at all. You go right ahead and stay here as long as you wish. I'll see you both around three thirty." He shook their hands and left the office.

Tom sighed and gazed at her. "I feel so much better than I have since the argument." He squeezed her hand, leaned toward her and gave her a quick, tender kiss. "I can't believe what a jerk I was."

Ann couldn't help bursting into laughter. He smiled and asked, "What?"

"That thing you said about Susan and me picking up rattlesnakes." She laughed harder, and Tom joined her. The last bit of disconnection from their angry words faded away. Tom stood, pulled her up to him and twirled her around in his arms. She giggled and he stopped, clasped her to him and rested his chin on top of her head.

"I almost called you a million times," he said. "First I was mad, and then I yelled at God for taking you away. I figured if you had to choose between me and God, you'd pick Him. Today I realized if both of us choose Him, we'll learn to cherish each other better. I stopped being afraid either I'd lose you or hurt your faith by marrying you."

His deep love and concern filled her with warmth. She pulled back to look at him. What a beautiful heart he possessed. "I almost called you, too, but I wasn't sure how to talk to you if I did. I've been praying for God to help us."

"Me, too."

Ann ran her fingers over the contours of his face.

"Oh, Ann." He gripped her tight. "I love you so much. I wish we could get married right now and never be apart. He gazed at her for a minute and said, "Let's go eat lunch at the Thai place."

She grinned at him as he took her hand and led her over to where their coats hung. His eyes traveled over her. "You're mine."

"I sure am. And you're mine."

ON THE WAY back to the church after lunch, Ann told him, "You don't have to go today if you don't want to."

"I know. None of us has to. But I want to come with you. I understand why you and Susan feel like you need to do this." He cuddled her against him for a few moments after he parked outside the building. They entered, and she spotted Jim with Susan and Eric. Jim motioned for them to come and sit.

"All right," he said and sat in a chair facing them. "I've already been to visit Doug Miller myself, and I can tell you he's an extremely defensive, hostile person. He might say things which are meant to disturb you, and I think it may be why he agreed to this meeting. So I'm asking if you're not sure you can remain calm, please don't go today. We can't do any good if we play into his angry world."

Eric asked, "What should we do, Jim?"

"Don't take anything he says personally. Be in a prayerful state of mind at all times, and keep Jesus' example foremost in your head and heart. If you can't think of a response to fit with that, stay silent but don't look away from him. Let him be the one who looks away. And try to show compassion in your eyes. It helps sometimes to picture men like Doug as the little children they once were."

Jim's eyes filled a little. "Some people who commit aggressions have endured cruelties and conditions in childhood that we couldn't imagine. I'm not making an excuse for the choices they make or their awful actions. Many people endure horrible things and don't act as Doug has. He's responsible and will be required to answer for it to God."

Jim reached for something in his pocket as he continued. "But in order to hope to reach him, I believe we need to show him the more excellent way. His brother told me a good deal about their family, and I can tell you he hasn't always been as he is now."

He showed them a picture of a small boy hugging a stuffed toy, his features shining with happiness. Jim scanned their faces. Silent tears tracked down Susan's cheeks when she viewed the snapshot. Eric swallowed hard and took Susan's hand. Tom and Ann shared a solemn glance.

Jim rose and handed a tissue to Susan. "This is serious business, as much a life and death matter as if he needed a blood transfusion to live. Many people wouldn't understand it, but I can tell all of you do. To me, a true believer is like a medic on the battlefield."

He sat down again as Susan dabbed her eyes. "It's not the medic's job to stop the war. It's his responsibility to try to save life, no matter what side the soldier he's treating is on. Spiritually speaking, this man is almost dead, and only true repentance will begin his reviving process."

Jim reached out and patted Susan's hand. "If we can somehow reach him with the truth of God's love and forgiveness, he may decide to choose life. Let's join hands now and pray before we go. Each of you ask whatever is foremost in your thoughts."

They joined hands and bowed their heads. Jim ended the prayers with the hope that Doug's heart would begin to turn. They looked up and Jim said, "Well, let's go. We can all fit in the van."

They were silent during the short ride to the county jail. Jim led the way inside. Tom held Ann's hand in a firm grasp while they waited to enter the room used for the meeting. Ann's gaze flicked to Susan after Doug Miller was led in. A quick flash of fear crossed her features, which gave way to a calm outer aspect.

Doug seemed surprised at the number of them, and his jaw clenched as he fixed them with a hard stare. He sat down with an almost jaunty attitude and flippant expression. He dispensed a brief, disdainful glance at Susan before his eyes traveled to Ann. He gave her a snide grin, and said, "Well, here's another one who got away."

Ann held onto Tom's hand and kept her features tranquil.

"So what do all of you people want from me?" His voice sounded bored, and he crossed his arms.

Jim said, "Well, Doug, we don't want anything from you. We came to give you something."

Doug barked out a sarcastic laugh. "Yeah, give me hell I bet. You religious people are all the same. I figured it'd be pretty funny to hear you try to chew me out or scare me with hell."

Jim glanced at Susan. "Actually we're here to offer you something quite precious."

Susan fixed Doug with steady eyes, and said in a clear strong voice, "I came to give you my full forgiveness for what you did to me."

A momentary attitude of confusion crossed his brow before he sneered and answered, "I didn't get a chance to do much, now did I? You were too busy trying to poke my eyes out and kick me in the gut."

"I protected myself. I'm sorry I had to hurt you."

He scanned all of them as his stare and demeanor hardened. He asked Susan, "What is this, some kind of a joke? Are you one of those dumb broads who like it rough, so now you're coming on to me?"

Susan stayed quiet while Eric kept his face straight. He tightened his hold on Susan's hand. Ann said a silent prayer for both of them. Tom shifted and cleared his throat quietly. The silence in the room grew as Doug Miller observed them. His discomfort increased as the stillness continued. All of a sudden he exploded. "Quit staring at me, you crazy bunch of church zombies. You don't fool me. You'd love to get your hands on me somewhere private and beat the life out of me."

Jim replied in a calm voice, "You're wrong, Doug. We came to offer you God's love and forgiveness."

Doug laughed. "I've got no use for Him, and He's got none for me. You're a pastor or something, aren't you? Why don't you ask Him what He thinks of me?"

Jim's voice held compassion. "I have. More than once. He wants you to turn away from evil and come to Him so He can help you."

Doug's eyes widened and appeared almost frightened. He darted a brief glance at all of them and got up. He stood next to the guard at the door and spoke in a rough voice, "Let me out."

"Think about it, Doug," Jim said. "I'll be back to visit again."

Doug said nothing and didn't turn around before he left. As soon as Doug exited, Eric took a deep breath and blew it out. "Whew."

Tom rubbed his forehead and stared into Ann's eyes.

Jim stood. "I think this was a good start. What about you, Susan?"

She nodded at him. "I agree. He knows we meant what we said. Now it's up to him to think it over."

They rose and followed Jim toward the door. He turned and addressed them. "Let's all keep praying for him. He's got a rough road ahead no matter what he decides."

They left the jailhouse and on the drive to the church, Tom asked Eric, "What does your partner think of all this?"

Eric grinned. "He's convinced we're off our rockers, but I expected it. I was surprised he didn't ask for a different partner after I first told him. He was disgusted, but his temper wears off pretty quickly where I'm concerned. Guess I'm the older brother he always wanted."

Susan smiled at him. "He's lucky to have you. He needs a good example around him of what a man is."

"Amen," Jim agreed as Eric appeared embarrassed. Tom patted Eric on the back and grinned at him.

Outside the church, before Ann and Tom left, Tom turned to Jim. "Would you be willing to marry us?"

Jim studied them. "I'd want to have a small talk with you both first, but yes, I'm willing. When do you plan to marry?"

Tom laughed. "As soon as possible."

Ann chuckled and looped her arm through Tom's.

"Well, you let me know and I'll be thrilled to do it." Jim waved and stepped inside the building.

"I need to get home and do chores pretty soon," Tom told her as he started the truck. "How about I take you somewhere for a cup of tea or something, and we'll come back for your car?"

"I can come and help with chores," Ann offered.

"This is your only day off, sweetie. I figured you'd want to take a nap after the couple of days we've had."

Ann snuggled against him. "I'm quite contented right now and not at all tired. So if you don't mind me probably getting in your way, I'd love to come with you."

"Okay, good. Snow's in the forecast for later, and I'd be more comfortable if I drove you home in case it gets nasty. So why don't you drop the car off at your place now, and I'll follow."

"Are you sure? I can drive in snow, you know. I have for a long time." Ann shot him a grin.

"Yes, but my snow tires are on and all you've got are those all-weather ones. They seem a little worn." Warmth spread inside. He even noticed the state of her tires.

"You're so sweet." She kissed him before she climbed out.

After they dropped her car off at her apartment, some light snow began while they rode out to Tom's place. He squeezed her hand. "Jesse will be thrilled to see you."

"Pretty soon, I'll be around him a lot more. And I should get familiar with how the farm works anyway, shouldn't I? I'll need to know where I fit in."

Tom clasped her with his free arm. "You'll fit in no matter what. I'll let you decide how much you want to learn, and you can go at your own pace. Dad and I've got everything pretty well nailed down. Especially this time of year when the pace lets up. Plus now that Jesse's older, he helps with chores, too."

"Susan and I discussed again how my hours would change once we're married. When we start closing the front at noon, she

[285]

said maybe some days I could be back home by two, depending on the day."

Home. Their home.

"How soon until it happens?"

"She'll set up more new restaurant standing orders this week." Ann traced the side of his face. "She said she'll look over the books. If everything works out according to plan, we'll make all the changes within two weeks."

"Sounds good to me. Do you think your family will lose it if we get married so soon?"

"I guess we'll find out." Ann rolled her eyes while Tom laughed. He pulled into his driveway, parked, and drew her to him for a long kiss.

"I'll do the milking first," he spoke near her ear and nuzzled her hair. "Then we can go up to my folk's house and eat dinner with them and Jesse. Afterwards, I'll take you back."

"Okay." She smiled at him, and he kissed her again. She sighed. "I wish we were married now."

"You said it." Tom flashed an expression of resigned longing before he touched the tip of her nose. "Let's go milk, my lady."

"You lead, I'll follow." She jumped down and walked with Tom along the path. Their feet crunched the newly fallen snow. Ann breathed in the cold fresh air and gazed up at the sky. Its blue shade deepened toward dusk. The gray clouds, heavy with moisture, moved slowly overhead. Pine trees scattered throughout the landscape were the only green left in sight and wore a light coat of snowflakes. Ann thought they looked as though they'd been dusted with powdered sugar, like the topping on the chocolate cherry cake she and Susan made.

Tom turned on the barn light and closed the door. He grinned at Ann while he pulled on a pair of coveralls over his clothes, stepped into large rubber boots, and walked toward the cows. He patted all of them and pitched some fresh hay into their bins. He showed Ann how he attached the milk machine.

His efficiency and calm, cheerful attitude while he worked captivated her. Once he finished and the milk was stored in the steel tank, he gave each cow another pat and filled a large bowl with warm milk. He set it down in the corner and said, "For the wild barn kitties. They'll show up after we leave."

They walked to the area of the barn where the goats were. Tom stopped at the gate. "We milk these by hand since we don't have so many of them."

She stretched forward to pet the goats. They clustered next to the gate and sounded their distinctive bleats. Ann giggled in delight at their friendly demeanor. "Their pupils are sideways, not up and down. How different looking."

"They're smart, too, and I think they have livelier personalities than the cows. Plus you can earn more money selling the milk and cheese from these girls." He climbed over the low gate and started working. She admired the deftness of his hands. No wonder they were so strong. Finished with that task, he led her to the area of the barn where the chickens were housed.

"The birds go outside most days when the weather's decent. See the door?" He pointed at a door across from them. "It opens out to a big fenced-in area. They almost always lay their eggs in here, though." The chickens milled around while Tom scattered cups of grain down for them.

"Don't fight girls, we've got plenty," he admonished as one pecked another to get at the food and she let out a loud squawk. Ann chuckled at the sound and the funny way the hen looked when she sounded her displeasure. "Want to feed them?"

"Sure." Ann copied what she'd seen him do. She grinned as some of the birds rushed over to peck and swallow. Their murmured clucks created a pleasing music. She followed Tom back near the door. He took off the boots, then the coveralls, and hung them up. They both washed their hands at the sink next to the milk tank, and Tom embraced her before they shared some long caresses. He sighed and hugged her to him.

He spoke in a low voice into her ear. "So you don't mind the barn smell?"

"Nope." She melted against him while he nuzzled her ear. Prickles of delight ran down her neck. "Kiss me again," Ann urged. "Oh," she breathed when he broke the kiss off. She sensed a slight tremble in his arms when he held her tightly.

After some quiet moments, Tom cleared his throat. "We better go eat now. They always wait dinner for me. Won't they be excited to see you with me? Especially Jesse."

They walked hand in hand up his driveway and across the street, toward his parents' house up the road. The bright outdoor light his father loved so much lit up the snowflakes as they fell to the ground in silent swiftness. Ann sighed. "How beautiful it is."

"I never get tired of seeing it. One of the best things about farming is I don't need to try to drive to work in the winter, so I can appreciate the beauty of the weather. I love the quiet that comes with the snow. It's like the whole earth is pacified by it."

Ann imagined how fulfilled she'd be once the three of them were together all the time, sharing the little special moments of each day.

"Annie!" Jesse beamed when they walked in. He ran to her and hugged her.

"Smells good in here, Mom." Tom hung up their coats.

[288]

Joe and Kathy greeted them with obvious pleasure and led the way to the living room. Jesse picked up the open picture album resting on one of the chairs.

"Daddy, we need some pichers of Annie in here." He scooted himself in between Tom and Ann and pointed at a picture.

"She's my first mom," Jesse told her while they studied Tom and Judy's wedding portrait. She'd seen a copy on the wall upstairs at Tom's house. Jesse had her smile, and her hair and eye color.

"She's beautiful, Jesse," Ann murmured.

"Yep," Jesse chirped. "Pretty soon I'll have another beautiful mom."

Ann swallowed hard so she wouldn't tear up.

Tom squeezed her hand and said, "You're right, buddy."

Kathy rose. "I need to go check on dinner."

Ann stood, too. "Let me help you."

"Okay." Kathy gave her a smile, and they walked together to the kitchen while Jesse tagged along. At a small doorway off the kitchen, Kathy stopped and turned on the light. "This is the pantry. I don't think you saw it the other night."

Ann couldn't help but be impressed with the large variety of home-canned foods on display. The various colors in the glass jars were beautiful, and Ann thought they shined like lines of jewels along the shelves.

"Did you do all this yourself?"

"Joe and Tom help when I need it. Even Jesse helps sometimes, don't you, baby?"

Jesse tilted his head and looked at Kathy with a serious expression. "Grandma, 'member we said I wasn't a baby now?"

Kathy laughed. "Oops, you're right, honey. I'll try to remember."

"Okay, Grandma." He ran over to her and gave her a hug. He dashed back to the living room and announced, "Grandma made chicken and dumplings, Dad, our favorite."

Ann and Kathy chuckled as they entered the warm, fragrant kitchen.

"I love your big stove." Ann said.

Kathy opened it and took out a steaming pan with lightly browned biscuits on top of the chicken stew. "Ooh, it looks good. I'm always thankful Joe got me this oven. Especially on holidays, when everyone's here. I can bake six pies at once." Kathy removed another steaming casserole dish and set it on the stovetop next to the chicken. "This looks just right."

"What is it?" Ann asked.

"Glazed sweet potatoes cooked with ginger and orange juice. Jesse loves it." Kathy slid serving spoons into each dish before she sniffed the yams. "Mmm."

"Sounds wonderful."

"The rolls and butter are already on the table," Kathy said, "along with the tiles to set the hot food on. If you want to take in the yams and the chicken, I'll put the broccoli and cheese sauce in a dish, and we can eat."

"Will do." Ann plucked some potholders from a hook on the wall.

As they ate the lovely dinner and laughed together, Ann experienced a depth of happiness filling her soul, more satisfying than any meal could be. She sensed a quiet strength inside while she waved good-bye to Tom after she arrived home. In her room, she whispered to God after she settled her head on the pillow. Grateful amazement washed through her. "Thank you so much...for all the miracles today."

CHAPTER TWENTY-FOUR

THE FOLLOWING DAY Ann stopped at her parents' house before she rode out to Tom's after work. She shut the front door and called out, "Mom? Dad?"

"In here, dear. We're watching the news," Mom's voice answered. Ann made her way to the living room, kissed both of them and sat on the couch.

"What's up?" Her father asked.

"Well," Ann stretched her legs in front of her and glanced at her boots before she regarded them. "We decided yesterday. The wedding will be in two weeks. I thought I'd tell you today so you can get used to the idea."

"Ann." Her mother's brow furrowed. "Dear, this doesn't feel right. Why? Why that soon? It worries me. You're always so careful about your decisions."

"Then you should trust me, shouldn't you?"

"Good point," Dad agreed and Mom scowled at him.

"Ann, you've never lived on a farm or cared for a child. How will you manage?" Mom threw her hands up. "Can't you wait until summer and give yourselves more time?"

"Mom, I know people who were engaged for years and did everything by the book and ended up divorced. You need to have faith in me. I'm sure about this, so what's the point in waiting?"

Mom sighed and fixed her with a puzzled expression. "You've changed so much lately. I hardly know what to think sometimes. It confuses me."

"I'm not that changed, Mom. I just see things with a different perspective. I used to be so nervous about what might happen to hurt or scare me. I tried to protect myself from anything bad. But now I know for sure God is real, love is real, and no matter what happens, those things never fail and never will. I can't explain it any better because I'm still learning."

Tears formed in Mom's eyes.

"Mom, I know you're worried I'll get hurt somehow. I'll go through difficulties, but everyone does. I'll hold on to my faith, as Tom will, and I'll have Tom and Jesse to work through the rough times with. And I've got you guys. I want you to be happy for me."

Mom wiped her eyes. "Of course I'm happy for you. I worry it will be too hard for you to get used to so many changes so quickly."

Ann shrugged. "I'm sure I'll mess up sometimes, but all I can do is my best." She grinned and gave out a chuckle. "And I can't wait to try."

Mom sighed. "How will we ever get everything organized in such a short time?"

"With a small, simple ceremony, we don't have much to organize. It's just both of our families plus Susan and Eric. Then some simple refreshments and Susan wants to make my cake."

"Will you at least let us buy your dress and flowers?" Mom asked with her head tilted as though exasperated.

"Yes, Mom," Ann agreed laughing. "Nothing too fancy. Tom and I are pretty plain as far as fashion goes."

"You find out what he's wearing and we'll come up with something to go with it." Mom bit her lip and crinkled her brows as she glanced upward.

I bet she's already decided the different stores we'll go to.

Ann embraced them both and left to drive to Tom's house.

Our house.

TWO DAYS LATER, at a dress shop, Ann exclaimed, "Mom. I think this is it. Tom's suit matches his eyes, and I think the trim around the neckline on this one is the same color as my eyes."

Mom held it next to Ann's face. "It's a match. Try it on. I spotted a nice veil to go with this. I'll go get it."

Ann adjusted the gown and studied her reflection. Her dress was white with soft blue-gray trim at the neckline. The fit was smooth but not too tight, the way she liked it. The calf-length skirt of it moved fluidly when she walked. The saleslady arrived with the veil, positioned it on her head and beamed at her. "Let's show your mother."

They stepped out of the dressing room. Mom's attitude of delight, coupled with tears, sealed the choice.

"Guess this is the one, eh, Mom?" she joked as the saleslady grinned at her. Mom nodded and gave Ann a wistful smile.

TOM AND ANN brought Jesse to meet her family the following Sunday after church. The house smelled of pot roast and apple pie.

[293]

Ann asked after they introduced Jesse, "Gram, did you make the pie?"

"I certainly did," Grandma replied while Ann hugged her.

"Oh, goody."

"Ah, the famous Jesse at last," Dane shook Jesse's hand.

"What's famous mean?" Jesse tilted his head up.

"It means you are a very important young man," Dane replied with a grin.

Jesse nodded. "I take care of Batman. And Abner, too."

Dane laughed. "I know who Batman is, but who's Abner?"

"He's my kitty. He's got seven toes, and if you play with his paws too much he does this." Jesse acted out a hiss and a small bite on his arm.

Everyone laughed, and Ann smiled at the delighted expressions on their faces. Jesse's charm was irresistible.

"Well, let's sit down and visit a bit," Mom said. "Now, Ann and I got her dress all picked out." She glanced around the room. "It's lovely on her."

"Thanks, Mom." Ann squeezed Jesse when he sat on her lap.

Tom ruffled Jesse's hair. "We won't need a rehearsal dinner for such a small family wedding, but my mother wants to bring some sandwiches and little appetizers for after the ceremony."

"And Susan will contribute sparkling cider and cake," Ann added.

"You're not leaving all of us much to do," Margie complained. "You don't even want us to buy gifts."

"Well," Tom replied, "We've already got more than enough between us to set up housekeeping, so we don't need anything. Neither of us is much for accumulating extras, so this kind of wedding suits us both. I hope you don't mind."

Dad shook his head. "Of course not. You should have the kind of ceremony you want."

"All you need to do, Dad, is walk me down to Tom and lift my veil." Ann shot him a grin.

"I can handle it," he chuckled.

"When is your meeting with Jim Cortland?" Greg asked and hooked his arm around Glenda's shoulder.

"Tomorrow night," Tom answered.

"How many more days now until you're my Mommy?" Jesse piped up.

Ann held up seven fingers. "Count them, Jess."

"Seven. That's not too many. Not even ten anymore." Jesse turned and gave her an excited cuddle.

Mom cleared her throat and said, "Well girls, let's get the food on. Bet Jesse wants to eat."

Jesse gave a vigorous nod, and Ann smiled to herself.

I knew Mom would fall for Jesse.

Tom ROLLED UP at her apartment. "Meet you here tomorrow. I'll pick you up, and we'll grab a meal at the Thai place before we go to the church, okay?"

He gave her a quick brush of the lips. She hugged sleepy Jesse, and waved to them from the door. Ann hung her coat and took a slow, contemplative stroll around her small apartment. Some of her things were already packed, but most would wait until she got back from her honeymoon. No rushing was necessary. Her lease wasn't up until the end of December.

"I don't think I'll miss you," Ann said to the walls. She realized she'd never done much more than exist here. "I have a real life now." *Thank you, God.*

"Well, hello, you two," Jim greeted them when they walked into his office the next evening. "Take a seat."

"Any questions?" Jim raised his brows at them.

Ann breathed in the familiar church smell of pine cleaner. She darted a glance at Tom and asked Jim, "What's the most important thing I need to know about being a wife and a mom?"

"Good question." Jim smiled. "First I'll answer, and then Tom should as well."

Ann grinned at Tom's wide-eyed look of surprise. Jim answered, "Every relationship is different, and the people involved find their own ways of creating it. I think the most important thing to keep in mind is not to be quick to assume you know what the other person thinks or feels. *Ask* them, and listen closely to the answer. As the Scripture says, "Be swift to hear and slow to speak.""

He studied them, his countenance serious and kind. "Even when you think your spouse is being unfair or wronging you, keep in mind they love you, and you chose each other. Don't let yourselves stay angry, but calm down first before you talk. Always, always pray for guidance and understanding. Sometimes it's best to be silent and wait. As for the mom part, be patient and loving, but firm when Jesse needs it. The greatest thing you can give Jesse is parents who love one another. So, Tom, how would you answer Ann's question?"

"I agree with what you said, Jim. I think Ann's got a pretty good handle on some of it already. I'm the one who tends to sound off too fast." He gave Ann a fond look and took her hand. "I want you to trust me and confide in me. If I do or say anything you don't like or don't understand, we need to talk about it. Don't hold yourself away from me or let me make you feel like you can't speak your mind. All I want is what's best for you and for Jesse."

"Another thing," Jim said. "You're both going to go through stressful, bad days, sometimes a string of them together. Try to remember you're human and not to expect you won't say and do things you wish you hadn't. The most important thing to learn from troubles is what you should do differently. Then you'll begin to exercise patience and forgiveness. You need to forgive yourself as you do others."

"That's the hardest part, sometimes." Tom shook his head.

"Don't I know it," Jim chuckled. "Now remember, every mistake is a chance to learn how to do better next time. So don't waste your efforts with recriminations or fault-finding in yourself or with each other. Forgive and go forward. Study the Word to learn a better way to be."

He reached into his desk and pulled out a small leather-bound book with a plain brown cover. "Evelyn and I wrote down many of our favorite Scripture verses for newly married couples in this. There are lots of blank pages after them, waiting for you to add your own as you discover them."

Tom accepted the little volume, his demeanor serious as he surveyed some of the pages. "Thank you, Jim."

Tom handed it to Ann. Her heart filled with warmth while she leafed through the first few pages and scanned the careful, hand-lettered words of Scripture. They'd penned the verses about the characteristics of love on the last written page, followed by their signatures and a wish for their marriage to be long and blessed.

"Jim, this is precious. Thank you." Ann wiped away quick tears, overwhelmed at the thoughtfulness and care the pages revealed.

Jim told them, "Evelyn is sitting with a sick friend tonight and asked me to tell you, Ann, any time you want to speak with her about anything, let her know, and she'll be glad to talk with you.

She's got a lot of wisdom and will be able to help you whenever you want."

"Tell her thank you. Bet I'll need plenty of advice."

They hashed out the few details about the ceremony before Jim said, "Well, unless you can think of anything else you two want to ask or say, I guess we've got everything covered."

Tom and Ann stood to shake Jim's hand.

"Ann, I never figured when you bumped into me this summer I'd be doing your wedding ceremony in the fall." Jim grinned and shook her hand.

"And if you'd said it, I'd have thought you were insane." Ann chuckled.

After Tom parked, they sat together in the truck outside Ann's apartment. Tom kissed the top of her head. "No doubts or worries?"

Ann snuggled closer to him and sighed. She listened for a moment to the slight whirr of the heater on the dashboard. "Just now and then. A thought will pop in my head, and I'll think, 'What if I do something to make him upset...or what if I make mistakes with Jesse?' Stuff like that. Nothing big."

He tipped her face up, and they kissed for long moments. He stroked her cheek. "Are you nervous about the honeymoon?"

Ann's face heated, and she closed her eyes. "Sometimes, yes."

Tom waited a moment and whispered, "Look at me."

She met his intent gaze.

"I'll be careful. I don't want you to be scared." She laid her head back on his chest. "I love you, Ann...so much. You go on in now. I'll see you tomorrow after work."

"I love you, Tom." She kissed him, walked to her apartment and waved from the doorway.

THE FOLLOWING NIGHT, Ann drove to Tom's and marveled how in five days she'd be his wife. She stepped out of the car into cold rain mixed with snow and rushed inside. The wind gusted and made it hard to shut the door.

"Whew. It's nasty outside." No answer. The house was warm yet silent.

"Tom? Jesse?" She walked through the downstairs rooms before ascending the stairs. Nobody upstairs, either. Tom's truck had been in the driveway. Maybe they were in the barn? She paused at the entry to Tom's room and stepped in. Her eyes traveled over a closet, chest of drawers, a wicker clothes hamper, and a large bed next to a nightstand. Pictures of Jesse were on the walls, along with what must be some of Jesse's artwork.

Ann closed her eyes and let the aura of the room fill her. Eyes open again, she stepped to his bed. Giving in to impulse she lay on it, her face turned to the pillow. Ann inhaled his scent and imagined him next to her. Her cheeks grew warm. Sounds from outside jolted her, and she hopped up, smoothed the covers and rushed downstairs.

Tom and Jesse traipsed in, with a swirl of fresh cold air behind them. Both their expressions lit up at the sight of her. Jesse sped over.

"It's going to snow a lot, and Daddy says maybe it will be enough so we can sled."

Tom gave her a kiss. "I listened to the weather report on the radio in the barn. It might get icy before the snow starts, so we'll need to keep an eye on it."

"Hey, I brought some coconut cake for dessert."

"Yippee," Jesse jumped up and down. "Daddy and me are making pizza for dinner. I get to put the toppings on."

"Remember, Jess, it's 'Daddy and I,' not 'Daddy and me.'" Tom corrected him with a smile.

"Daddy and I," Jesse repeated.

"Can I help, too?" Ann asked as they filed to the kitchen.

"Sure you can, right, Daddy?"

Tom nodded and chuckled.

"Ooh, you started already." The large pizza on the table sported sauce and cheese. Next to it on a plate were chopped black olives, onions, peppers, and slices of sausage. Ann and Jesse took turns placing the toppings, leaving an area onion-free for Jesse. Tom handed Jesse the Parmesan cheese, and showed him how to sprinkle it on top.

"Ta-da," Tom exclaimed and slid the pizza in the oven. "I love pizza for dinner, well, because I love pizza, but also because you don't need anything else with it, except maybe some salad."

"Let me make it," Ann offered. "I'll throw in the leftover black olives with it."

She opened the refrigerator and brought out lettuce and spinach while Tom washed the dishes he'd used. Jesse pulled a toy mouse on a string in front of Abner, and squealed whenever the cat batted and caught it.

Ann carried the finished salad to the table. "The pizza smells so good."

"Sure does." Tom clasped his arm around her. "The hard part is waiting for it to cool enough to slice. I've burned my tongue before because I couldn't wait."

Ann giggled and touched his face. "Poor, hungry fellow."

Their gazes locked until Jesse laughed and called out, "Watch this, Daddy and Annie."

Jesse darted with the toy trailing behind as Abner chased it. Jesse peered over his shoulder and yanked the mouse away just as Abner pounced. Jesse chortled and declared, "He almost got it."

Ann clapped her hands and grinned at Jesse's proud expression.

Tom strode to Jesse and scooped him up. "I got you." He pretended to bite him on the shoulder. Ann beamed at Jesse's delighted squeal.

As soon as the pizza cooled, Tom rolled the cutter over it and served the slices.

"Look, Annie." Jesse pulled the piece he ate away from his teeth and let the cheese stretch out. He and Ann giggled.

"Mmm." Ann smacked her lips. "I could eat this every night."

"Me, too." Jesse nodded.

"I'm not sure why more people don't make their own pizza." Tom reached for another piece. "It's really not hard and it doesn't cost much, either. At least not compared with what you pay at a pizza place."

"I think that's because of the dough part. I've always been nervous about bread dough. At home, we made biscuits and muffins, but bought all our yeast bread. I want you to teach me how to make dough."

"Yes, ma'am." Tom saluted her with a grin.

After they put Jesse to bed and settled in front of the fire, Tom glanced at the window and said, "Sounds like sleet. Wonder how long it's been going on."

He rose and made his way to the door. "Oh, man. Not good."

Ann rushed over and stood next to him. Her car already had a coating of ice, and the driveway shone with it. The wind spat some sleet toward them, and Tom shut the door.

"You're not driving in this." He turned to face her.

[301]

"But I need to get home and go to work tomorrow. As soon as the plows go through, it'll be fine." Ann placed her hand on his arm.

"Ann, you're used to the roads in town where they plow and salt right away. They might not be out here for hours yet. By then it will be even worse than it is now." He reached and drew her to him.

"I'll be okay. I've driven in sleet before." She gazed up at him.

"What if you slide into a ditch? Or some other car bashes into you? No, you're not driving in this."

The stern expression on his features frustrated her. "Tom."

"If you think you absolutely have to go, I'll drive you."

"But you'd need to ask one of your parents to come over here in this mess to sit with Jesse so you could take me. Then I'd be worried about *you*." Ann stroked some of the hair on his forehead. He took her hand and walked with her back to the living room and they sat down.

"Ann, why don't you stay here tonight and sleep on the couch? Once the sleet switches to snow and the trucks go through a few times, you'll be able to get to work, or if it's still bad, Jesse and I will drive you in."

She thought about it. She'd be living here soon anyway. It would be a relief not to go out in the storm. "Well, okay, if you think it's all right."

"Of course it is. I'll get you some bedding and a pillow. Do you want a t-shirt of mine to wear for pajamas? I doubt anything else of mine would work since you're so much smaller than me."

"Sure." A thrill tingled through her at the thought of staying overnight.

Tom returned downstairs with everything and set in on a chair. He added log pieces to the fire and they lazed together on the couch. She cuddled onto him and listened to the slight hiss of the burning wood and the tinkling sound while sleet struck the windows.

Tom sighed. "Five more days."

"Five more days," she echoed. Relaxed and warm, she let herself drift off and woke to see his gaze fixed on her, a deep expression in his eyes. Ann blinked a few times and smiled. He kissed her gently and when he drew back, she pulled him to her into another kiss. Tom's arms tightened around her as the contact intensified. He stopped abruptly. She stared into his magnetic gaze and ran her fingers over his lips. His breath caught.

"Ann, don't." He closed his eyes. She had a sudden realization. He became as breathless by her touch as she did from his.

Tom's self-control amazed her. "I'm sorry. I am."

He took a deep breath. "It's okay. I'm going up to bed now. What time should I wake you up?"

"Is five all right?" she asked when he stood up.

"Sure. Goodnight, sweetie. Sleep well."

"Goodnight." Ann sat a while and stared at the rhythmic motion of the flames. She imagined him in his room. Was he still awake and picturing her down here as she pictured him? She roused herself, got up, changed into his t-shirt, and made up the couch.

Ann snuggled under the covers and smiled to herself. The slight sounds of the storm and the fire lulled her. Tom and Jesse were upstairs. Soon she'd be up there, too. They'd be a real family.

Ann woke to the smell of coffee and slight noises in the kitchen. She stretched, yawned and lay there waiting. Tom strode into the room.

"You're awake." He beamed at her. His hair was all tousled and he hadn't shaved yet. He looked marvelous. "It's about five fifteen and I've got some oatmeal and coffee ready if you want some. I'm going to go wake up Jesse. The road's been plowed, so all we have to do is clean off your car. I already shoveled behind it."

"You're amazing." She wished he'd stand right there and let her stare at him for the rest of the day.

"So are you." He sauntered over, kissed her forehead, and gave her a fond gaze before he headed upstairs.

She hurried into the downstairs bathroom with her clothes and dressed with speed. As they ate together, Jesse asked, "Are you my mom now?"

They both laughed, and Tom said "Almost. Four more days."

"Oh." Jesse appeared puzzled.

"She stayed here last night because of the storm," Tom explained.

"Did it snow enough for sledding?" Jesse's eyes widened.

"I think so, pal." Tom smiled and ruffled Jesse's hair. "We'll try it after our chores."

"Okay," Jesse dug into his oatmeal.

CHAPTER TWENTY-FIVE

ANN BLINKED HER eyes open. *My wedding day.*

A mix of nerves and anticipation drove her fully awake, and she sat up. Mom and her sisters would arrive soon. Gram and Dad planned to meet them at the church with everyone else. She stood, stretched, shrugged on her robe, and plunked in her chair to wait and think.

Well, Father, here I am again. Another big change. Help me relax, please.

The bell rang. She took a deep breath and got up to answer.

"The big day is here," Mom announced as they filed in.

"Nervous?" Margie asked her.

"Not too much," Ann answered and sat down.

Take deep, slow breaths.

"I was, a lot." Margie laughed.

"Me, too," agreed Glenda.

"Maybe it's because you both had bigger weddings. I'd probably be more nervous thinking about lots of people being around. But it's just the families and Susan and Eric, so I'm fine."

"Well, good." Mom held up a bag. "I brought some scones and hot chocolate for us to have before we get dressed."

"Thanks, Mom." Ann wondered if her nervous stomach would let her eat. They sat together and enjoyed the treat. Ann half-listened to the three of them reminisce about their various wedding memories while she finished part of a scone and set down the rest.

"Don't you want anything more to eat?" Mom asked.

"I'm not very hungry." Ann took in a breath and her mother patted her shoulder.

"Well, girls, we'd better get ready." Mom got up and washed their cups and plates.

"Are you sure you don't want to wear any make-up at all?" Glenda asked when they walked to Ann's room.

"Yes," Ann answered. "I always forget it's on, and I rub it off. I tried more than once in high school, but it doesn't work for me. Tom says he likes me the way I am."

Margie chuckled and opened the closet. "Which shoes will you wear? I'll shine them up for you."

"The white ones with the blue trim. Mom picked them out."

"We were lucky to find a pair to match the dress so well." Mom smoothed out Ann's veil on her bed and murmured, "This is so sheer and pretty."

"Sure you don't want me to do your hair?" Glenda asked. "We could kind of pile it up and pin the veil to it."

"Tom likes it down the way I wore it on our first date. I braided it last night after I washed it, so it would be wavy like it was then."

They changed into their dresses in Ann's room while Ann dressed alone in the bathroom. She knew Mom and her sisters never understood her modesty.

I guess I am who I am.

She shrugged at her reflection and brushed out her hair. A quick smile in the mirror and she headed back to the bedroom. Mom placed her veil in a small bag. After Ann slid on her shoes and stood up, she glanced around at everyone.

"Oh, Ann," Margie said.

"All right?" she asked.

Mom and Glenda both had their lips pressed together and nodded, their eyes moist.

"I guess I look pretty good," Ann grinned. She donned her coat and grabbed her suitcase. Tom had made reservations for a honeymoon cabin in the Catskill Mountains not far away.

A whole week with Tom, Ann thought with bliss and nervousness while they drove to the church and parked near the door. Mom set the suitcase in Tom's truck, and handed the bag with the veil to Ann. Though the morning was cold with a slight wind, the sky showed a clear, bright blue. The sun was warm on her face while she gazed up and stood still a moment before she entered the side door.

In a small room next to the bathroom, someone had placed a handful of chairs and a mirror. Gram rose from one of the chairs and greeted them. Ann drew back from her embrace. Gram's eyes were full of tears.

She patted Ann's cheek. "I'm so thrilled for you, my sweet girl. I don't think I've seen you this chipper since you were little. I'm proud of the woman you've become."

"Stop now, or you'll make me cry." Ann swallowed hard and smiled at her.

"When you get back, I'd like to come to church with you and Tom." Gram's expression lit with a smile. Ann returned it and glanced at Mom's widened eyes. Maybe Mom would visit someday.

Anything's possible.

[307]

"Well, guess we better get this show on the road." Ann shook the veil out and handed it to her mother. "Here, Mom, you do the honors."

Mom smiled and arranged it over Ann's head. She stepped back and gazed at her. Her eyes were dry though her smile trembled a bit.

She stretched her arms and hands toward Ann and asked the others, "Beautiful. Don't you think so?"

Margie and Glenda nodded, eyes soft. Gram's still held tears.

Mom cleared her throat. "I'll go see if your Dad and Tom and his brother are all set. C'mon Mom." She stretched her hand out to Gram. "I'll show you where your seat is."

Evelyn arrived in the little room and greeted them while they left. She studied Ann.

"Ann, don't you look wonderful."

"Thanks so much." Ann beamed at her and introduced her sisters.

Evelyn said, "I'll begin the music once I get the nod from your dad. He's waiting for you at the front door near where we hang the coats. Everyone's here, so we'll start as soon as you're ready."

"I'd like a short time alone to pray first," Ann told them.

Glenda and Margie exchanged a glance. Margie asked, "Do you want to do that now, or is there anything else you need us for?"

"I'm all set except for prayer. Tell Dad I'll be out soon."

Both of her sisters kissed and hugged her. Ann closed her eyes when the door shut and relaxed into a prayerful state. She thanked God for all the blessings He'd given her, especially Tom and Jesse.

"And of course, getting to know You," she added with a tearful smile. "Be with me always, please." Ann stopped speaking and bowed her head. Peace and a poignant joy spread through her, and when she knew it was time, she stood up and said, "Well, here I go."

Dad paced near the door. She gave him a smile, and his features relaxed. He handed her a small bouquet to carry, red and pink roses with ferns, baby's breath, and tiny blue-gray flowers. "Ready?"

"You bet," she answered, and they shared a grin.

He stood at the doorway to the main room and nodded. The music began, he took her arm, and they stepped in. Both families were seated, along with Susan and Eric. Tom waited at the front with his brother and Jim Cortland. Her eyes fastened on Tom. His intent gaze and handsome, serious face almost stopped her breath.

She couldn't take in anything else but Tom as she and her father walked to him. She heard Jesse's little voice when he chirped, "Hi, Annie."

Ann's eyes found him, and she shot him a smile while everyone chuckled. She answered, "Hi, Jesse."

She gazed up at Tom's beaming face as Dad lifted her veil, took her hand, and placed it in Tom's. Dad kissed her cheek and sat down next to Mom, whose eyes already glistened.

Jim said a prayer for their life together with a hand on each of their shoulders before he read some Scriptures about marriage. He smiled at the family members and looked at Tom and Ann. "I'm very honored to join these two together. I've been heartened by their level of faith and commitment to God and to each other. They're well-matched and stand ready for this wondrous, challenging journey."

Jim closed his Bible. "I've spoken with both of them, and though they haven't known each other as long as some couples do before marriage, I can tell their commitment is true and strong as is their love. They wanted this ceremony to be short and sweet like their courtship," he added as everyone chuckled, "so I'll read the vows now."

Once he pronounced them man and wife, Tom leaned his head down and whispered, "Our first married kiss." After a slow, tender one he murmured, "With lots more to follow."

Ann's face heated, and Tom chuckled. Jim patted their shoulders and said, "Ladies and gentlemen, I'm pleased to present Mr. and Mrs. Tillman."

Tom and Ann exchanged grins, turned and walked hand in hand toward their families. Jesse jumped into his father's arms, and the three of them shared an embrace. Soft music on a stereo played in the background while everyone chatted and waited to congratulate Tom and Ann.

It didn't seem real yet.

I'm Tom's wife. Jesse's mother. Me, Ann.

Moments passed almost in a blur as she tried to wrap her mind around her new reality. Did every newlywed experience this?

After they'd all eaten appetizers, tiny savory sandwiches, and cake, and toasted the bride and groom more than once, Tom stood.

"I hope you folks don't mind, but I'd like to take Mrs. Tillman here and leave for our honeymoon. All of you stay and visit and get to know each other. Ann and I want to thank you so much for being part of this wonderful day. We love each one of you."

Tom retrieved their coats and helped Ann with hers. He and Ann gave Jesse a last hug and kiss. They stood at the back of the room and waved.

"Good-bye," they said as everyone chorused their farewells and Jesse piped, "Bye, Mommy and Daddy. I love you!"

Ann gazed at Tom, touched to her core. She couldn't speak. Tom answered, "Bye, Jesse. We love you, too."

Tom flashed a playful grin as they walked out. "C'mon, Mommy."

He opened her door, helped her step up and hurried around to climb in. Once inside, he pulled her to him and kissed her for long moments. He started the truck and teased, "What now, Mrs. Tillman?"

"Let's drive by the bakery before we leave town." She grinned at his quizzical expression. "It's where we met. But first, kiss me again."

ABOUT THE AUTHOR

Nancy Shew Bolton is a wife of 41 years, mother of five grown sons, and grandmother to a boy and girl. Ever since she learned to write, she would jot down her thoughts and impressions in little snippets of inspiration in the form of poetry, song lyrics, or short essays. About six years ago, she decided to try her hand at writing a full-length book. She's since written five works of fiction, two non-fiction, and is working on an idea for a children's book, as well as more fiction manuscripts. Writing a full-length work is much more challenging than she thought, and she has received so much valuable assistance from other writers, especially from the ACFW critique groups. Her husband has been supportive of her long hours spent at the keyboard. Many thanks to her beloved Johnny! She thanks God and His Son for her life, her loved ones and the spark of creativity inside every person. She believes each person is a unique creation, with their own special voice and place in this amazing universe. God's handiwork amazes her every day!

Thank you for your Prism Book Group purchase! Visit our website to enjoy free reads, great deals, and entertaining, wholesome fiction!

Made in the USA
Lexington, KY
04 June 2015